Change Up

The Homestand Series | Book 1

Michael Geraghty

Hold Fast Publishing

Chapter 1

Wes

In years past, spring could never come around fast enough. I would spend all winter getting myself ready, staying in shape and prepping the new baseball gloves I would use that year. I'd watch out the window from my home in Pennsylvania as the snow and ice would slowly start to melt. Eventually the winter would give way to the signs of spring that erupted from the trees and ground. That joy has been with me since the time I was a teenager up until now.

As much as I wanted the winter months to end, it was also the only time I would get to spend with my daughter, Isabelle. Time with family when you are a professional ballplayer can be fleeting, and I wasn't even there the day Izzy was born. I was still young, only twenty years old, and was working my way through the minor leagues. We were on a road trip in Texas, heading to Round Rock or Corpus Christi, or any one of another dozen minor league towns that I passed through over the years, when I got the call that Rachel had gone into labor and was on her way to the hospital. Back then, players didn't get the opportunity for paternity leave, especially if you were a minor league player. You hoped you would be nearby when it happened so you could jump home for a day and then get back on the road. With my luck, I was 2,000 miles away and didn't get to see my daughter until weeks later when we had a day off.

When I turned twenty-two and finally made it to the major leagues, I had a bit more security, could take better care of my family, and saw how important those few months in the winter were to be with my daughter. It became even more significant to me when Rachel left me after seven years of marriage, taking off with an old high school boyfriend and leaving Izzy in my care. Thankfully, my parents stepped up to help me out, caring for Izzy at their home in Pennsylvania while I was off playing. It took some real adjustment on all our parts, and Izzy went through some times of real resentment with me, hating that I was gone for months at a time, that she was uprooted from the life she knew to live with her grandparents, and to basically be apart from her parents all the time.

I did my best to make up for it when I had the time to do it. Playing in the majors gave me a lot of perks, including a very good paycheck so I could provide well for Izzy and make sure she had everything she needed and then some. There were times when I clearly overcompensated, buying her things that she never really needed to make up for not being there, but I felt like it was something I had to do.

Years go by too quickly for all of us, and it seems even more so when you are a professional athlete. Now I look around and see that Izzy is fifteen, growing into a young woman, and I am thirty-five, an old man by baseball standards. It takes a little longer for me to get going when spring rolls around now. It's harder to get out of bed, my muscles ache after a workout, and coming off a second left knee surgery over the winter certainly didn't make things easier.

By the time I got to Bradenton, Florida for spring training this year (the spring home of my team, the Pirates), I knew things were going to be difficult. I had been the starting first baseman for the last thirteen years, putting up good numbers along the way. I was no Hall of Famer, but my bat and glove had done a steady job, and I even got to go to an All-Star Game one year. This year, however, things were different. The team knew I was coming off an injury, my contract was up at the end of this coming season, and all I kept reading about in the newspapers was how it was time for the team to move on from me and give some younger guy a chance.

I tried not to let it all get to me – the constant hounding by reporters, the blog articles on the Internet saying I was done – but in the back of my mind, I could feel myself questioning whether they were right. Those feelings affected my play, and I had a terrible first few weeks of spring. Every time I was in the lineup, there were more strikeouts or soft outs, and more aches and pains to deal with afterward.

When the end of March came, I had hit .150 for the spring with no home runs. Most of my playing time had gone to a couple of young kids that the team management was high on. Even teammates I had for years shied away from talking to me about it, unable to come up with the words of encouragement that things would be alright.

And then the day came where I was called into the office. The manager, Tim Newhouse, who I had played with in the minors years ago, was there with the new general manager, Steve Goodson. He was a smug, young guy in his twenties who was glued to his laptop all the time, looking at figures and numbers that meant nothing to guys that played the game.

"Have a seat, Wes," Tim said to me, pointing to the single chair positioned in front the small, wooden desk that was crammed into his office. Steve Goodson stood, his laptop resting on the file cabinet in the office. He stared at the screen, glancing over at me after I sat down.

"We're coming to the end of spring training Wes," Tim started, barely able to look at me as he spoke.

"I know Tim," I said to him, hunching forward, closer to his desk. "I know where things are at. You know what I can do and have done for the team for years now. Spring training numbers don't mean anything."

"You've always come through for us Wes, year after year, and I'm sure you could do it again with more time..." Tim's voice started trailing off before Goodson interrupted.

"The fact is Wes that from a numbers standpoint, Bill Thomas is a better investment for us at this time, so we're going to have to release you today," Goodson said to me bluntly.

"You feel that way too, Tim?" I said, trying to get Tim to look me straight in the eyes while he spoke. I saw him rubbing his hand over the stubble on his chin, searching for an answer that would appease Goodson and me, but we both knew there wasn't one there.

"It's alright Tim, I get it," I said to him, standing up from the chair. Goodson walked over and stood in front of me.

"It's nothing personal, Wes," he said to me with a grin that I wanted to punch off his face. "The organization thanks you for all the years you have given us." Goodson extended his hand to me, and I just stared at it.

"Nothing personal?" I said angrily. "It's personal to me since you just took my job away."

I stormed out of the office and went to my locker. I began to clean everything out while the few teammates left in the locker room watched on. Hank Swan, a pitcher that had come up just a year after me in the organization, walked over to me as I packed the last items away in my duffle bags.

"Wes, you okay?" Hank said to me, putting his arm on my shoulder.

"It'll be fine Hank," I told him, giving him a hug.

"I'm sure you'll land someplace," Hank replied, trying to lift my spirits. "I'll be pitching against you in no time."

"We'll see," I said to him as I carried my bags out into the hot Bradenton sun and over to my Lexus SUV. It was the only luxury car I ever bought with the money I made. I tossed my bags into the back and slammed the trunk closed. A couple of kids ran up to me, holding baseballs in their hands, asking for autographs. I gladly signed the balls.

"Thanks, Mr. Martin," one of the young boys said excitedly to me as they looked at the ball with my signature scrawled on it. "I can't wait to see you playing up in Pittsburgh this year."

I just smiled and nodded at the kids as I climbed into my car before heading out towards the hotel I always stayed at during spring training so I could collect the rest of my things. I reached over and pressed the autodial button on the steering wheel and called my parents' house. The phone rang once before it was answered.

Hey, Wes," my father said cheerfully. "What's going on? You usually don't call until the evening."

"I'm coming home Dad," I said to him as I pulled out of the stadium lot for the last time.

Chapter 2

Kristin

Springtime in Western Pennsylvania still carries quite a chill, so the walk to the library from my apartment on Main Street was a bit brisker than I would have liked. It was days like this that made me long for the warm weather I always felt growing up in Georgia. In Georgia, it never seemed to matter what time of year it was; you could always count on it being warm, even sultry. Many times when I was younger there were days in March where we wore our shorts to school. Life in Pennsylvania was proving to be much different.

Working as a librarian in a small town like Chandler has certainly had its perks. I only started here back in February, when the previous librarian decided to retire. I had found the job online as I scoured both job search websites and forums for libraries that might be looking for librarians. Being a librarian may not seem like the most glamorous job, particularly for a young woman today, but I have always been drawn to books, reading, and libraries since I was a little girl. Growing up in a small town in Georgia where we didn't have a lot of money to spend on things meant spending many days at the library. I was able to borrow books, read, and take part in the programs they offered. The library gave me things to do that didn't cost anything. My sister Lucy and I spent more time at the library than at home just so we had something to do.

When we started to get older, Lucy came with me more as an excuse to leave the house and go and meet boys. I, on the other hand, had fallen in love with the library by then. I volunteered there, helping with programs throughout the year and working there during the summers all through high school. When the time came to graduate high school, Mr. Driscoll, our local librarian, pushed me to search for programs offering library science degrees. I did, and I was accepted at Valdosta State University. With the help of some scholarships, and hard work, I was able to put myself through and graduated in January.

At that point, I was willing to accept the first job that was offered to me just to get my foot in the door somewhere. Weeks of searching, sending applications, conducting interviews on the phone and online, and even driving hundreds of miles to different locations for interviews had led to nothing... until I spotted this job in Chandler. I had never even heard of Chandler, Pennsylvania, and had to Google it to find out where it was. I saw it was a small town about an hour north of Pittsburgh with a population of just under 2,000. It might not have been the ideal fit for me, but it was an opportunity, so I applied. I heard back right away from Marion Harris, the director of the library, and soon had a phone interview that I worked my way through nervously. Surprisingly, just a few days later, I was asked if I could come to Chandler for an in-person interview.

I flew into Pittsburgh and drove the hour to Chandler, shocked to see that it was even a smaller town than where I had grown up in Georgia. There was plenty of snow on the ground and cold in the air, something I was woefully unprepared for as a lifelong southern girl. After parking nearby, I walked quickly to the library, wearing my thin coat and braving the wind that whipped up the skirt of the navy suit I had bought for interviews.

Marion Harris was impressed by my education and background, and loved the ideas that I had for a library that was a bit outdated and crying out for a new space. She offered me the job on the spot, though admitted she was a bit embarrassed that they could only offer me a starting salary in the $35,000 range, but I was eager to jump at it and said yes.

I quickly uprooted my life from Georgia, packing my belongings from my parents' house and driving up to Chandler. Marion helped me find an apartment that was both right down the street from the library and very affordable. While it was a modest place at best, it suited me just fine. With the help of some borrowed furniture from family and finding deals from local sources, my one-bedroom place was a nice, comfortable home in no time.

Starting a new life so far from home was not easy. I had learned to become somewhat more outgoing thanks to my library experiences when I was younger, but I still thought of myself as shy and quiet. I was just as happy reading a book at home as I was going out with friends or going on a date. That doesn't mean I never had boyfriends. I had a few steadies in high school and then again in college, but nothing I would ever call serious. Since I had arrived in Chandler,

I had not seen too many eligible bachelors in the area. There isn't a lot of industry going on around here, with mostly retail stores filling the town. Most of Chandler's residents were employed at either the hospital or college that were nearby, just outside of town. There was also plenty of farmland around that people worked. With a small, mostly aging population, I had not come across anyone that seemed like good dating material.

My companion at the library was Karen Manning. She had worked as an assistant here for a few years and was now in her late twenties. She didn't have the degree they wanted for the head librarian job, so she never applied for it, but Karen was more than welcoming to me when I started, and we became fast friends. Karen was tall, much taller than my short stature at 5'4", and she carried herself well. She kept in great shape, running every day that she could as well as walking to work every day from her place. Karen was perhaps the most confident and outspoken person I had come across in Chandler. More than once when Marion would be in the library with us I could see her shaking her head at the things that would come out of Karen's mouth. Nevertheless, she was a good friend that took me out and around town, as well as introduced me to everyone that came in the library so that I quickly became familiar with the community.

When I had arrived at the library, Karen was there at the front door waiting for me to open things up. I could see her breath in the cold air of the morning as I approached, and her red cheeks indicated to me that she had been there for a few minutes waiting for me.

"It's about time you got here!" she chastised, hopping up and down as I unlocked the front door. I quickly went inside and shut off the alarm system we had installed recently. In the past, the library never had the need for an alarm, but I had recently obtained us some funding so that we could add a couple of new computers. With the new technology, Marion felt the need for extra security.

Karen and I walked in and went through our morning routine: switching on the lights, checking the return bin, checking books and materials back in, turning on the computers and the like. I went into the small office I had just behind the front desk and turned on my computer to check my email. Most days, the email was just questions about books and when they would come in. Karen came into the office and handed me a cup of coffee she made at our coffee maker and sat across from me.

"How was your night?" she said to me as she flipped her short brown hair back.

"Nothing special," I told her. "I was just working on coming up with some ideas for spring programs. Spring break will be coming up for the schools soon, and I want to have some things in place for the kids to do. I have ideas for the younger kids, but I haven't been able to come up with anything the high schoolers might like."

"The high school kids?" Karen replied, shocked I would even mention them. "Have you seen many high school kids come in since you have been here Kristin? If we get one or two a month, it's a shock."

"Maybe it's because we don't have anything they might like," I answered. "We need some ideas that will get them interested in coming here."

"I don't know," Karen said skeptically as she leaned back in her chair and took a sip of her coffee. "Kids today just want to do stuff on their smartphones and not much else."

"Let me think about it for a bit," I told her. "I'll come up with something. I used to love coming to the library when I was a teen," I said proudly.

"No offense Kris," Karen said, putting her feet up on the corner of my desk so I could see the black boots she was wearing, "but most teens don't see going to the library as something fun to do. You might have been out of the ordinary in that way." Karen smiled at me as she sipped her coffee some more.

"Okay, so I was a little geeky," I replied meekly. "That doesn't mean we can't make fun things that teens might like. There's stuff out there we can try, we just have to work at it."

"Okay Boss," Karen said to me, giving me a salute. She then heard someone milling around out in the library and got up to see if anyone needed help.

I went back to scanning my computer, reading the few emails I got. One message caught my eye. It was a request for a copy of Dracula. It wasn't the request for the book that was unusual, but the circumstances for the request made me take notice. The email asked if there was any way we could mail the book to the address. It seems the request came from a young girl who wanted the book to read to her grandmother, and she had no way to come down to the library to get it during the day. The email struck a chord with me, and I wanted to find a way to help the girl out.

I walked out of my office to the front desk and saw Karen helping someone check out one of the latest best-selling thrillers we had.

"Karen, do we have a copy of Dracula on the shelf?" I asked her.

Karen punched the information into the computer. "Sure do," she replied. "We have a couple of copies. Are you looking for light reading tonight?" she said with a smirk.

I smirked back at her and walked over to the small horror section we had and grabbed one of the hardcovers off the shelf. I walked back to my office and printed out the email and grabbed my coat.

"Where are you off to?" Karen asked as I walked by her.

"To make a delivery," I said to her. "I have to walk back home and get my car first. I'll be back in a bit."

I tucked the book under my arm and walked quickly back to my apartment so I could get my car. It rarely left its parking spot these days since I walked everywhere, so I was a little worried if the car would start in the cold weather. It whined at me a little bit before finally turning over and I tried to get the heat going as quickly as possible.

While the car warmed up and the heat slowly transitioned from ice cold to tepid warm, I looked at the email to grab the address to bring the book to. I was still getting used to where everything was in Chandler, and the address seemed like it was one just on the outskirts of town since it was given as 2 Martin Way on Route 5. I looked down at the name on the email, and it was Isabelle Martin. It was a bit unusual for someone to live at a house on the street with their own name, but in small towns anything is possible. The drive was just a few minutes, so I pulled out of my parking spot and headed out.

Hopefully, this brings a smile to someone's face, I thought as I moved down Main Street and made a left to head out to Route 5.

At the very least it gives me something different to do today and create some goodwill with the community, I considered as I smiled to myself in the rearview mirror, looking forward to this little adventure.

Chapter 3

Wes

After taking the time to explain to my father just what had happened at spring training, and then gathering my belongings from the hotel, I knew I had to make a call to my agent, Randy Miller. Randy has been my agent ever since I was signed out of high school to play ball, and he has always done right by me. Some people may think that he is pushy and arrogant, and he is, but that's what helps to make him so good at his job. As I drove up through Florida and Georgia, heading back home, I gave him a call at his office in New York. He knew what the call was about as soon as I got him on the line.

"Wes, I heard what happened, and I'm sorry," Randy started off the conversation. There was sincerity in his voice, and I knew he felt bad about my getting released.

"Thanks, Randy," I said to him as I tried not to sound like this was the worst day of my life.

"I've already started making some calls, pinpointing teams that may need a first baseman or a DH, so I've got some feelers out for you already. I don't think it will be too long before we hear from someone about an offer."

"I'm in no rush Randy," I said to him resignedly. "To be honest, it feels good to be able to go home for a few days and spend some time with my folks and Izzy. I think I can use the break physically and mentally. It's been a rough spring."

"I know it has bud," Randy answered, trying to reassure me. "Take a few days to get yourself together, and I'll see what I can come with for you. Once word gets around that you are available, I don't think you'll be hanging out for too long. Sit tight, and I'll get to work for you. In the meantime, enjoy the ride home. The weather's a little chillier up this way than what you had in Bradenton, so be prepared. I'll talk to you as soon as I hear anything."

"Okay, Randy, thanks," I said as I hung up the speakerphone. I turned the radio on to listen to something, anything to get my mind off what had happened, and I made the mistake of putting on a sports radio station. I heard them mention that I had gotten released today, so close to the end of spring training. They went on and on about how it might be tough for me to latch on somewhere else or that maybe my time was over in baseball.

The thought that I was done had crossed my mind as well, and now that I had all this alone time on the ride home, it was becoming more and more of something for me to obsess over. Perhaps my time was over after spending half my life playing ball. It certainly was a possibility, but at thirty-five I wasn't exactly ready to just sit around for the next fifty years of my life doing nothing. I had made a lot of money playing, and I was always careful with my spending, saving, and investing. Izzy and I could live quite comfortably without an issue. The problem would be finding a way to fill that empty hole in my life if I wasn't getting up to play ball each day.

Sure, I could spend time with my daughter, but Izzy was fifteen now. How much time does she really want to spend with her father? She's gotten so used to not having me around for nearly ten months out of the year that I didn't know how thrilled she would be to have me there all the time. She has school, her friends, her hobbies, and in a few years, she will be ready to go off to college. It will be great to be there for her, but then what happens when she is gone?

My parents were getting older, and even though Dad was in pretty good health, Mom was not. Cancer has been her main battle for the better part of a year now, and it was going to be difficult to deal with. Dad has had a lot of the burden on him, but with Izzy's help, they have been able to make things work. With everything going on, maybe having me around would be a good thing right now. Dad has been tasked with taking care of Mom, Izzy and the horse farm that was a big part of the land they lived on.

Dad has run the horse farm since I was little, and it has been his pride and joy. I learned to ride at a pretty young age and spent my formative years working alongside him, tending to the horses. But once baseball became a bigger part of my life, I spent less time there to focus on playing. After I made it to the majors, it afforded me the money to make sure that the farm was there for him and my mother. I bought the land adjacent to theirs and expanded the area for them, as well as built a home for me, Izzy and Rachel, at the time, just on top of the hill beyond their home. I always knew that this was where I was going to return to, I just never thought it would happen now.

I guess somewhere in the back of my mind I knew retirement came for ballplayers at a much younger age than people in other careers, but as a player, you always think that day is further off than it may really be. No one likes to hear they aren't wanted anymore, can't perform as well as they used to or that they won't be missed when they leave, but the reality is that we're all replaceable when it comes to working. I've only been gone from the team for a few hours, but I am sure they are already focused on the new, younger kid that will make a bigger impact than I would.

I heard a few phone calls on the talk radio show mention me, and how it was about time they got rid of me or how my time had passed. Fans are passionate in many ways about the game, and they want to see their team win, something that hasn't happened in Pittsburgh in a long while now, so I can understand their frustration. As a player, you grow used to hearing both sides of the argument. You love the cheers you get at the stadium or when people come up to you in public and say how much they love you as a player, but just as often you hear the jeers, boos and far worse from fans that are frustrated and want you to be better. It's never easy no matter how you look at it.

Getting lost in my thoughts had allowed me to get much further along on my drive than I thought I would when I left Florida. Typically, the drive home from Florida would take roughly seventeen hours, so as much as I wanted to make it home in one day, I knew I would not be able to do it in one shot. All the coffee in the world wouldn't let me get there. I had left Bradenton around ten in the morning, and as it was now approaching seven in the evening. The sun was starting to set, and I knew I wouldn't be driving much longer. I was still in Virginia and had about eight hours of driving left, so I got off the highway and stopped at the first hotel I could find to see if I could get a room for the night.

The first place that came along was one of the big chain hotels, and while this hotel wasn't large, it was going to suit my needs just fine. I pulled into one of the parking spots, and saw that the lot didn't have a lot of cars there other than mine, probably the norm for a Thursday evening in March. I stepped out of the car and immediately felt a chill in the air. There was probably a twenty or thirty-degree difference from when I left Florida to now. I grabbed one of my small bags out of the trunk and my leather jacket off the back seat before I walked to the entrance and through the automatic doors of the hotel.

The hotel itself was clean and bright, with pleasant lighting throughout the lobby area. There was a young man behind the front desk, dressed in the jacket and tie appropriate for this hotel branch. His nametag read Bruce, and he looked no more than twenty-five. He smiled at me from the time I got within fifteen feet of the front desk until I stood right in front of him, a toothy grin that seemed almost robotic in nature. His short neatly cropped brown hair looked like it never moved or grew at all.

"Good evening sir," he said to me cordially. "How can I help you tonight?

"Hi," I replied. "I was looking for a room for tonight."

"Do you have a reservation?" Bruce asked me dutifully.

"No, no I don't," I told him. I assumed by the lack of cars in the parking lot that getting a room wasn't going to be a problem, and I saw Bruce typing away at his keyboard as he worked to locate a room for me.

"I have several rooms you can choose from tonight," Bruce said with his customary smile. "I have rooms with double beds, queen beds or king beds, your choice."

"I'll take one of the king-size beds, please," I said to him as I go out my wallet from my front jeans pocket. I handed over my credit card to Bruce, and he ran it through the card system. He took a look at the card and handed it back to me, presenting me with the hotel slip to sign along with it.

Bruce then handed the small white keycard over to me. "Here's your key Mr. Martin," he told me. "You're in room 304, on the third floor. The elevator is just to the left here in the lobby, and there is complimentary breakfast in the lounge in the morning starting at 7 AM."

I peered over into the lounge and saw the bar there along with some tables, a couch, and a large screen TV.

"Is the bar open?" I asked Bruce as I put my credit card away and picked up my bag.

"Yes sir, until 12 AM. You can also get food there until 11."

"Great, thanks, Bruce," I said as I nodded and smiled at him.

"You're very welcome Mr. Martin," Bruce answered. "You have a great night."

I walked over to the elevator and pressed the button. Within a few seconds, the doors slid open, and a man who looked to be about my age walked out with his young son. The boy was wearing a baseball cap, and the man took a long look at me as I smiled at both of them. I was pretty sure he recognized me and was probably wondering what I was doing hundreds of miles away from where I should be. I was still wondering the same thing. As the elevator door closed, I could see the man still looking at me, pointing and saying something to his son.

The elevator arrived on the third floor and I moved out into the hall. I found my room just two doors away from the elevator, pushed the keycard in, and opened the door. I placed my bag on the obligatory chair across from the bed and sat down on the bed. It felt like the typical hotel bed to me, one I had been on in thousands of places over thousands of days. It was firm, but not too firm, a bit saggy in spots, and it had the same floral bed cover that every other hotel has. I pulled out my phone to give Dad a call and let him know where I was at.

"Hey," I heard his voice answer right away. "I was wondering when I would hear from you. Where are you at?"

"I'm in Virginia," I told him. "I'm about seven hours away. I was getting punchy, so I stopped at a hotel for the night."

"Good idea," Dad said in his fatherly tone. "So you'll be here by tomorrow afternoon."

"I should be," I told Dad. He was never much at small talk or conversation on the phone. "How's Izzy?"

"Oh, she's fine," Dad said to me. "I didn't tell her you were coming home; I didn't want to worry her. She's been in with your mother all day. She stayed home from school today. I needed to get out to the stable with Dr. Walters to check the horses, so she stayed home with your mother. I hope that's okay."

"It's fine Dad. What's wrong with Mom?"

"Oh, you know, same old stuff. Some days are worse than others. Your mother just had trouble breathing today is all. The oxygen helps, but it doesn't always do the trick. I just wanted someone there in case she needed anything while I was out."

Dad's voice never wavered. It always had the calm, monotone to it, whether he was happy, sad, or angry, so I could never tell when things were bad or not.

"I can get home tonight if you really need some help, Dad," I told him, letting him know my concern.

"Stop it, Wes, everything is fine. Get a good night of rest, and we'll see you in the afternoon tomorrow. You want to talk to Izzy?" Dad asked me.

"No, it's fine," I replied to him. "Just... just tell her I was tired after practice and that I love her. I don't want her to worry about me."

"I'll let her know. Talk to you later," Dad told me as he hung up.

I put the phone in my shirt pocket and felt my stomach grumble a bit. I hadn't bothered to stop for any food along the way and was starving at this point. I pulled myself up off the bed and went back to the elevator, pressing the call button. Again, the elevator arrived quickly, and I stepped in and went right down to the main floor.

I walked past the front desk, with Bruce smiling that same smile at me as his eyes followed me all the way over to the lounge. I walked over to the small bar area and sat at the bar. There was no one else around, but within seconds the bartender appeared from a door behind the bar.

He was an older man, looking older than me. He was balding, with a few stray gray hairs on top, but he was tall and had a proud stature. He stood in front of me and smiled, as he slid a small cocktail napkin in front of me.

"Evening," he said with his slight southern drawl. "What can I get for you?"

I glanced over at the selections of beers behind him and then decided to have something a little stronger. I spied a bottle of Grey Goose behind the bartender, my favorite vodka.

"I'll have a Grey Goose martini, on the rocks, please," I said to the bartender. I glanced at his nametag and saw his name was Gary.

"Coming up," he said as he turned and grabbed the bottle of vodka off the shelf. I watched him expertly mix the vodka and vermouth in his shaker, using just the right amounts of each. He shook the mixture slightly, and I could hear the ice rattle in the shaker for a few seconds before he poured the drink out into the rocks glass filled with ice. He tossed in a couple of green olives on a toothpick and placed the drink in front of me.

"Thanks, Gary," I said as I raised the glass and took a sip. I could feel the lovely burn of the vodka and vermouth hit my tongue. It was the first martini I had in a while, and it was perfect. "Very nice," I said to him.

"I'm glad you like it," Gary told me with a smile. "Can I get you a menu?" he asked me, reaching beneath the bar for one.

"Please," I said as he handed the paper menu over to me. It was typical hotel and bar fare, with soup, salads, sandwiches, and burgers on it. I didn't really have to be careful about what I ordered for dinner tonight since I didn't have to worry about workouts or a game the next day, so I decided to order the pub burger with onion rings and French fries.

Gary took my order and entered it into his register while I continued to sip on my martini. I glanced over at the big screen TV, and it was broadcasting the big sports channel with sports news. They showed a highlight of the spring training game between the Pirates and Phillies, and how Bill Thomas, the young twenty-one-year old that replaced me, hit a big home run today. I turned away from the TV and took a long sip of the martini, draining the glass.

Gary saw the glass was empty and walked over. "Get you another?" he asked as he picked up the glass and dumped the ice into the sink below the bar.

"Please," I said emphatically. I turned around the stool and looked to my left and saw the man from the elevator walking with his young boy again. The boy was wrapped in a towel now, so I figured that they must have used the indoor pool. As they were walking by, the man stopped and saw me again. I smiled and nodded as he and the boy looked on. They began to approach me, unsure of what they should do.

"Are you... Wes Martin?" the man asked, unsure if it was me.

"I am," I said to him quietly.

"Robbie," the man said turning to the boy, "this is Wes Martin, from the Pirates... oh, I'm sorry," he said, embarrassed that he had mentioned the team that cut me early in the morning.

"It's okay," I told him. " Nice to meet you, Robbie. I'm Wes." I extended my hand, and the young boy came up and shook it.

"Would it be okay if we got a picture with you, Mr. Martin?" the man asked. He seemed more like a young boy now than his son did.

"Sure," I told him as I stood up off the stool. The man fumbled with his cell phone, trying to angle it so he could get all three of us in the picture before Gary offered to take the picture for him. He handed the phone to Gary, who snapped a couple of photos of the three of us.

"Thanks so much Mr. Martin," the man said to me, shaking my hand again. "I'm sorry to disturb you."

"No disturbance at all," I told him, as I watched them walk away, both staring at the photos on the phone.

I sat back down at the bar and Gary appeared with my burger, sliding the full plate in front of me. I turned and looked up at him and smiled.

"You must get that all the time," Gary said as he handed me a napkin that wrapped a knife and fork.

"Not as much as you think," I said as I picked up an onion ring and ate it. "Most people don't recognize me when I'm not wearing a uniform." I took a bite out of the hamburger, seeing it was cooked nicely to a medium. It tasted like the best thing I had eaten in weeks.

"Raw deal you got today," Gary said to me as he wiped down the bar. "You deserved better after all those years."

"That's the way it goes sometimes," I said in between bites. "It's a business too, so I get it, even if I don't like it."

"Well, I hope you catch on with someone else and then stick it to the Pirates," Gary said with a smile.

I wiped my face with the napkin after another bite and stifled a laugh. "I'll do my best."

The rest of my brief meal passed quietly as I finished up. By then, a blonde woman had come into the lounge and taken a seat at the bar a few down from mine. She sat down, wearing a red button-down shirt and blue jeans, and ordered a rum and cola. She glanced down at me and gave me a brief smile. She looked to be about my age, well-tanned as if she too had just come from Florida, and her shirt was open just enough to show a hint of cleavage beneath it. A quick glance at her hand indicated no wedding ring (something as a ballplayer I had become accustomed to looking for on women; married women were always off-limits to me).

"How are you tonight?" she said to me as she raised her glass to me, flashing a bright smile. Her voice had a bit of a gravelly tone, giving her a sexy note to her inflection.

"Doing well, thanks, and you?" I said to her as I politely raised my glass as well and took another sip of martini.

"Great," she told me, "Just relaxing after a long day."

I could see there was a glimmer of hope in her eyes that I would jump in and do some flirting, and on any other day I might have spent some more time with her, but today I just didn't have it in me. I placed my glass down on the bar and pushed my empty plate away. Gary walked over and pulled both away from me.

"Anything else?" Gary asked me.

"That's it, Gary, I'm calling it a night," I said to him. I could see the disappointment on the lady's face as she turned away from me now, focusing her attention on the TV. Gary slid the check over to me.

"I can charge it to your room if you like," he said quietly to me.

"I got it," I told him as I pulled some cash from my wallet. I handed Gary the cash for the meal and drinks and then handed him two twenties. "Take the lady's drink from this, and the rest is for you," I told him. Gary took the money in his left hand and then presented his right hand to me.

"Thanks, Mr. Martin, it's greatly appreciated," he said to me with a big smile. "I hope to see you playing again soon," he said softly.

"Thanks, Gary," I told him as I got up from the stool. I gave a congenial nod to the lady at the bar, and she gave me a passing smile as she finished her drink. Gary began walking down to her as I walked away and back to the elevator.

I walked passed Bruce, who was still positioned at his station, and he followed me with his smile as I went to the elevator. Once I was back in my room, I stripped out of my shirt and jeans and just climbed under the blanket, wearing only my briefs.

My head was spinning a little from the martinis, and as I closed my eyes, I could see flashing colors in front of me. Once they subsided a bit, I drifted off to sleep quickly, feeling spent from a stressful day and hoping that tomorrow would bring better things for me.

Chapter 4

Kristin

I hadn't had many occasions to venture out onto Route 5 since my arrival in Chandler, and I tried to take in the beautiful scenery around me. Much of this immediate area was dotted with forestry and farms, and there were some signs of greenery and budding trees pushing up, letting me know that springtime really was closing in on us.

I watched the street signs for Martin Way and found it just a mile or so up on the left of Route 5. I turned up the street, which was just a long driveway surrounded by white, wooden fencing. The drive up was longer than I had anticipated, and I could see some horses walking freely on the farm to the left of me. As I got further along, there was a large house looming up at the top of the hill, the largest I had seen in Chandler. Further down the hill was a smaller, ranch-style house on the left with a larger barn area well behind the home.

I slowly pulled up to the home on the left and saw the number 2 posted on the front porch. I pulled my car into the small driveway behind the pickup truck and turned the car engine off. I reached over and grabbed my copy of Dracula off the front seat next to me and got out of the car.

I walked up the front steps of the porch and looked for a doorbell but didn't see one. There was a bell you could clang to the right of the door, but to me, that seemed a bit loud to ring, so I knocked on the door instead. I could start to feel some chill on my legs as I stood waiting outside when a voice seemed to come out of nowhere.

"Who is it?" I heard a voice say over some type of intercom. I looked around to see where the voice was coming from and it was then that I noticed a camera perched at an angle above the door, pointing down at me.

I turned and looked at the camera, getting closer to it. "I'm Kristin Arthur, the librarian at the Chandler library. You sent me an email about a book." I held up the copy of Dracula closer to the camera so it could be seen.

"Hold on," the voice replied to me. I stood nervously, glancing at the camera and the front door, wondering why a horse farm in Chandler would need so much security.

Moments later, the front door opened and there stood a young girl. Her long brown hair was braided into a ponytail that hung over her shoulder. The girl was striking, much taller than me, with piercing blue eyes and the soft, beautiful skin girls that age would die for. I smiled at her through the screen door between us.

"Hi," I said to her happily, holding up the book. "Are you Isabelle?"

"I am," she told me, seeming a bit wary as to why I was here. "I thought you would just mail the book to me," she said, surprised to see me standing there.

"Well, you weren't far from the library, so I thought I would just bring it over to you. I hope that's okay."

"No, it's fine," she said as she opened the screen door. "We don't get a lot of people out this way is all." I handed the book over to her.

"It's probably none of my business," I said to her, "but why did you want Dracula?"

"Oh, well my grandmother is sick, and I read to her sometimes," Isabelle said, looking down at the book. "She's trying to go over some of the classics that she read when she was younger and looks for ones I haven't read already. It's getting harder for her to find books I haven't read, so she picked this one."

"Well it's a great book, I'm sure you will really enjoy it," I told her, trying to make some conversation with her.

"When do you need it back?" Isabelle asked me.

"No rush," I told her, brushing my blonde hair out of my eyes. "Just bring it to the library when you are done."

"Okay, thanks," Isabelle said. She smiled at me, giving me a radiant smile. She seemed grateful to have the book. "It was really nice of you to bring it out here."

"Well," I said to her, "I'm new here, so I'm trying my best to get out, meet people, and let them know that the library has a lot to offer the community. I'm happy to bring you anything else you may want to read if you want something else for your grandmother, or you."

"Great," Isabelle replied. "I'll keep that in mind. I need to get back to my grandmother," she said as she took a step back into the house.

"Sure," I said to her as I walked back towards the steps. "You have a nice day," I told her as I turned and walked down the steps towards my car.

I got into my car and backed out of the driveway and headed towards the exit. I could see Isabelle standing by the door, and she gave me a light wave as I drove away.

The whole situation seemed a little peculiar to me. It must be difficult to have to take care of a sick relative at a young age, and I wondered where the rest of her family was.

I was back at the library in minutes and decided to leave my car there instead of driving it back home. I parked in the small lot next to our building and I walked back into the library, feeling proud of my delivery. Karen was behind the counter, sitting idly while a few patrons were at tables reading.

"Where did you go?" Karen asked me as I took off my coat and walked into my office.

"I dropped a book off to someone who wanted it for a sick relative," I told her. "It's good if word gets around that we're willing to help out people like that."

"I suppose so," Karen answered. "Where did you have to go?"

"Martin Way on Route 5," I said to her as I sat at my desk. "Do you know them?"

"The Martins?" Karen said as she sat down opposite me. "Everyone in town knows the Martins," she said, shocked I didn't know who they were.

"Why is that?" I asked her, picking up my now tepid cup of coffee.

"Well, the family has been around here forever. Wyatt and his wife Jenny own the horse farm, but it's Wes that everyone knows," Karen said to me.

"Who's Wes Martin?" I asked, still confused.

"Seriously Kris?" she asked me incredulously. Karen stood up from her chair and walked over to me, nudging me out of the way so she could use my computer. She typed Wes Martin into the search engine, and up popped pictures of a man in a baseball uniform. I looked closely at the picture, and I could see the same incredible eyes in front of me that I had just seen on Isabelle. Wes Martin had a rugged look to him on the close-up picture I saw. He had heavy stubble on his face, and even though he was flashing a small smile, you could see the serious and stern look of an athlete there.

Karen scrolled down the page to find other pictures, including one of him in a swimsuit by a pool. The man was well put together, muscles in all the right places without an ounce of fat to be seen, so you could see that he clearly took good care of himself.

"So, he's a baseball player?" I asked, feeling awkward because I never really followed baseball at all.

Karen rolled her eyes at me. "Yes, Kris, he's a baseball player. He's basically Chandler's claim to fame. He's played for the Pirates since he was a teenager with their minor league teams, so he's the 'local boy made it big.' He's not around here much, but that big house on Martin Way is his, and he gives a lot back to the community. He built the local Little League fields, and he gives money wherever he can to help Chandler."

I sat back in my chair still looking at his picture. "Well, his daughter seemed very nice. I guess his wife was up at the house and they help out with the grandmother?"

"Oh no," Karen said, sitting on the edge of my desk, glad to hand out some gossip. "His wife left him about eight years ago. I guess she didn't like the life of being a millionaire baseball player's wife. I heard she packed up and went to New York and hooked up with some hedge fund guy worth a ton of dough. What a gold-digger. Jenny, Wes' mother, has been fighting cancer for a while now. She's such a sweet woman. I guess Wyatt and Isabelle take care of her."

Someone rang the small bell at the front desk and Karen scurried out of the office to help whoever was there. I sat at my desk and stared at the pictures of Wes Martin, captivated by his looks and wondering how tough it must be for him, juggling a life where he is never home, acting as a single dad, taking care of his family, and having a career in the spotlight. I admired him for how he was able to do everything and keep smiling in these pictures, and wondered what went on behind those captivating eyes.

Chapter 5

Wes

When I woke up in the hotel, for a moment I thought I was still in Florida. It felt like any other morning as the alarm on my phone went off at 7 AM, telling me it was time to get up and head to the field for morning workouts. Only today it was just an alarm to get me up and remind me I had nowhere I needed to be right away. I rolled over to my left and could see the sun just peeking through the closed blinds in the room. I groaned as I rolled so that I was looking at the ceiling as I contemplated what to do next. Even the patterns on the ceiling seemed to be like baseball diamonds to me, and the frustration caused me to get out of bed and get my day going.

I went into the bathroom to give myself the hot shower I badly needed right now. I washed off, letting the shower get nice and steamy. Even though the flow from the hotel shower was less than strong, it did the job for me. My achy knee felt a bit better today, more than it had in a while, perhaps because I didn't spend all day yesterday running around on a baseball field.

I wiped the fog off the mirror in the bathroom to look at myself. Scratching the stubble on my chin, I decided now was a good time to get a fresh start and shaved off what semblance of a beard I had growing. My hair length looked fine, and was shorter than it had been in years since I went for a haircut while in Bradenton just a few days ago. Wiping the last of the shaving cream off my face, I looked at my reflection and felt better about what I saw.

I quickly dressed and threw everything into my overnight bag so I could get on the road early.

Maybe I can get home by two before Izzy gets home from school today, I thought to myself, happy that I would be able to surprise her a bit.

I went down to the lobby to check out, a little disappointed that Bruce wasn't behind the front desk as he was yesterday when I arrived. A lovely woman, Ava, helped me check out and asked if I wanted to grab any breakfast before I left. I decided to go in by the buffet in the lounge and just get some coffee for the road. I was surprised there were as many people there getting breakfast as there were, but I guess the hotel was a stopping place for many business people. The woman I saw at the bar last night was there, sitting at a table drinking coffee and reading the newspaper. I decided to move quickly through and fill my to-go cup and get moving, hoping to avoid engaging in any conversation that was going to be embarrassing for either of us.

I filled up my mug with some regular coffee and scooted out the door to my car. The air was still crisp, and there was some condensation on the car when I got to it. I climbed behind the driver's seat and decided to check my phone messages before I took off. There were a few messages from former teammates and from a few reporters that had my number, but I didn't really want to talk to any of them now. There was one message on there from Izzy, saying she was sorry she missed my call and hoped to talk to me the next day. It lifted my spirits a bit knowing she missed me and I would get to see her again.

As I got on the highway headed towards Chandler, I thought more about Izzy. I must give my parents a lot of the credit for how well she has grown up. I missed many of the typical events that parents are part of over the years – concerts and plays at school, parent-teacher meetings, dance recitals, you name it – but they were always there to pick up the slack for me, especially after Izzy's mom left us.

I always knew deep down that Rachel wasn't happy with the way things were. We got married at a very young age when I was still coming up through the minors, and it seemed like a fun life at first for her. Then, when I made the majors a few years later and did well, she seemed happy living the high life for a while. Eventually, I think she got tired of living life in a small town, tucked away from everything with no husband around. I don't think it was the life she envisioned it would be. It all changed when I came home after the season eight years ago. I had been home for two days and went out to do some work on the farm with my Dad. When I got back, Rachel was gone. She had left a note saying she couldn't do it anymore and had been having an affair with an old boyfriend who was now a hedge fund guy in New York making billions.

I was panicked at first, worrying about my marriage, but more worried about what would happen with Izzy. She was only seven at the time and when she came home from school her mother was gone. It took some explaining, but she seemed to grasp things well right from the start and was okay with it. We spent some time together that off-season and put the plan together for my parents to help take care of her while I played.

In all the years since then, I've never really had a steady girlfriend or anyone stable in my life. Sure, there have been flings and dates over the years. You hear lots of stories about groupies and fans stalking players at hotels and stadiums, and a lot of that is true. It was not always easy to say no, but you learn after a while that it is the safest bet to stay away from trouble like that. The few women I did meet and date for a little bit never worked out very well, and it had been a few years now since I really saw anyone on a steady basis.

Do I get lonely? Sure I do, sometimes. When you're out on the road all the time, you have your teammates with you, so there isn't a lot of alone time. However, as you get older, you tend to let the younger guys go running around to bars and clubs or stay up late playing video games, and you head out for an early dinner and get to bed. It's on those days that you wish you had someone with you, a companion, someone you could trust to be there with you or just to talk on the phone.

All these thoughts flying through my head seemed to consume me for hours, and it wasn't too long, a little after one, before I was getting off the exit to head towards Chandler. It had been many years since I was back in town at this time of year and even though I had only left for Florida back in early January, things seemed different now. When you live in a small town, you notice everything, like the paint store on Main Street that isn't there anymore or how Fleming's Department Store had changed their window displays. As I drove down Main Street and headed out towards my home, I could see the subtle differences that had occurred in that month I was away, and it made me wonder what differences I would find at home.

I pulled up the road and drove down the driveway to my parent's house. Both the pickup trucks were in the driveway, which meant Dad wasn't out on the farm and was at home. I stepped out of my SUV, leaving the bags in the car for now, and stretched my legs before I went to the porch. I took a quick glance over at my house up the hill and wondered how it was. I had hired a cleaning company to come in once a week to keep the place looking good while I was away since Izzy spent most her time down here with my parents. It was likely I would have to spend some time doing typical homeowner things that I hadn't done in a long time, like grocery shopping and household repairs.

I walked up the porch steps and opened the door to go inside. My parent's house hadn't changed much over the last twenty-five years, though they did have an addition put on after they started taking care of Izzy, giving her a space of her own in their home. It was a basic ranch-style home with a couple of bedrooms, though my Dad had converted my old bedroom into an office long ago, so he had space to work. The front door opened into the living room, and I looked around and saw no one in the area. I could smell a pot of coffee brewing, something that was always going on in the house, so I knew Mom and Dad were around somewhere.

"Hello," I yelled out, waiting for a response. My Dad peered around the corner into the living room from the kitchen and smiled at me.

"We're in here, Wes," he said to me, waving me over.

I walked into the kitchen to see Mom and Dad sitting at the table drinking coffee, each reading. Dad was dressed in his typical plaid shirt and blue jeans while Mom was just in a t-shirt and sweatpants. Dad looked good and always kept himself in fantastic shape. He had a long, wiry frame that was perfect for running a horse farm. He always reminded me of a cowboy from the time I was little, with his bushy mustache and stringy hair, though both were a bit grayer now than ever before. He stood up from the table and gave me a hug, welcoming me home.

Mom looked over at me, surprised to see me, and she went to get up from her chair, struggling a bit to get her strength and balance.

"Mom, sit," I told her as I came over and gave her a kiss on the cheek. Ever since she was diagnosed with cancer, things have been rough for her. The surgery and treatments helped at first, but the cancer returned a few months ago, and she has been struggling ever since, ending up on oxygen lately to help her keep her strength up. Her face and arms looked a bit thinner than they had when I saw her just a few weeks ago, causing me some concern.

"What are you doing here?" she said to me. "What's wrong?" Mom glanced back and forth at me to my Dad while I poured myself a cup of coffee.

"Jenny, relax," my Dad told her, patting her hand.

"Everything's fine Mom, don't worry," I said as I sat down at the table across from her.

"If everything were fine you wouldn't be sitting here right now Wesley," she said sternly. Mom never called me Wesley unless she was upset.

"The Pirates released me yesterday," I told her as I took a sip of coffee.

"Oh Wes, I'm so sorry." Mom gave me a look of concern.

"It's fine, really. Randy was making some calls to see if any other teams are interested."

"Well for all the money you pay him, I would think he would finally do something for you," Mom said in a huff. She never understood what Randy did as my agent and why he was worth ten percent of what I made each year.

"Have you heard anything yet?" Dad asked me, folding up his newspaper and looking at me.

"Dad, it's been one day."

"I know Wes, but you would think everyone knows by now. Hell, we've gotten calls from friends and relatives since yesterday afternoon."

"Why didn't you tell me people were calling?" Mom chimed in, looking at my father.

"Jenny, you had a rough day yesterday, and I was out with the doctor tending to horses, so I really didn't think it was a good idea..."

I could see Mom rolling her eyes at him as she waved her hand. "Does Izzy know?" Mom asked.

"No, not yet," I said, drinking some more coffee. "I thought I would surprise her and pick her up at school. She gets out around now, right?"

"She does," my Dad told me as he stood up from the table, "but she was going to the library after school. She had a book to return and wanted to look at something."

I was surprised to hear that she was going to the library. I knew Izzy was a voracious reader, but she pretty much ordered whatever book she wanted online these days.

"Well," I said standing up, "maybe I'll really surprise her and be at the library when she gets there. Do you two need anything while I am out?"

"We're good Wes," Dad said. I saw Mom had already returned to the magazine she was reading. Dad walked with me out into the living room and to the front door.

"Is she doing okay?" I whispered to Dad. "She looks a lot gaunter than just a month ago."

Dad looked at me with a bit of concern on his face. "Dr. Gilmartin says she's doing well, and I trust her. The medications and treatment have really taken a lot out of her lately, but she's tough, and she's fighting through it."

We walked out the front door and down the steps and stood in front my SUV.

"And how about you, Dad? Are you alright?" I could see he was looking a bit tired himself.

"I won't lie to you Wes, it's been tough," he told me as he sighed. "Running the farm, taking care of the house and your Mom, it takes a lot out of me. Thank God Izzy has been here to help. She's quite the young lady."

"Well, I have you and Mom to thank for that," I said to him, slapping him on the back.

'Don't sell yourself short Wes," Dad said to me. "There's a lot of you in her, and it shows."

"Is that a compliment Dad?" I said with a smirk.

He smiled back at me. "Today, it is. When she was eight or nine, maybe it wouldn't have been."

I climbed into my SUV and turned the engine on. I pressed the automatic button for the window to go down.

"I'll be back in a bit," I said to Dad. "Maybe we can have a good dinner tonight, as a family."

"That would be nice," Dad said. He backed up a few paces as I pulled the car out of the driveway and headed down the road.

I worked my way over to the library, seeing it was still only about 1:45. I guessed I had about thirty minutes before Izzy would be there, and I smiled thinking about what a great surprise she would find.

I parked in the small lot for the library and got out. I hadn't been to the Chandler library in many years, probably since I was back in high school and before I started playing ball, so I wasn't quite sure what to expect inside. It always seemed small, cramped and run down to me, and it was not the ideal place to go to find what you needed. I wondered how libraries could even compete for patrons with the electronic age we live in today.

I pulled open the front door to the library and stepped inside. There was no one I could see immediately in the lobby. Unless someone was back in among the rows of books that encompassed the far end of the library, it was empty. I figured a good place to stake myself out was right at one of the tables near the entrance, so I picked up the local newspaper to check it out and see what was going on in Chandler and waited for my daughter to arrive.

Chapter 6

Kristin

It was late afternoon and I was alone at the library. Thursday was always the day we stayed open late, and Karen and I traded off working Thursday nights to keep things fair. This was Karen's week, so she had taken off early and would come back around 3 PM to pick up the evening shift. The library was often quiet between two and five anyway, with only the occasional person coming in to do some research or read.

I was able to get work done in my office and kept an ear out to hear if anyone came in or needed help at the desk. I started mapping out some ideas to get teens to come down more often to the library and see we had a lot to offer, like movie nights they would like, or getting guest speakers on topics of interest to them. It would take some work, but I was sure I could cultivate some interest in the place.

All the while when I was typing or researching on my computer, I kept up in the background the information on Wes Martin. I wasn't exactly sure why I left it there, but there was something about him that I found intriguing and, well, attractive. It had been a long while since I had a date or a boyfriend, and there was something about this man I was drawn to, even if he was thirteen years older than me.

I was staring at the picture on my computer, daydreaming, when I heard a cough out in the library that startled me. It startled me so much that I spilled coffee down the front of my white blouse. It wasn't hot, but it was enough for me to take notice right away.

"Shit!" I yelled in aggravation and reached for tissues on my desk to blot up the coffee seeping through my blouse.

"Everything okay in there?" I heard a deep voice ask from out in the library.

I froze for a moment, realizing whoever was out there just heard me swear and I was going to have to find a way to cover for it. I found myself wiping faster and faster on my blouse as I stood up to walk out there and offer help to this person.

I walked through the doorway, still wiping my blouse, and looked around, not seeing anyone standing at the front desk. I then looked over at the tables and saw a gentleman sitting there with the newspaper. He peered over the newspaper and looked at me.

"I'm sorry about that," I mumbled, still lightly wiping my blouse. "I heard you cough, it startled me and I spilled my coffee. I didn't think anyone was out here."

The gentleman placed the newspaper down and stood up, walking towards me. He was tall, wearing a black leather jacket and blue jeans. He did not look like the typical patron here at our library. He was what my mother always called a "manly man" – he was tall, looked rugged and strong, and had the walk and demeanor of someone that was confident.

He stood in front of me while I was behind the front desk, still furiously wiping my blouse, and suddenly I felt like a nervous schoolgirl in front of him. Even the smell of him, the mix of the cologne he wore, the soap he used, and his leather jacket, was making me feel weak in the knees. I got a closer look at him, and while he seemed somewhat familiar to me, I could not place him at all.

"I didn't mean to startle you," he said to me nicely. "I just had a tickle in my throat is all. Must be the air in here."

"Well, it is a bit dusty in here sometimes," I replied.

Really, talking about dust? Get with it, Kristin! I thought to myself.

"I hope it didn't ruin your blouse," he said to me as he looked down at me. It was then that I realized the coffee stain was right on my right breast and had soaked through the white blouse enough so that my shirt was a bit see-through, revealing the lacy cups of my favorite bra. I now felt even smaller and blushed a bit.

"Oh, I'm sure it's fine. No worries, it was my fault completely," I said as I reached over and grabbed Karen's red cardigan sweater that was hanging on the back of a chair and quickly put it on so I could cover up. "Is there something I can help you with?" I asked, looking to change the subject. His deep blue eyes now moved up from the sweater to meet mine.

"I'm just meeting my daughter here after school," he told me. I saw him look around the library. "I haven't been here in a long time," he said to me. "It looks like there have been some changes." His eyes came back and rested on me once again. He was much taller than me, perhaps almost a foot, and just having him standing there talking to me was making me feel giddy.

"Yes," I said, clearing my throat, "I have tried to update the place a bit since I have been here," I said proudly.

He turned to me again after looking around some more. "Oh, you're new in town?" he asked me.

"Well, I have been here for about two months, so I guess I am still new. I'm the librarian, Kristin Arthur," I said to him, holding out my hand.

He reached over and took my hand in his to shake it. I could feel the warm, strong grip of his hand right away, and it sent shivers through my body.

"It's nice to meet you, Kristin," he said with a smile. "I'm Wes Martin."

I mindlessly kept shaking his hand, enthralled by his look and touch. I felt even more embarrassed that I did not recognize him right away, but with the clean-shaven face and short hair, he did not look like any of the pictures I was just ogling on my computer.

"The... the baseball player, right?" I said as I gently pulled my hand away.

"That's right," he said as he looked down, almost as if he felt embarrassed by his fame. "Do you follow baseball?" he asked me.

"No... I mean not really... I was never a big sports person. I'm sorry," I said, feeling flustered.

Wes let out a light laugh. "Don't apologize," he said to me. "You don't have to be a baseball fan. It's kind of nice to meet someone in this town who isn't."

I could feel my feet shuffling on the floor as I looked for something else to say, and then it dawned on me.

"You said you're meeting your daughter here?" I asked him. "Is that Isabelle Martin?"

He looked surprised that I knew who she was. "Do you know Izzy?" he asked.

"Well, not really, we just met yesterday," I said honestly. "I brought a book out to her yesterday that she asked about."

"You brought a book out to her? Is that some new policy at the library to make deliveries?"

"She... she had sent me an email asking about Dracula and that she wanted it to read with her grandmother, and I thought if she couldn't get here..." I was fumbling for words again, not sure if he was upset I went out there or not.

Wes laughed again. "It's okay, really," he said as he looked into my eyes again. "Izzy and my mother read a lot. It was very nice of you to do that."

I could feel myself blushing again as my body felt a warm rush go through it. Wes stepped closer to the front desk.

"Now that I know you deliver, I may take you up on that service," he said, smiling at me.

I couldn't believe he was flirting with me. The line was a little lame, but he clearly was flirting to see if I was interested.

"I'd be happy to help," I said quietly, gazing up at him.

Just then I heard the front door open and close.

"Dad?" a voice questioned. I saw Wes turn quickly towards the front door, and I looked over as our gaze broke.

Isabelle ran over to her father and gave him a big hug around his waist. Wes hugged her tightly back.

"What are you doing here?" she said as she kept hugging him. She broke the hug quickly and looked up at her father. "Is everything okay? Is it Grandma?"

"Everything's fine Izzy," he said, comforting her. "There's nothing wrong with Grandma. And if there were, why would I be at the library?" he said.

"Why aren't you in Florida?" she asked, looking up into his face. He looked over at me, and I moved to try to busy myself with some work behind the counter so that it seemed like I wasn't intruding.

"It's a long story; I can explain it to you at home," he said as he started to move her towards the door.

"Wait," she said to him. Isabelle walked over to me at the counter and handed me a book. "Here's your book back," she said to me with a smile, giving me the copy of Dracula.

"You finished it already?" I said to her, shocked she read it that fast.

"Yeah," Isabelle told me. "I read some with my grandmother, about half, and then she fell asleep, so I just kept reading it until I was done. It was really good. Thanks for bringing it out to us."

"Sure, no problem," I said to her as I put the book to the side. I watched Isabelle walk back over to her father, giving him an admiring look as she put her arm around his waist.

Wes looked back over at me and smiled. "Thank you for your help, Kristin," he said to me.

"You're welcome," I replied. "Come back again soon," I told Wes. "I mean... the both of you." I was feeling flustered again.

"I'm sure we will." Wes and Isabelle walked out the front door, passing Karen just as she was walking in. She smiled at them as they passed, and then shot me a look as she raced over to me at the desk.

"That was him!" she shouted.

"I know it was him," I said to her casually. "What are you doing back here already? You're not due back here yet."

"I was running errands and thought I would come in and grab my sweater," Karen told me then narrowed her eyes. "Why are you wearing my sweater?"

I looked down at the sweater and blushed. "I spilled coffee on my blouse as soon as Wes walked in, and... well..." I pulled the right side of the sweater open to reveal the stain on my shirt.

"Nice look," she said to me sarcastically. "Cute bra, by the way," Karen told me. "I am sure 'Wes' liked it too."

"That is his name Karen," I said, trying to justify my words.

"Oh, I know it is. Funny how you call Clyde Stuart 'Mr. Stuart' when he comes in, and not Clyde."

"Clyde Stuart is seventy years old," I replied.

"My point exactly," Karen answered. "You are completely crushing on Wes Martin right now."

I stood there, trying to think of a defense for myself, but I couldn't come up with anything. "So, what if I am?" I said defensively. "You saw him, and he seems very nice, and he was so sweet with his daughter... and... and I think he was flirting with me," I said shyly.

Karen moved behind the counter and gave my shoulder a light push.

"Get out!" she shouted.

I let out a little laugh. "He did," I told Karen. "It was a little corny, but it was definitely flirting. I am sure he does it all the time with women."

"Not that I know of," Karen said as she sat down in the chair, spinning it around. "Kris, I've lived here my whole life, and I grew up with the legend of Wes Martin. I've seen him around town after his wife left him, and I never saw him flirt with anyone. He's always polite and cordial, but that's about it. If he was flirting with you, he's got some interest."

Hearing Karen say that made me feel pretty good about myself, and it made me wonder if I would see more of Wes Martin anytime soon.

Karen cleared her throat to snap me out of the haze.

"What?" I said to her.

"You might want to go home and change your blouse before Clyde Stuart comes in and lets the rest of the town know you're putting on a show at the library today," Karen said with a laugh.

I turned red and took off her sweater, handing it to her. I quickly grabbed my coat and put it on to cover up, and hustled out the door.

Part of me was hoping I would run into Wes again in the parking lot, but when I got out to my car, they were nowhere to be found. I climbed into my car and drove back to my apartment, still thinking about those blue eyes looking at me.

Chapter 7

Wes

Isabelle seemed genuinely surprised to see me, and we made our way out of the library back to my SUV. She climbed into the front seat next to mine, and as I started the car, she immediately jumped into a conversation.

"Really Dad, why are you home?" She had a worried look on her face like I was keeping something from her.

"It's nothing to worry about honey," I said to her as I backed out of the spot and turned left down Main Street to head back home. I glanced over and could see she was still staring at me, waiting for an answer. "The team released me yesterday," I finally said to her.

"Why would they do that?" Izzy yelled.

"Well, I can give you a lot of reasons that might not make much sense to you or to me either, but none of that matters. The fact is that they did it, and for now, I don't have a team to go to."

"Does this mean you are done playing baseball?"

That idea hadn't set in as a final fact just yet, and I paused for a moment before I answered her.

"I don't think it does; not yet anyway," I told Izzy. "We'll just have to wait and see how things play out."

Izzy still looked worried, and I was trying to take her mind off it. "For now, we get to spend some time together. You get to have me at home." I smiled over at her, but I didn't see the smile I had hoped for come right back to me.

"What's the problem?" I asked as we turned towards our road.

"It's not that I'm not happy you're here Dad," Izzy stated. "But I have my routine here of what I do at school and at home, and, well, having you here changes all that."

"I'm sorry if I'm disrupting your schedule," I said, feeling a little hurt.

"I knew you were going to take it the wrong way," Izzy said with a huff, crossing her arms.

I drove the SUV passed my parent's house and up the hill to our house.

"Where are you going?" Izzy asked me.

"I'm going to our house. It's where we live," I said, trying to exert some control of the situation. I pulled the SUV around the circular drive, so it was parked right in front of the front door.

"All the stuff I need is at Grandma and Grandpa's," Izzy told me.

"Like what?" I asked as I got out of the car.

"Stuff for school, my laptop, my speaker for my music, clothes I like to wear. It may surprise you to learn that I live THERE most of the year, remember?"

"Isabelle, don't take that tone," I gave her a stern look as I grabbed a few bags out of the trunk and started walking up the stone steps to the house. I searched around in my pockets for my keys before I realized I didn't have a key to the house with me. I always left them with my parents when I left for spring training, and they were still down there. I turned and saw Izzy standing next to the SUV with a defiant smirk on her face.

"See, you don't even have keys to your own house!" she screamed. She grabbed her backpack off the front seat of the car and stormed down the hill towards my parents' house. I picked the bags I had taken to the door and hurtled them into the trunk, slamming it closed loudly. I saw Izzy flinch as she heard the slam and she looked back at me, surprised I could get that angry. I marched down the hill to catch up to her, but she kept moving faster so I couldn't quite get to where she was. As we got to my parents' house, she started in a full run and ran up the porch steps and inside. I followed right after her, but she was already inside, and I heard her slam the door to her bedroom. Mom and Dad both came into the living room to see me standing there.

"What was all that?" my father said to me.

"Izzy," I said, catching my breath. "You can see she's thrilled to have me home."

"I'll talk to her," my mother said as she walked slowly down the hall towards Izzy's room. I sat down on the couch, and my Dad sat in his recliner to my right.

"I take it you caught her off guard," Dad said to me as he popped the recliner back a bit.

"Everything seemed to be okay until I told her I was going to be home for a bit, and then she freaked out, saying I was disrupting her routine." I shook my head in disbelief as I looked at my father.

"Well, you are disrupting her routine Wes."

"Thanks for the support Dad."

"Look at her from her view," Dad said to me. "Eight years ago, her life gets thrown into turmoil, and she starts living with us for most of the year. She loves the time she gets to spend with you, but for all intents and purposes, she lives here... this is what she knows. She gets home from school, does her homework, does chores, spends time with her friends, goes out and does things... all the things a teenager is supposed to do. Having you around means changing all that again."

I sat back on the couch and looked at my father. I knew he was right as much as I didn't want to admit it to myself.

"So, what I am supposed to do, Dad? Just let her stay down here while I'm in the house by myself?"

"I'm sure we can work something out," he said confidently. "Besides, you don't know how long you're going to be here. It could be a day, a week, a few weeks, who knows? Why cause upheaval today only to do it again right away?"

"I guess you're right," I said, admitting defeat. "I guess I was just hoping Izzy would be happier I was here."

"I'm sure she is happy you're here, but the initial shock of it all might take away from that. Give her some time."

My mother came walking down the hall, Izzy following close behind, her eyes a little puffy from crying. She still scowled at me a bit. My mother looked back at her, arched an eyebrow at Izzy, and Izzy came over to the couch and sat next to me.

"Izzy, I'm sorry," I told her. "I know you have your life established here, and I don't want to cause a problem, so how about we work something out where you can spend time down here and then, if I am still here after a few days, you come up to the house and stay with me? Is that fair?"

Izzy looked at me and sniffled. "Okay," she said quietly and leaned over against me. I put my arm around her, feeling better we had worked things out.

"Isabelle," my mother chimed in, "don't you have something to say to your father?"

She looked over at my mother and then at me. "I'm sorry for yelling, Dad."

"It's okay," I said, pulling her to me. "I guess we're all going to need some to adjust and get back into the swing of things."

"You looked like you were getting into the swing of things the way you were flirting with the librarian," Izzy said with a teenage giggle.

I looked at her quickly. "What are you talking about? I wasn't flirting."

"Oh please Dad," Izzy said, rolling her eyes. "The two of you were making goo-goo eyes at each other. Anyone could see it."

"What happened?" my mother asked, sitting in her lounge chair, taking a greater interest in the conversation than before.

"When I walked into the library, Dad was there talking to Ms. Arthur, the new librarian. They were, you know, flirting."

"How do you know what flirting is?" I asked Izzy.

"Dad, come on," she said to me, aghast that I couldn't believe she would know what flirting is. "I'm fifteen, Dad, not seven. I see flirting on TV, in movies, in books. Boys flirt with me all the time." She quickly put her hand to her mouth, wishing she could take back that last part.

"What boys?" I asked, feeling my paternal protection kick in.

"Just boys at school Dad, it's nothing."

"Let's get back to you flirting with the librarian," my mother said to me.

Izzy took the opening and got up off the couch. "I'm going to do my homework!" she yelled and tore off down the hall.

I looked at my father, and then my mother, and back to my father again. They were both looking at me, waiting for an answer.

"So?" my mother said to me.

"I was just talking to her Mom," I said in my defense. "I would hardly call it flirting."

"Is she pretty?" my mother asked.

"Oh yes," I replied, and heard my Dad reply at the same time. Mom shot him a look.

"Well, she is," my father said, fidgeting in his chair.

"When did you see her?" my mother said, turning the heat up on Dad instead of me.

"I met some of the boys down at Harding's Diner for breakfast one morning, and she walked by on her way to the library. Clyde Stuart was talking all about her the whole time. She seems like a very pretty girl. Everyone in town says she's been great for the community."

Mom sat there silently for a moment, and then seemingly satisfied with Dad's answer, turned back to me.

"Wes, it's none of my business what you do with your personal life," Mom started. I already knew where the conversation was headed. "But, it's been a long time since you have seen anyone or gone on a date, and if Izzy noticed a little "something" between you, then maybe it's worth exploring."

"Mom," I answered, "she looks like she's not much older than Izzy."

"She's twenty-two," Dad interjected. Mom gave him another glare. "That's what Clyde said, I swear," Dad said, putting his hand over his heart.

"All I'm saying is if you're going to be around town for a little bit that you might want to see what's out there for you. You don't want to be alone, Wes."

Mom was right; I didn't want to be alone. Kristin Arthur was an incredibly attractive woman, and I did sense there was some chemistry between us during our brief conversation. Honestly, I knew I was flirting with her, even though it was a lame attempt at it. But, she didn't shoot me down, which was a good thing.

"I'll certainly give it some thought, okay?" I said, hoping this would appease my parents.

"Thank you," Mom told me. "Now, what are we having for dinner tonight? I'm hungry!"

I looked over at Dad to see if he had an answer, but he just looked back at me.

"Don't look at me," I told him. "I might have a bottle of ketchup at the house, and that's it."

"I guess we're taking a ride down to Wally's," Dad said, referring to the local supermarket. He got up from the recliner and looked at me.

"We'll be back with dinner," I said as I got off the couch and followed Dad to the front door.

"Stay out of trouble, you two," Mom said with a smile. "And Wyatt?" Mom said to Dad. Dad turned to look at her.

"You stay away from Clyde Stuart," she offered.

Dad blew her a kiss as he walked rapidly out the door with me.

Chapter 8

Kristin

It only took me two minutes to get back to my apartment. I rushed inside and went into my bedroom looking for a clean shirt that was suitable to wear back to the library. I found a nice green blouse that I liked, and I had just stripped out of my soggy white blouse when Karen sent me a text message. She said since I was already home and it was quiet, she could cover the rest of the day at the library. I flopped back on my bed and relaxed for a minute, thinking about how I would spend the rest of the day.

My first thought was to just put my pajamas on, crawl into bed and see what movies I could watch on Netflix for the rest of the day. I could enjoy a nice bowl of soup or a sandwich and just be a vegetable for the rest of the day. I threw on a pair of my plaid sleep pants and an old t-shirt and wandered out to the kitchen to see what I could fix for a meal.

I opened the fridge, and it was like a ghost town in there. I realized then that I hadn't been shopping for about ten days. Other than a couple of half-eaten Chinese food containers, some yogurt and what may have been some vegetables that were now past their prime in the vegetable drawer, there wasn't anything in there that would do.

I guess I'm going shopping I thought to myself. I walked back into my bedroom, feeling defeated because I would have to get dressed again so I could go down to Wally's for some food. I grabbed a pair of jeans from my dresser, took off the pajama pants, and put the jeans on. I looked in the mirror over my dresser and decided to give myself a more relaxed look and tied my hair up in a ponytail. It would be a quick trip out, so I didn't feel that I needed to look my best.

I took my lightweight, blue windbreaker from the hook by the door and picked up a couple of my canvas bags that I used for shopping and decided to head over to Wally's. Wally's was just a few short blocks away, so walking was never a problem there for me. One of the great things about living in a small town is that nearly everything is within walking distance. As I got more familiar with where everything was in the town, like the post office, movie theater, places to eat, and so on, Chandler began to feel much more like home to me.

The sun was still shining nicely, and the day had begun to warm up from the chill that was there this morning, making it feel much more like a spring day that you could enjoy outside. I walked down the street and I went passed Harding's Diner, where I could see the usual group of older men gathered at their regular table by the window. Clyde Stuart was busy holding court there, and he smiled at me as I went by the window. The other men at the table all turned and waved to me as well, and I gave them back a friendly smile and wave as I went.

Just down the block from the diner, beyond the flower shop and antique store, was Wally's. Wally's was a lot smaller than the typical supermarket I had grown used to seeing in Georgia, but it was representative of what you might find in a smaller town. It was owned and run by the Walters family, and the third generation of Wally Walters was now in charge. The store always had everything you could need, including a great assortment of fresh local vegetables and meats.

I grabbed a shopping cart from the row by the door and began to make my way through the market. I was still feeling in the mood for some soup tonight, so I grabbed some carrots, celery, and zucchini from the produce section. I picked up some greens as well so I could have something for salads later in the week as well.

I wandered around from aisle to aisle, picking up things here and there that I might need for dinner both tonight and in the days ahead, but my mind wasn't really on shopping. I kept thinking back to meeting Wes Martin in the library and what that was like. He was this famous, eye-catching, older man that I know I felt some attraction to right away, something that did not typically happen to me. I thought back to the guys I had dated in college, and they were always all about my age. I would have never even consider dating a guy that was barely older than me back in school, let alone someone that was thirteen years my senior. But here I was, mooning over this man I barely knew other than that one brief interaction and some cyber-stalking on the Internet.

I turned up the next aisle and walked over towards the meat department so I could get some beef or chicken to go with my soup. As I was walking past the corner of the aisle, my cart rammed into another coming from the left. I was startled and jarred and looked over quickly to see who I had hit. There stood Wes Martin with an older gentleman, both standing behind the cart that I had just hit.

"Fancy meeting you here," Wes said to me with a smile.

I felt completely embarrassed and turned red.

"I'm so sorry," I said to him, looking at our carts. "I guess I was daydreaming," I said and wanted to take it back as soon as I heard the words come out of my mouth.

"Not a problem," Wes said to me. "I hope you were dreaming of something good at least."

I laughed, hoping to cover up what I was thinking. The older gentleman, a distinguished looking man who was just a bit shorter and thinner than Wes, but looked just as strong, elbowed Wes as we stood there.

"Oh, Kristin, this is my father, Wyatt Martin," Wes told me.

"Nice to meet you, Mr. Martin," I said, shaking his hand. He had the same firm, strong grip Wes had in his hands.

"Please, call me Wyatt," he said as we shook hands. "It's nice to meet you. I've heard great things about what you have done with the library."

"Oh, thank you," I replied. "I'm doing my best, trying to make things better for all of us here in Chandler."

The three of us stood in awkward silence for a minute.

"Out doing some shopping?" I said to Wes.

Nice Kristin. Of course, he's doing shopping; you're in the supermarket! I felt like slowly slinking away.

"Well," Wes began, "I haven't been home for a while, so there's not much in the way of food at the house right now. We thought we would have a nice dinner tonight since we're all together."

"That sounds nice," I said, still trying to think of things to say that were at least interesting, or made sense.

I heard a man clear his throat and looked up and saw Vince, the butcher, behind the meat counter, looking at us.

"Can I help either of you?" Vince said politely.

Wes waved me ahead of him politely, and I walked over to the counter. I asked for some boneless chicken breasts and a sirloin steak I planned to use either for either steak or soup. Vince wrapped everything up nicely for me and handed it to me quickly so he could get to the Martins.

I placed my items in my cart and went to move on.

"That's all you're getting?" Wes asked me.

"It's just me, and I don't need much I guess," I told him. "I just kind of shop when I need to get stuff, and I'm only making soup for one tonight."

"Okay," he said as his father talked with Vince, ordering some steaks. We stood looking at each other again for a few seconds again. I didn't know how long I could stand there with him before starting to shake.

"Enjoy your dinner tonight," I said to him as I moved away.

"Thank you, Kristin," he said to me politely as he turned to go over towards his father.

I worked to finish up the rest of my shopping as quickly as I could, getting the rest of the things I needed for my dinner so I could get out of there without feeling completely lost and tongue-tied again. After gathering the rest of my items, I got up to the checkout counter and waited on line.

Mrs. Findley, a kindly, older woman, was on the line in front of me with quite a full cart, so it was taking a while to get rung up. She was chatting idly with the cashier about the prices of nearly everything that got scanned, and then she had her stack of paper coupons to get through as well. I glanced around at the impulse buy items up near the register and found myself tossing a candy bar or two into my cart while I waited. I noticed the register next to me had just opened, and Wes and his father were already unloading their cart at it. I tried not to look at them, instead focusing on the celebrity scandal magazines at the counter so I could see who was cheating on who this week.

Finally, Mrs. Findley finished and moved on, so I could get my items up on the belt and get finished. I tried to get everything done quickly so I could get out of the store and back home. I cordially smiled at the woman who was the cashier while piling my items up to get scanned. There wasn't much there, so the work was done fast, and I even sped things up by putting the items in my own bags. I paid for my groceries and when I looked up I saw that the Martins were already gone, letting me breathe a bit of a sigh of relief.

I walked out of Wally's, bags slung over my shoulder, ready for my walk home. I got up the street just before the diner when I saw Wes loading the items he had bought into the back of his pickup truck. He glanced over as he was shutting the tailgate, saw me and smiled again.

He walked up on the curb and leaned on the side of the truck.

"Got everything you need?" he asked me.

"I think so," I told him. "How about you?"

"It was more than enough to get started, but I'm sure I'll be back to restock things." I tried not to stare and broke my gaze at him, looking down at the sidewalk.

"Do you... do you need a ride home?" Wes asked me.

I felt butterflies in my stomach for some reason.

"Oh, no, thanks; I only live right over there," pointing to the small apartment building two blocks away.

Why would you say no?

"Oh, okay," Wes said, seeming almost like he was disappointed I said no. I struggled to come up with something else to say to him, but I couldn't think of anything, so I started slowly stepping away.

"Kristin," Wes called out to me. I turned and looked at him and saw he was walking closer to me. I looked up at him as he was in front of me. His broad shoulders blocked out the sun that was slowly setting behind him, keeping the glare from my face but framing him in a radiant glow.

"Yes?" I answered.

"If you're not busy, I thought, maybe... maybe you would like to get together tomorrow night, maybe for dinner, or a drink?" Wes looked impossibly adorable at this moment, like a teenager approaching a girl for the first time.

I don't know how long he was staring at me, waiting for an answer, but I finally snapped out of my frozen state.

"I would love to," I replied quietly.

"Great," he said, looking relieved. "We can go to Angelo's if you like. Say around seven?"

"Sure, that's perfect," I told him. "Angelo's is only a block away from my place. I can meet you there if you'd like."

"Okay," Wes looked at me and saw his father coming out of the diner behind me. I turned to look as well and saw the group of men staring out the diner window at the two of us.

"I guess I'll see you tomorrow night," I said as I started walking up the street again. I tried hard to contain the big smile on my face as I walked past Wyatt Martin. Wyatt tipped the cowboy hat he was wearing to me.

"It was nice to meet you, Wyatt," I told him as I walked by.

"Same here, Kristin," he said as he smiled. I glanced up at my viewers in the diner window, all of them still smiling down at me.

I couldn't help but feel that Wes was watching me as I walked down the street, and I took a quick glance over my left shoulder, catching him looking at me as he was climbing into the passenger seat of the truck.

I guess I have a date tomorrow, I thought with glee, my mind racing about how I would have to get ready for tomorrow.

Chapter 9

Wes

S hopping at Wally's, or anyplace in Chandler for that matter, was never something that I relished. Don't get me wrong – I love people that are fans, and I am more than happy to stop and pose for pictures or sign autographs. After all, it's the fans that allow me to do what I do, and I am appreciative. But, the problem with being in your hometown is that everyone feels like they are an integral part of you and what you do, and they all want to give you advice regarding what to do. When I became a free agent years ago, everyone in town had advice about where I should sign, what I should do, what to ask for, and so on. I never had any intention of leaving the Pirates, and the team knew that from the start, so it was just a matter of time before I signed with them, but I would still get people coming up to me in a panic over it.

Things were not going to be any better now that I had been released from the team, and I wasn't looking forward to having to deal with all the questions and advice. Dad drove us to Wally's in his pickup, and he could see some concern on my face.

"You know, Wes," he said as we pulled up in front of the diner to park the truck, "there aren't going to be a lot of people in Wally's this time of day anyway. You don't have to worry about getting bombarded. Besides, at some point, you are going to have to deal with it. It might be better to get things over with sooner rather than later."

"I know Dad," I told him as I took off my seatbelt to get out of the truck. "I just hate having to listen to it and talk about it." I got out of the truck and closed the door, stepping onto the sidewalk. I looked over at the diner and saw Clyde Stuart and his gang at their table, arguing over something, and they quickly pointed when they saw Dad and me. I gave a wave and walked right into Wally's so I didn't have to deal with them, and Dad quickly followed.

To be honest, I had no idea what I needed at the house since I hadn't been there since January. During the season, if I knew I was going to be home either for a day, during a break, or when the season was ending, Dad would stock the house for me or I would have the service that cleans the house do it for me. But, since no one knew I was coming home this time, it wasn't prepared. I figured I would just get some basics and what we needed for dinner and that would be it.

"How about some steaks tonight?" Dad said as we walked in and right towards the meat counter.

"Sounds good to me," I answered, looking around briefly to see what was going on in the store. Dad was right; there weren't many people in the place at this time of day, which was a relief to me. We walked down one of the aisles, and I grabbed just a few things on the way to the butcher. As we get to the end of the aisle, we collided with another cart. To my surprise, it was Kristin.

She seemed just as shocked as I was to see her. Her blonde hair was pulled back nicely into a ponytail, and she wore a simple pair of jeans, and a t-shirt that was barely visible underneath the windbreaker she wore. To me, she looked even more attractive than when I had seen her in the library in her work clothes.

Kristin apologized for the cart collision, and we both tried to make some small talk, but we both seemed to fumble for our words. I introduced her to Dad, who was his usual affable and charming self. Dad had a much better way of talking with people than I ever did and seemed more at ease with everyone. It didn't matter if it was a friend he had for forty years or someone he just met – he still could engage with them right away and make them feel at ease.

I did the gentlemanly thing and let Kristin order from the butcher before us. I found I couldn't take my eyes off her as we waited, and Dad noticed this, especially when I saw her reach over to the top of the counter where the butcher had placed her packages. Her reaching pulled her windbreaker and shirt up just a hint to reveal a bit of bare flesh between her shirt and jeans.

"Don't stare, Wes" Dad whispered as he elbowed me. He then went over to order our steaks while I talked with Kristin again briefly. I was watching her walk away again when Dad returned to the cart with the steaks, a big smile on his lips.

"So?" he asked me.

"So, what?" I said, oblivious to what he was asking.

"Did you ask her out?"

"No, I didn't," I said as I pushed the cart towards the produce so we could get some vegetables to go with dinner.

Dad just shook his head at me. "I went to get the steaks to give you some time to talk to her. Jesus, Wes, you are bad at this. I saw the way she was looking at you. Izzy was right about what she said. You should just ask her out."

"I didn't realize I needed dating advice from my father," I said as I walked over to grab some Russet potatoes to go with dinner.

"Well someone needs to get you moving in the right direction. You can't seem to do it yourself."

"Thanks for your confidence in me, Dad." I picked up some other vegetables to go with dinner and saw Dad looking around.

"Okay, I think we're done," Dad said to me, taking control of the cart and pushing it towards the registers.

"Dad, I didn't get anything for the house," I said as he moved away from me.

"You can order stuff from the service tomorrow; let's go," he said as we pulled into a register that was just opening.

I helped him put the few things we got on the conveyor belt as a young man scanned our items. The cashier looked to be in high school, and I could see that he recognized me, but I just went about my business. I could see Kristin was on the register line next to ours, but she was occupied looking at the magazines at the register.

All our items were scanned and packed before Kristin even got up to her cashier. Before I even had a chance to pay, Dad had already taken care of the bill and was grabbing the bags to take them out to the truck. I followed him quickly, saying a fast thanks to the cashier, who beamed a big smile back at me.

Dad was placing the bags next to the truck when I got out there.

"What was that all about?" I asked him.

"Strategy, boy," Dad said to me. "Now, listen to me closely. You load the bags into the truck. I am going to the diner to talk to the guys for a few minutes. Kristin walks by here on her way home so she will have to pass you. You will have your chance then to talk to her, so take advantage of it." Dad then walked away, going to the diner and greeting his friends.

I opened the tailgate of the truck and placed the few bags we had in the truck bed. Sure enough, moments later, Kristin was walking out of Wally's with her bags. She looked up and saw me as I was closing the tailgate.

"Got everything you need?" I asked her.

"I think so," she told me, "How about you?"

"It was more than enough to get started, but I'm sure I'll be back to restock things," even though I knew we barely bought anything because Dad rushed me out of the store. We both stood there not saying anything as I tried to come up with conversation.

"Do you... do you need a ride home?" I asked, even though from what Dad told me, she lived nearby. I was just trying to buy myself some time to think of what else to say.

"Oh, no, thanks; I only live right over there," she told me, pointing to the apartment building right along Main Street.

I was disappointed she said no since it would have given me more time with her. I had never felt this inadequate speaking with a woman before. I saw that she turned as if to start walking away, so I had to make a move if I was going to do something today. I looked up to see Dad and his cohorts staring out the diner window at us and Dad frantically waved his arm at me, indicating I should move closer to her.

"Kristin," I called out to her. I moved over onto the sidewalk, standing in front of her. She looked up at me, waiting to see what I would say.

"If you're not busy, I thought, maybe... maybe you would like to get together tomorrow night, maybe for dinner, or a drink?" I could feel myself shifting on my feet. It brought me back to that first time I had asked Rachel out when we were teenagers and how nervous I was about that.

I could see Kristin looking up at me, squinting a bit because of the sun from behind me. I waited for an answer that seemed like it took hours to give.

"I would love to," she said to me with a smile.

I huge feeling of relief washed over me.

"Great," I said to her. "We can go to Angelo's if you like. Say around seven?" I had looked beyond her and saw the sign for Angelo's down the street, and it was the only place I could think of spur of the moment.

"Sure, that's perfect," she said to me. "Angelo's is only a block or so away from my place. I can meet you there if you like."

"Okay," I said to her as I looked at her. I took a quick glance and saw Dad coming out of the diner behind Kristin. The old guys in the window were all giving me thumbs up signs. Kristin turned around and saw the group of men staring out the diner window at the two of us, and they all had put their thumbs down before she turned and gave congenial smiles to us.

"I guess I'll see you tomorrow night," Kristin said as she turned to walk away. I saw my Dad tip his hat to her as she walked past him.

Dad reached my position on the sidewalk.

"Always the suave gentleman cowboy, Dad," I said to him quietly. He walked around to the driver's side of the truck. I stood by the passenger's side, watching Kristin walk away. She took a brief glimpse over her shoulder back at me before I climbed into the truck.

"Suaver than you'll ever be, son," Dad said to me with a sideways glance as I closed the truck door. "That was like watching someone get a tooth pulled."

"Well, you and your cronies didn't have to watch the whole thing."

Dad drove the truck towards Route 5 to get to the house.

"You must have dates when you're playing during the season, Wes. How do you ask them out?" Dad asked me as he drove.

"I don't know, it just seems easier then," I said to him. "I feel more confident at that time. The surroundings are different. And I know most of those women I would only see once or twice, and that's it. Kristin... I don't know... she throws me off track."

Dad just smiled as he drove and laughed a little.

"What's so funny?"

"Nothing," he said, still laughing. "I just thought if those guys at ESPN or some sports channel could see you. The big, burly, baseball star getting all tongue-tied and twisted up over a woman half his size."

"You're a riot, Dad. I can see I am going to love being at home."

As we pulled onto Martin Way, I knew Dad was right. Kristin Arthur was twisting me all up, and we had just met hours ago. It made me nervous to think about what might happen tomorrow.

Chapter 10

Kristin

I felt like I floated home the two blocks back to my apartment. By the time I got inside, I didn't even feel like making my soup for dinner or doing anything else. I wanted to burst inside and had to talk to someone. I thought about texting Karen at the library to let her know, but I knew if I did that she would be completely distracted for the rest of the night while at work. I decided I would let her know the good news in the morning.

I quickly realized I didn't have any other girlfriends in Chandler that I could talk with and confide in about stuff like this. I made a resolution that this was something I was going to work on, but for now, I had to get a hold of someone to let them know what was going on.

I grabbed my laptop and made a video call to my sister Lucy. Lucy was still living in Georgia and loving life there. She had received her nursing degree and was working at a hospital not far from my parents. She normally worked the night shift so I thought I might just catch her before she left to go to work.

I opened the program and clicked on her name to make the call to her. The call rang for what seemed like an interminable number of times, and I was getting ready to disconnect and close my laptop when the screen finally opened, and there was Lucy. I could see she was dressed in her pink scrubs top, with her blonde hair pulled back into a ponytail similar to mine. No one could ever doubt we were sisters.

"Hey, Kris, what's up? I was getting ready to leave for work. Everything okay?" she said to me.

"Everything's fine, I just wanted to call you and see what was going on."

"No, you didn't," Lucy said to me, getting that serious look on her face. "I can see the way your eyes are bouncing around. You have something you want to share, so spill it."

I was glad she noticed because I wasn't sure how long I could contain myself. "I met someone," I said excitedly, "and we have a date tomorrow night."

"Great," Lucy said as she slipped the lanyard with her hospital badge on it over her head, seeming not nearly as excited as I hoped she would be.

"Well you could be more excited for me," I said, disappointed in her reaction.

"No offense, Kris, but it's just a date," she looked back at the screen at me. "Unless it's more than a regular date? I can see it on your face. Give me details."

I explained to Lucy that it was with Wes Martin. Lucy, who was always much more into sports, knew who he was right away. Lucy was always an avid Braves fan and followed baseball closely, and now she was excited.

"I didn't realize he lived there," Lucy said to me.

"I didn't either," I told her, trying to act like I knew who he was. "We just met today."

"You know why he's home, don't you Kris?"

"I have no idea why, but I'm glad he is."

"Kris, he got released by the Pirates yesterday. It means he's off the team. You may want to be careful with how you approach this."

I sat back on my bed as I talked to her. "Why do I need to be careful?"

"First, he just lost his job, and may not take that too well. Second, he could sign with another team at any moment and end up a thousand miles away from you by the weekend and be gone for eight months. Third..." Lucy hesitated for a moment before going on.

"What else?" I said, wondering what other problems there could possibly be.

"Kris, he's thirty-five and a professional athlete. He's a lot older than you, has seen and done a lot more, and probably has a laundry list of women around the country that he sees, dates and beds. Maybe you don't want to be just another notch on his belt."

I considered all that Lucy just said to me. I knew she was trying to help me and protect me, but it was hurtful to pop my balloon just like that.

"I don't think he's like that Lucy," I said, defending Wes. "He seems very... genuine. And I know he's older than me, but that doesn't matter. You've dated doctors older than you."

"Fair enough," Lucy said to me. "I just don't want you to get your hopes up and then get hurt. I'm just trying to look out for you Kris. You're up there by yourself, maybe you're lonely, a little vulnerable, and this famous guy comes along and asks you out... it just sounds like..."

"Sounds like what?" I said angrily.

"To be blunt, it sounds like he wants to lay a cute twenty-two-year-old and brag to his buddies about it. I'm sorry, but it does."

"Thanks for your support, Lucy," I said as I went to slam my laptop shut.

"Kris, wait!" Lucy yelled. I stopped short before I closed the laptop and pulled it open again. "I'm sorry. I hope I'm wrong about him. Just go into the date with the right frame of mind, okay?"

"I will, I promise," I replied.

"Okay," Lucy said, feeling better. "I have to go to work. Let me know how the date goes. I miss you, sis. Love you."

"I miss you too," I told her, feeling misty-eyed now. "Love you too."

The screen went black as Lucy hung up. I closed the laptop and got up to put it on my desk. I walked into the kitchen and started chopping vegetables for my soup, thinking the whole time about what Lucy had just said. There were a lot of factors to consider here about Wes Martin. I really didn't know him at all, and not nearly enough to feel as caught up in him as I was feeling already.

Maybe Lucy was right, and I needed to be more cautious. He could leave in a few days, and I would never see him again. Or maybe he was just looking to add another woman to his list of those he slept with. I was lonely sometimes here, and it was nice to get some attention from a man, especially one that found me attractive and wanted to spend time with me. Maybe that did make me more vulnerable than usual and cloud my judgment.

Even with all those questions, part of me still felt Lucy was wrong. Wes didn't seem like the guy she was describing. He seemed much more unsure of himself when he was with me, not like some of the confident, cocky athletes that you read about on the Internet that are dating different models all the time.

As I finished making my soup and poured some into a big cup so I could sit on my couch and watch a movie, I decided I was going to have to form my own opinion of Wes. No matter what Lucy said, Karen said, what the Internet said or how much older he was than me, I had to see for myself what he was like on this date tomorrow to see where things would go.

I was the only one that could decide what Wes Martin was like and what he might or might not mean to my life.

Chapter 11

Wes

Dinner with my parents and Izzy was just what I needed to help me put the stress of the last few days behind me. We smiled, laughed, told stories, and I got caught up on everything going on around them for the last two months that I had missed. Just this one dinner made me realized how much I missed having them all as part of my life each day when I was out on the road.

Naturally, Dad couldn't pass up the opportunity to mention my interaction with Kristin, and how he managed to save the day so that I could have a date tomorrow night. Izzy seemed quiet through the whole conversation about the date, and I took some good-natured ribbing from Mom and Dad throughout dessert and cleaning up the table.

After we finished cleaning up, Izzy went to her room quietly. I decided to go and talk to her to make sure everything was okay. I gently knocked on her bedroom door, and she invited me in.

Izzy was sitting at her desk, her laptop was open with some music playing quietly. Her room was decorated much like the room she had in our house, though this room was smaller than what she had in the main house. Still, she had managed to make it her own space, decorating it the way she wanted. My parents had consulted her along the way when building the room for her to be sure it was just what she needed.

I sat down on the edge of her bed while she sat in her desk chair.

"You okay?" I asked her. "You were awfully quiet at dinner and during clean up."

"I'm fine," Izzy said nonchalantly, typing away on her laptop before closing the lid and turning to face me. "It's all just a lot to take in one day I guess."

"I know, it's a big upheaval having me here," I said to her taking her hands in mine.

"It's not only that, Dad," she said as she looked at me. "It's the whole date thing too. Don't get me wrong; I'm glad to see you going out on a date, I really am. You spend way too much time alone or with just me or Grandma and Grandpa. You deserve to go out and have some fun and find someone you like. But..."

"But what?" I prodded, curious to see what she was going to say next.

"But Ms. Arthur... don't you think she's kind of young? I mean, she's only a few years older than me."

"You're only fifteen, Izzy. She's more than a few years older than you."

"I'll be sixteen in May, Dad," she defended. "She's not that much older than me. It just feels a little weird is all. Besides, you just met her."

"That's how dating works, Izzy. You meet someone you're interested in, you go out, learn more about each other, and see what happens. I'm not marrying her; it's just a dinner date. I get that you're not used to seeing this side of me. I never dated anyone when I was home with you. I wanted that time for just you and me. But I have dated other women since your mother left, when I'm out on the road or down in Pittsburgh."

Izzy nodded her head. "I know. I guess none of that ever seemed real because I never saw or met any of them. Ms. Arthur is right here... I don't know, it's silly, I suppose."

I put my arm around her and gave her a little hug. "It's not silly, honey. Believe me, I take your feelings into consideration with anything like this. And I appreciate your concern. I know she's younger than me, but there's nothing wrong with that."

"So you would be okay if it was me dating some guy who was almost thirty?"

"Hell, no," I said quietly. "I would break his legs with one of my bats. But when you're twenty-two, that decision is on you. Right now, stick to the boys in your high school. I'm even a little uncomfortable with them. Maybe just forget about boys for now and concentrate on school."

"You're funny, Dad," Izzy said to me. She stood up from the bed and placed herself in front of me.

"Are you going up to the house?" she asked me.

"Yeah, I really should get my stuff unpacked and try to get settled there and see what we need." I rose and gave her another hug and kissed her on the top of her head.

"Good night, Dad. Love you," she said, hugging me. "I am glad that you're here, you know."

"Love you too, Izzy," I said to her, holding her. "I'm glad I'm here too."

I left her room, closing the door behind me, and walked out into the living room. Dad was sitting in his recliner, reading the newspaper.

"Where's Mom?" I asked him as I stood next to his chair.

"She was tired, she went to lay down. The day took a lot out of her."

"I'm going to head up to the house. Do you have the keys?"

Dad fished the Pirates keychain out of his pocket and handed the keys to me. "You can always spend the night down here if you want," he said to me. "We have the extra bed in my office."

"Thanks, Dad, but I think I want to be in the house and sleep in my comfy, king-size bed instead," I told him. "Besides, I have the stuff to unpack and things to get to at the house. I'll stop down in the morning."

"Okay, good night, Wes," Dad said, going back to his newspaper.

"Goodnight Dad," I told him, "and thanks for your help."

"I do what I can, son," he said to me with a smile.

I walked back up the hill towards my house. The air was much cooler now that night had arrived. I could hear the quiet of the farm as I paced my way over the blacktop. When I reached the top, the motion lights came on and lit up the circular drive. I walked over and got a few bags out of the trunk, leaving my baseball gear in the back for now.

No reason to bring that in I suppose, I thought to myself.

I took the keys and unlocked the door. I heard the familiar beeping of the alarm system and punched in the code to shut the alarm off. I flipped on the lights in the foyer, and the living room area lit up. Everything looked just as it did when I left in January. The cleaning service did a great job if keeping the house dust-free and looking its best. I would have to remember to contact them in the morning to let them know I was in the house for now, so they were aware.

I carried my bags into the master bedroom, which was located downstairs and down the hall to the left of the living room. I left the bags at the foot of the bed and walked out and to the left to go towards the kitchen. I flipped the lights on there and walked over to the large refrigerator to see what was in there. Sure enough, it was empty. I then remembered the game room downstairs and decided to go there. I walked back down the hall past my bedroom and opened the door just to the right of the bedroom. The stairway there led down to the game room I had set up.

Turning the lights on down there, I could see that everything was nicely in place. The pool table was ready to be played, and the big screen TV hung nicely on the wall over the row of leather recliners and couch. I walked over to the mahogany bar at the far end of the room and picked up the remote sitting on the edge of the bar. I pointed it towards the TV, curious to turn on the sports network to see if they had anything to say about me, but then I thought better of it. Instead, I pressed the button for the sound system and turned on some music.

I looked at the beer taps on the bar, knowing they were not currently connected to anything, but the refrigerator beneath the bar would have some bottles and cans of beer in it. I reached in a grabbed a cold bottle of whatever was there first and popped the top off with the bottle opener screwed to the bar. I took a long swig and then went and sat in one of the leather recliners and looked around.

The game room was pure luxury, one of the things I treated myself to when I had the house built. It wasn't a space I used often. In fact, Izzy and her friends used it more for sleepovers than I did for entertaining friends, but I still thought of it as my space.

I sipped the beer and wondered what the next few days would hold. A quick look at my smartphone told me there was nothing from Randy, and the house phone wouldn't have any messages on it since I had it shut off whenever I left for the season.

Another thing I must remember to take care of, I suppose, I thought to myself.

I felt like I was caught in limbo every which way. I was without a team or job, but that could change at any moment. I was without Izzy, even though she was only a hundred yards away. There were more questions than answers going on in my life right now, and that included Kristin Arthur.

Just what am I expecting with Kristin? I considered.

It had been a very long time since a woman struck me like she did. There was something about her that got to me inside. Maybe it was because she wasn't fawning over the fact that I played baseball or had a lot of money. Maybe it was because she was a smart and attractive woman that showed some interest in who I am. Or maybe part of it was because she was younger than me and part of me liked the fact that a woman that age might still be attracted to me at this age.

Whatever it was, I was looking forward to finding out, more than I had looked forward to any date I had in years.

Chapter 12

Kristin

The excitement was running through me from the moment I got out of bed Friday morning. It had been a while since I felt like I had something to really look forward to for the weekend. While I had tried to venture out with Karen and do things on the weekends here and there, it's not quite the same as having a date with a handsome man. Even though the date wasn't until seven in the evening, I found myself taking extra time primping as I got dressed for work that morning. I spent a little more time making sure my hair looked right, and I wore a nice pair of black slacks to go with my white ¾-sleeve blouse.

I took my usual walk to the library that morning, feeling great about myself. When I passed Harding's Diner, naturally the men were there in their window seats, and I made sure to give them a smile and a wave as I went by. I even got to the library a little bit early, allowing me to open, get the coffee going, turn my computer on and even check in some books before Karen arrived.

I was sitting in my office doing some paperwork when Karen strolled through the door. She came into my office, amazed to see me sitting there with stuff done already and with a smile on my face.

"What got into you this morning? Did you get here at 6 AM?" she said, surprised.

"I was just feeling good this morning, so I got here a little early and got some things done. The coffee is ready if you want some," I told Karen with a smile.

Karen went and poured herself a cup and came in and sat down in my office. She saw me typing away, still smiling and feeling good.

"Okay, what's going on?" she said, leaning forward and putting her coffee down on my desk.

"I don't know what you mean, Karen," I replied, barely able to contain myself and smile.

"You're one of the few people I know that are always in a good mood Kris, but today seems even extreme for you, so something must have had happened yesterday after you left here."

"Nothing much really," I said casually. "I just went and did some shopping at Wally's yesterday and ran into Wes Martin. We chatted a bit, and he asked me to dinner tonight." I kept typing, glancing up at Karen to see her reaction. She had a look of disbelief on her face.

"Are you serious?" Karen said, shocked at my statement.

"Yep," I said, showing more excitement now as I stopped typing and put my feet up on my desk. "We're going to Angelo's tonight at seven."

"I can't believe he asked you out after meeting you for just a few minutes," Karen said, standing up now. "You must have really knocked his socks off. That's great, Kris!"

"It is great, isn't it?" I said proudly. I stood up, and Karen came over and gave me a hug.

"Do you know what you are going to wear?" she asked me. I could see the excitement in her eyes now too.

"I have a pretty good idea," I told her. "I don't want to wear something that is too dressy or formal or something that is too revealing. I have this great red dress that I think will be perfect. It's not too fancy, it fits me really well, and I think Wes will like it."

"Oh, I'm so excited for you," Karen said.

We spent the next few minutes discussing details about going to Angelo's before the first patrons of the morning came into the library. Karen went out to the desk to help them while I tried to busy myself with my work in my office.

It was difficult to concentrate on the work I had to do: answering emails, placing book requests and setting up programs for the upcoming spring break, but somehow I managed to get through it all. I was even too keyed up to worry about eating lunch and completely skipped over it. That last hour in the library before five seemed to drag on forever, but by the time it rolled around, I eagerly shut down my computer and grabbed my things to go.

I walked out into the library as Karen was checking out the last visitor of the day, a young woman and her child checking out a few children's books. Once they were set and walking out the door, Karen turned and looked at me with a smile. I looked back at her with nervous excitement and shrugged my shoulders and smiled.

Karen gathered up her things, and we walked out the door together. I locked up for the night as we strolled up the street a bit.

Karen, your place is the other direction," I said to her as we kept walking.

"I thought you might want some help getting ready," she said. Karen may have been just as keyed up about the date as I was. I decided that I could use a friend's advice as I got ready to make sure I looked my best.

"That would be great, thanks," I said to her. We walked by the diner, and a few of the gentlemen were perched in their spot to watch us. Karen gave them a big smile and blew them a kiss as we went by.

"Enjoy your dinner guys!" she yelled as we were going by. She then took my hand, and we ran up the street together.

We went to my apartment and headed straight for my bedroom so I could get out the dress I had chosen to show to Karen. I walked over to the closet and pulled out the garment. It was a cap sleeve red dress that was fitted at the waist and then flared out at the skirt. The neckline was not very deep but was not conservative either.

I held the dress up for Karen to look at and she seemed to like it.

"Do you want help with makeup?" she asked me.

"I don't think I am going with any," I told her. "I want Wes to see me, not a caked-up version of me. Maybe just some lipstick and my nails." I looked down at my nails and realized they were not in the best shape to start with.

"Could you help me with my nails after I shower?" I asked her.

"You bet, I'm on it," Karen replied. She reached over to her large handbag and pulled out a variety of nailcare items.

"Go shower, and I'll get everything ready," she ordered, pointing over to the bathroom.

I turned on the shower, making it nice and hot, and stripped down and climbed in. I even took some time to shave my legs carefully, something I didn't do that often recently. I found that when you live in a colder climate, no one sees your legs for months. I made sure to avoid any nicks and took long, slow strokes with the pink razor in my shower to make sure I did a good job.

After getting out of the shower, I made sure to put moisturizer on my legs, making them shiny, soft and smooth. I wiped the fog off the mirror and took a good look at myself, happy with what I saw. I smiled and winked at myself as I wrapped a towel around my body and worked on drying my hair. My hair always had a little bit of curl and wave to it towards the ends, and I thought this would lend a great look for the night.

I walked out into the bedroom and saw Karen had laid out all her nail supplies on the bed. I sat down across from her, and she set to work like an expert, trimming and smoothing my nails, so they were all just the right shape and uniform. Karen then buffed my nails so that they were looking great, and then set about putting a clear base coat on each nail.

"Wow, you really know what you're doing," I said to her as we waited for the base coat to dry.

"My mother owned a salon, so I picked up all the tricks along the way," she said with a smile. "I think this red will be great with your dress," she said to me as she picked out a deeper red than the color of my dress.

It had been a while since I pampered myself and felt "girly" like this, and I was having fun just getting ready. Once my nails were dry, I was ready to start getting dressed. It was already a little after six, but Angelo's was only right down the street, so I didn't have far to go to meet Wes.

I went over to my dresser to pick out some underwear for the night. I actually gave some consideration to what I would wear for the first time in a while, and Karen could see me studying the drawer.

"What's wrong?" Karen said to me.

"I don't know what to wear," I said, tossing aside some items as I searched around.

"Well," Karen said as she got off the bed and stood next to me, staring into my underwear drawer. "I guess the question is, do you think this is anything he is going to see tonight?"

I did blush a little at the thought. I honestly hadn't considered whether things would actually get that far on this date. While I certainly didn't anticipate that happening, I guess the truth is I wasn't sure. I decided to go with something in-between, choosing a pair of red lace boyshorts I had. I held them up for Karen to see, and she approved. I then went with a red lace bra to match, figuring that was the right way to go.

I put on the bra and panties and looked in the full-length mirror I had to the right of my dresser. I was happy with the way things looked, and Karen nodded in approval in the background. I then chose a pair of black patterned pantyhose that would complement the dress nicely and carefully slid them up my legs. I slipped the red dress over my head, and Karen helped me with the zipper on the bodice. I turned to her and asked her what she thought.

"You look fantastic," she said to me.

I went over to my closet and grabbed my black strappy heels and put them on. I hadn't worn heels like this in a while since I didn't have any dressy places to go, so I made sure to walk around a bit to get used to them. I figured they gave me a little boost in height as well since Wes was so much taller than me.

"I think I'm ready," I said confidently to Karen.

I glanced down at my watch and saw it was nearly 6:45. I still had a few minutes before I could walk down to Angelo's. I realized would need to wear something for a coat since it was still getting chilly at night here in Chandler, so I went back to the closet to see what options I had. I grabbed a black shawl I had in the closet that I thought would both look nice and provide me with the extra warmth I was seeking.

Karen gathered up her things in her handbag, I grabbed my purse, and we were ready to head out the door. As we slowly walked up the street towards Angelo's, I could feel butterflies building in my stomach.

"You okay?" Karen said, sensing something might be wrong.

"I'm just feeling nervous all of a sudden," I said to Karen as we moved along.

"You've got nothing to be nervous about, Kris," Karen reassured me. "Don't take it too seriously. It's just a night out. Relax, be yourself, and have fun. That's all you can do."

"Thanks, Karen," I said as I hugged her again as we reached the wooden front door of Angelo's restaurant.

"You make sure to give me all the details," Karen directed. She pulled open the door for me as I walked through the door and up to the server's podium.

I had never been in Angelo's before, but had heard plenty about it from the people in town. It was a nice Italian restaurant, nothing too fancy, but it was considered a special location by many in the area. The lighting was dim inside as I looked around and saw many of the typical trappings you find in restaurant décor on the walls. Music played softly in the background, and an older gentleman came up to the podium moments after I arrived there. He was dressed impeccably in a dark suit and tie and greeted me with a broad smile.

"Can I help you, Miss," he said to me politely, with just a hint of an Italian accent.

I looked around the restaurant and didn't see Wes sitting anywhere in the front part of the dining room, so perhaps I had gotten there ahead of him.

"I'm... I'm meeting someone here for dinner tonight, but I think I may be here before him," I told the gentleman.

"Oh, you must be meeting Mr. Martin," the man said to me with a smile. "Please, come right this way."

I followed behind the man as we wound our way through the main dining room. The restaurant was much bigger inside than it looked from the outside, and I didn't know there was even a back room to go to. We walked into a smaller room that had just three or four tables to it, and the gentleman led me over to the table in the corner where I could see the shape of a man in a dark suit with his back to us.

"Mr. Martin," the gentleman stated, "Your guest has arrived." Wes stood up right away as I arrived and smiled at me as I walked around to the other side of the table. The gentleman pulled out the dark leather chair for me to sit on, and I sat down. He then handed me the white linen napkin to place in my lap. I looked over at Wes in his nicely pressed black suit and gray tie.

"I'm glad you made it," he said, looking over at me.

"I am too," I said, softly, as our date began.

Chapter 13

Wes

Waking up in my own bed felt wonderful and odd at the same time. When I woke up, I half-expected there to be sun peering through the window of a hotel room. Instead, I had awoken to the abrupt sound of a text message coming to my smartphone. It took me a few moments to clear my head and reach over and grab the phone to see who it was from, and it was then I realized I had a few messages there.

A couple were from reporters still trying to get a hold of me for comments. I had put them off and planned to continue to do so, figuring Randy would take care of them on my behalf. One message there was from Izzy, simply wishing me both a good morning and day before she left for school. The final message, which had just come in, was from Randy. His message was simple and straightforward:

Just because you are unemployed doesn't mean you can sleep all day. It's 10 AM, get up and call me!

I can't remember the last time I slept until 10 AM. Even during the offseason I always up early, getting my morning routine and workout going. This morning didn't have that same motivation. I sat up in bed and pressed Randy's number on my phone. It only rang once before he picked it up.

"Hey there, it's Rip Van Winkle," he said to me. "Did I rouse you out of your beauty sleep?"

"You're hysterical Randy," I said to him as I stretched a bit. "How about taking care of these reporters who keep messaging me, asking me for comments?" I said grumpily.

"Forward the texts to me; I'll take care of them for you, no problem," Randy assured me. "Anyway, I do have some news for you. I've been sending some feelers out to see what might be out there right now. There's still a couple of teams that haven't made any final decisions yet, so there's nothing imminent. I've talked to some GMs, and they know you're out there and they have interest, they just don't want to commit to anything until they see their final rosters. You know how it goes."

"Yeah, I know," I said to him. I was a little disappointed no one had jumped right away to make an offer.

"Don't let it get to you buddy," Randy said. "I think we'll have something soon, but it might not be until after Opening Day. Are you okay with that?"

"Sure, that's fine," I said, glad he was confident about the prospects. That left me with a few days of waiting around for answers.

"At least it gives you some time to be with the family," Randy said to me. "Don't just sit around moping; get out and do some stuff to stay busy."

"I will... I mean, I have," I told him. "I... I even have a date tonight," I said to him.

"Really?" Randy said, sounding very surprised.

"Yes, really. Why are you so shocked?"

"I'm not shocked, Wes. It's just that I've known you for a long time. Since Rachel left, you've kind of been a bit of a loner. I know you've seen some women along the way, but I've never heard you say you have a date. 'Date' makes it sounds more serious. Anyone I know?"

"No, I just met her myself yesterday."

"Wow, well great. So go out and have a good time. A few days with someone else will help you get your mind off things. Have a good time."

Thanks, Randy," I told him. "Let me know if you hear anything."

"Will do, buddy. Take care," Randy said as he hung up.

I wasn't sure why I had even bothered to tell Randy about the date with Kristin, but I guess I didn't really have anyone else to talk to about it around here other than my parents. I didn't spend enough time here in Chandler over the last fifteen years to be able to say I had any friends in town. Sure, plenty of people knew who I was, but I didn't think I could say any of them were friends. I had some guys that I had played with over the years that I considered friends, but they were either still playing right now, or retired and living in other states.

I spent the rest of my morning and afternoon occupying myself, taking the time to work out in the exercise room I had in the house. I had gone to the expense of having an indoor batting cage installed just out behind the house and beyond the pool area, but I didn't feel up to swinging a bat today, so I just worked out instead. I did some stretching, time with weights and ran on the treadmill for a while, getting in a respectable workout that brought on some good sweat. I watched TV while I worked out, and there was a passing mention of me on the sports news, stating that I was exploring my options and there were several teams showing interest. I could see Randy kept his word and was taking care of things.

I showered and shaved after my workout and slipped into a pair of sweats and a t-shirt. I then set about making some calls to set things up with the house, like turning the house phone back on, letting the security company know I was here and talking to the house care service. I told them I was here and arranged for a food delivery so they could bring stuff to stock the fridge for about a week for now. I also gave Angelo's a call to make a reservation for seven. I had known Angelo for years and when I spoke to him I asked for a table in the back room so I wouldn't have people coming up to me all during dinner and disrupting things. He said he would be glad to take care of it and looked forward to seeing me.

I then spent some time looking through the stack of mail the service left for me in the kitchen. I still get quite a bit of fan mail each day, and since I had some time, I thought I would go through it and answer some of it. It was always nice to read letters from fans young and old, and I signed some cards and baseballs and packaged everything up to get returned in the mail.

The day went by pretty quickly, much to my surprise. Before I knew it, it was nearly five-thirty.

I guess I should get ready for my date, I said to myself.

Even just hearing it in my head sounded unfamiliar to me. I walked over to my walk-in closet and looked at the rack of suits I had to choose from. I picked out a nice black one I had made last year from a shop in Pittsburgh that a bunch of the other players used as well. A simple white dress shirt, black tie and black shoes seem to round the outfit out for me. I splashed on some cologne and brushed my teeth and got dressed for the night.

It was still just barely after six when I was ready, so I went out, got in the SUV, and drove down to my parents' house to see them before I went out. I walked in the front door and heard Mom, dad and Izzy all in the kitchen, having dinner.

I strode into the kitchen in my suit, and all eyes turned to me right away. No one said anything and just looked at me.

"So, " I asked, "Do I look okay?"

All three of them looked back and forth at each other before Izzy spoke up.

"Don't take this wrong way, Dad," she said to me, "but you look like you're going to a funeral instead of a date."

"What are you talking about?" I said, defending myself. "This is my best suit."

"The suit is fine son," Mom said to me as she put her forkful of meatloaf down. "You just need a little color is all. Wyatt, help your son."

Dad got up from the table and walked out of the kitchen. A moment later he reappeared with a tie in his hand.

"Take the black tie off and try this one," he said, handing me a muted gray silk tie. I sighed and dutifully took off the black tie and then tied the gray one on. Dad reached over and straightened it for me to make sure it looked its best.

"Better?" I asked the ladies at the table.

Izzy gave me a thumbs up while she ate mashed potatoes. "Looks good, Dad," she said with her mouth full."

"What time is your reservation?" Mom asked as she took a sip of iced tea.

"It's at seven," I said as I reflexively looked down at my watch to see it was nearly six-thirty now.

"You better get going then,"Mom said to me.

"Mom, Angelo's is five minutes away," I responded.

"I know, but you want to make sure you get there before her so you can get settled, have some wine at the table, make things nice for her. Tell him, Wyatt," Mom said, nodding to my father.

Dad put his arm around me and led me towards the door.

"Have fun Dad!" Izzy yelled from the table as we walked out of the kitchen.

"Don't mind your mother, Wes," Dad said to me. "She just wants to make sure you have a good time, treat the young lady right, and so on. Maybe it's all those romance novels she reads, I don't know."

We reached the front door and Dad fixed my jacket for me like I was a teenager going to the prom.

"Do you have cash?" Dad said to me, reaching for his wallet.

"Seriously, Dad? You're getting cash for me? I think I've got it covered," I said incredulously.

"Well I don't know if you have anything in your wallet," he answered, putting his wallet away. "Enjoy your night out, Wes. Have a good time."

"Thanks, Dad," I said to him as I went out the door to my car.

The drive down to Angelo's was uneventful, as expected. I parked in the side lot of the restaurant and walked in. Angelo was there at the podium to greet me. He was the epitome of the classic Italian restaurant owner. He had his roots in Italy and ended up in Chandler after having a restaurant in New York for years and then deciding he wanted a quieter life for himself and his wife. It had been a while since I had been here, and Angelo looked a little grayer, but he was still fit, eager, and smiling as he extended his hand to me.

"Always nice to see you, Mr. Martin," he said as he gave me a firm handshake.

"Hello Angelo," I replied. "I hope the family is well."

"Oh yes, they are great," he told me as he began to lead me towards the back room. "Grandson number three was just born a month ago. He is beautiful."

We walked past a few patrons in the dining room that looked up as we went by. I saw a few sparks of recognition from people as I went, but that was it.

Angelo seated me at a table towards the back of the room, a table set especially for two.

"A special guest tonight, Mr. Martin?" Angelo said with a smile as a busboy came over and poured some water into a glass for me.

"Yes, Angelo," I answered. " A young lady. Kristin Arthur. She's the librarian in town. I don't know if you know her. She's blonde, petite, very nice..."

"I haven't had the pleasure of meeting her yet," Angelo replied as he handed a napkin to me, "but I will keep an eye out for her and bring her over when she arrives. Can I get you a drink while you wait? A vodka martini on the rocks perhaps?"

"Your memory is impeccable, Angelo," I said with a smile. "A martini would be perfect. Could you bring a bottle of red wine to the table as well for when she arrives?"

"I'd be glad to pick something out for you," he told me and was off to find something appropriate for dinner.

I took a quick sip of my water and tried to calm myself down a bit before Kristin arrived. Perhaps it had been too long since I was on a date, but I wasn't accustomed to feeling this nervous around anyone. Confidence was always the one trait I thought helped me the most in my career, and I tried to carry it over into my personal life. But, for the first time in years, I found myself fidgeting around trying to get comfortable.

A young waiter dressed in a white shirt and dark trousers came over with my drink and placed it on the table in front of me. Angelo quickly followed with the bottle of wine he had retrieved from the wine cellar, a Cabernet Sauvignon that he highly recommended. Angelo opened the bottle expertly, poured some for me, and placed the bottle down on the table. I took a sip and saw it was a smooth and sweet wine and tasted great.

"Thank you, Angelo," I replied. "It's very nice."

"You're welcome, " he said with a smile and walked away.

I took a sip of my martini, savoring the flavor of it when I heard steps coming up behind me.

"Mr. Martin," Angelo offered, "your guest has arrived."

I stood up from the table and turned to see Kristin standing there with Angelo. She looked stunning in a red dress with a black shawl over her shoulders. I smiled as Angelo led her over to the other side of the table and pulled the chair out for her. Kristin sat as Angelo handed her a napkin.

"I'm glad you made it," I said to her.

"I am too," she replied to me.

We looked at each other across the table for a moment before Angelo presented us with the menus.

"Angelo, this is Kristin Arthur," I said to him.

"A pleasure to meet you, Ms. Arthur," Angelo said politely.

"Nice to meet you too, Angelo," she said as she took the menu from him.

"Can I get you something to drink?" Angelo offered.

"A glass of this red wine is perfect," she indicated to Angelo, pointing to the bottle.

"Excellent," he answered as he poured a glass for her.

"I'll let you two look at the menus and be back to tell you the specials and answer any questions." Angelo walked away from the table, leaving us alone.

I scanned the menu, not really paying much attention to what was on it. I was more captivated by the way Kristin looked tonight. She was beautiful and the light from single candle lit on the table danced light across her. I tried not to stare , but I found it difficult to take my eyes off her. She glanced up from her menu and saw me looking at her and smiled.

"What?" she asked me as I looked at her.

"I'm sorry," I said to her. " I didn't mean to stare like that; that was rude. You just look... you look lovely."

She looked down and smiled and then looked back up at me. "Thank you," she said shyly.

We sat quietly for a minute, looking at the menus, as I wracked my brain trying to think of something to say. Before I could, Angelo arrived back at the table to let us know about the specials, including a stuffed branzino that sounded great to me.

He turned to Kristin to see what she would like.

"I think I'll go with the linguine in clam sauce," she said, offering the menu back to Angelo.

"Wonderful choice," he told her. "All our pasta is made in-house, and the clams are very fresh; you will love it. And for you, Mr. Martin?"

"I'll have the branzino special, Angelo," I said as I handed him the menu.

"Very nice," Angelo offered. He backed away from the table, leaving us in our awkward silence again.

"This place is nice," Kristin remarked, looking around the room.

"Oh yes," I answered. "I've been coming here for years. Angelo's is the best place in town."

"So you've brought a lot of dates here?" Kristin stated as she took a sip of red wine.

I could feel my face turning red. "Oh, no, that's not what I meant at all. I just meant..."

"Relax, Wes," Kristin said with a giggle. "I'm just teasing you."

I tried to laugh a little, and then let out a sigh. "I'm sorry," I said to Kristin as I took a sip of my martini. "I don't mean to seem so tense. I... I don't go out like this very often. It might take me a bit to get into the swing of things."

"It's okay," Kristin said to me. "I haven't dated since I got to Chandler, so I'm a bit rusty too. Let's just try to get to know each other. Tell me a little about yourself."

"Well, I've lived in Chandler all my life, even if I'm not here much. I grew up here, went to high school here and played baseball here before the Pirates drafted me. I worked my way up through their minor leagues in a few years and then played with them ever since, up until a few days ago, that is."

"I heard about that," Kristin said. "I'm sorry. It must be hard after being with them for so long."

"It is hard," I said to her honestly. "It hurt when they told me, but I guess it was time for both of us to move on to something else."

We sat for another quiet moment before Kristin stated, "Your daughter seems very nice."

"Thank you," I offered. "Though you can actually thank my parents for most of that. They have pretty much raised her since... well since my divorce. They stepped in and took care of Izzy when I wasn't here. She has turned into a wonderful young lady."

"It must be difficult," Kristin said as she took another sip of wine, "Raising a child on your own with the kind of work you do."

"It's pretty challenging sometimes," I said to her. "I know I have missed out on a lot of Izzy's life, but I've tried my best to make up for it and be there for her when I could be."

The busboy came over and placed a basket of fresh bread on the table for us. I offered Kristin a piece, which she took, and then I took a piece myself.

"So what about you?" I asked as I buttered the piece of warm bread. "How does a southern girl wind up in the middle of nowhere in Pennsylvania?"

"How do you know I'm a southern girl?" she said to me with a smile as she took a small bite of bread.

I laughed when she said this. "I've traveled around enough over the years to know accents pretty well. If I had to guess, I would say you are from Georgia, perhaps Southern Georgia, close to Alabama."

"That's right," she said, impressed with my answer. "I was raised in Augusta. I've always had a love of books since I was a little girl. I followed my passion, went to school for library sciences and got my degree. I found this job listed and thought it sounded like a good chance for me to see someplace new. I have to say, I really like Chandler... and I'm growing to like it more all the time." Kristin smiled at me again.

We kept up the small talk all through dinner, in between bites of fish, linguine, bread and more. We finished the bottle of wine with ease and then enjoyed Angelo's famous tiramisu for dessert with espresso for me and cappuccino for her. We talked more about what it was like to play pro ball and be "famous", what it was like for her to grow up with a sister since I never had siblings, and how it was dealing with teenagers today, both as a parent and a librarian.

When the meal was done, I felt I had come to know Kristin pretty well, and had shared more about myself than I had with anyone else in a very long time. Angelo came with the check, and we could barely push ourselves away from the table we were so full. I paid the bill and thanked him for a wonderful meal, and he gave me a hug and proceeded to kiss Kristin on each cheek, saying how wonderful it was to have her.

I took a look down at my watch and saw it was nearly eleven and that the restaurant had long cleared out of other patrons. We stepped out into the cool air of the night, and Kristin immediately tightened her shawl around herself. We stood in front of Angelo's for a second, neither one of us sure as to what the next step should be.

"It was a wonderful dinner Wes, thank you so much," Kristin said to me kindly.

I felt like she was ready to end the evening, but I wasn't sure I was ready to do that just yet.

"Can I... can I walk you home?" I said with a smile, pointing to her building just down the block.

"That would be nice," she said as we started to walk together. Eleven at night in Chandler may as well be two or three in the morning somewhere else. Nothing was going on right on Main Street, and it was just us walking on the street. You could hear the music from Rusty's, the local bar two blocks over, echoing through the night.

There was a light breeze along the street, and Kristin put her left arm around my right as we walked. We reached her apartment building all too quickly, and we looked at each other in front of the steps that led up to her apartment on the second floor.

I turned to her and looked down into her eyes.

"Thank you for coming out with me tonight," I said to her. "I had a wonderful time with you." I hesitated a second, and then slowly bent down to give her a light kiss. I felt her right hand go behind my head to hold the kiss there for a few seconds longer before we broke. I could see a sweet smile on her face as I slowly began to pull away. Before I could get too far, she pulled me back down for another kiss, this one deeper and longer than the last. I kissed her back passionately, wrapping my arms around her tightly.

When we finally stopped kissing, Kristin seemed a bit out of breath. Her hands were pressed against my chest, and she held them there for a moment before she reached up and gave me another light kiss.

"Wes..." she said breathlessly, "I better go in before..."

"Before what?" I whispered as I kissed her again.

"Before I don't want you to go, and I don't think either of us is ready for that just yet. I... I don't want you to get the wrong idea about me." Kristin kissed me again, and I put an arm around her waist. She then broke the kiss again. "You're making this very difficult," she said with a grin.

"That's the idea," I said to her, grinning back at her as I went in for another kiss. She put her hands up to stop this time, giving me a quick peck on the cheek. She grabbed my cell phone from my jacket pocket and punched some information and then scampered up the steps to her apartment door.

"Call me or text me tomorrow if you want," she said to me as she leaned over the railing on the second floor. "I'm off on the weekends; maybe we can do something." Kristin then unlocked her apartment door and went inside.

I took the walk back to my car, glancing down at my phone to see that she entered her phone number with a smile emoticon next to it. I continued the walk to my car, and my phone buzzed with a text message. I had hopes that it was from Kristin, asking me to come back, but I saw it was from Izzy:

Hope the date went well. See you in the morning. Love you.

I opened my car, climbed in, and shut the door. I then quickly tapped a return message to Izzy:

The date went nicely. We had a great time. Talk to you in the morning. Love you too.

I sat for a moment before I turned the car on and tapped out one more text message, this one to the number Kristin left me:

Thanks for a great night. I really needed it. You're an amazing woman. Good night.

My screen lit up with a reply shortly after:

You're not so bad yourself. Thank you for making me feel special. Good night.

I started the car and began my short ride home, trying to figuring out what to do tomorrow and what would be next for me.

Chapter 14

Kristin

I threw myself onto the bed as soon as I got home, so pleased with how well things went with Wes. He proved to be such a wonderful man and was witty, charming and gentleman through and through. I felt like I would burst and had to talk to someone, and thankfully it wasn't long until Karen sent me a text asking if I was still out on the date. I told her I was home, and my phone rang about five seconds later.

"Hello?" I answered casually, pretending nothing important was going on.

"Don't hello me," Karen said smartly.

"Who is this?" I replied.

"Kristin, you better start talking, or I'm coming over there right now," Karen told me with a hint of annoyance in her voice.

I proceeded to tell her all about my dinner with Wes, how the meal was at Angelo's, and how much we talked so we could get to know each other more.

"He's a pretty incredible man, Karen," I sighed into the phone as I got undressed and into my pajamas. "I could have talked to him all night long. He has lived a very interesting life and seen a lot of places, a lot more than a little Southern country girl like me."

"Are you sure you could have only talked to him all night long? Is all you two did was talk?" Karen asked, hoping for some juicier details.

"Well, he did kiss me goodnight," I said honestly.

"Now we're getting somewhere," Karen said, anxious for specifics. "What else happened?"

"That's it," I told her as I sat down on my bed. "We kissed a few times, and then I went into my apartment."

"Really?" Karen told me, disappointment in her voice.

"Really, Karen. Did you honestly think I would do more than that the first time going out with him? That doesn't speak to well of your opinion of me."

"I didn't mean it that way," Karen said with a hint of ruefulness in her voice. "I'm just surprised is all, I guess."

"Surprised at what?" I answered. "That I'm not jumping into bed with him right away?" I was enjoying giving her a hard time.

"Not at you," Karen said, exasperated. "I guess I figured he would at least make a move to see if he could do anything. I mean, he is a rich sports star."

"I think everyone thinks just because he has a lot of money and is a good-looking sports hero that they assume he is just bedding women left and right. He's not like that Karen. He's sweet, sensitive, very polite and very much the gentleman. It's been a while since a guy has made me feel like a special woman, and he did that tonight, without having sex with me."

"Wow," Karen said to me.

'Wow, what?" I replied to her.

"I think you're falling hard for Wes Martin very fast," Karen said to me.

I thought about what she said for a moment as I laid back on my bed. I had never felt this emotional about any of the guys I had dated in the past. Granted, my dating history wasn't very long, but I had a few what I would call serious boyfriends in college. But even thinking about them didn't quite measure up to the way Wes made me feel, and we had only known each other for a day. All of a sudden, I felt a little scared.

"I think you might be right Karen," I said into the phone.

We were both quiet for a moment before Karen said something.

"Are you okay with that?" she asked me.

"I'm not sure," I said to her honestly. "There's so much about Wes to like, and I feel like he swept me off my feet, but there's a lot to be worried about too."

"Such as?" Karen questioned.

"To start with, there's his career. He could start playing for another team at any time and pack up and go. Where would that leave me? Second, he's got a teenage daughter in his life. How is she going to feel if her father suddenly has a girlfriend? Or how will his parents feel? Then there's the fact that he's thirteen years older than me. He's seen and experienced a lot more of life than I have.

Maybe I'm not enough for him. Or maybe he just wants someone to have a fling with."

Thinking about all those things made me realize there really was a lot to worry about. Maybe my sister Lucy was right about everything. But there was still a part of me, a big part of me right now, that didn't believe any of that. Spending those hours with Wes gave me the chance to get to see different sides of him that I didn't think many people had the chance to see, and I really liked what I saw there.

"You still there?" Karen said to me. I realized I had been quiet for a while.

"I am," I said to her, snapping out of my haze. "I guess I'm just tired. It's been a long day; a wonderful day, but a long one."

"Do you think you'll hear from him soon?" Karen asked.

"Well, I gave him my cell number, and he texted me right after I got inside to say thank you for the date, so I think I will. At least I hope I will."

"I'm glad you had such a good time tonight, Kris," Karen said with a yawn.

"I should go. I've had an exciting night too you know."

"Oh yeah?" I said, perking up a little. "What did you do tonight?"

"It was a big night. A man showed up at my door," she said in a hushed tone.

"Really? Who was it? What did he want?"

"He wanted $12.00 for the pizza and salad he brought me," Karen told me. "After that, I watched a movie. It was more excitement than I could take. I'll bet your date with Wes Martin can't top that!"

I laughed hard for a bit. "Thanks, Karen. Have a good night; I'll talk to you later."

"Good night Kris," she said as she hung up.

I put my phone down on my nightstand and turned off the light. I lay in bed for a few minutes, pulling the covers up to my chin, thinking about my date with Wes.

You're all wound up. What have you gotten yourself into Kris? I asked myself.

"Something good, I hope," I whispered out loud.

Chapter 15

Wes

I made sure to set the alarm for myself so I would get up early in the morning. I wanted to start getting myself into more of a routine, even if it was a Saturday morning, in case this was going to be my life for a few weeks more, or even longer. The home service had come and brought food to stock the fridge for me, and I made sure to get up at around 6:30 so I could get in an early morning workout. I needed to make sure I stayed in the best shape possible in case I got the call from another team. I didn't relish the idea of having to go to the minors for a few weeks to get myself in playing condition, but that could happen if the delays went on much longer.

After my workout and shower, I put on a pair of jeans and a black t-shirt and threw one of my plaid button down shirts on over it. I put on my favorite boots, a pair I had picked up years ago when we were in Texas, grabbed my leather jacket, and then took a leisurely walk down the road to my parent's house.

I knew at the very least that my father would be awake since he got up early to tend to the horses. Mom might still be asleep, depending on the kind of night she had, and I figured there was no way Izzy was awake this early on the weekend. If she didn't have to get up to go to school, she was probably up late talking to her friends and thus would end up sleeping late.

Sure enough, when I opened the front door, I could smell the familiar aroma of a fresh pot of coffee brewing in the kitchen. I walked over into the kitchen and saw Dad there, already dressed for the day and looking like he had already been out to the stables to do some work.

"Good morning," he said as he spied me out of the corner of his eye. "Want some coffee?"

"That would be great, thanks, Dad," I answered as I sat down at the table. Dad brought a mug over to me and then sat down in his chair at the table.

"Mom and Izzy still asleep?" I asked. I could smell the dark roast of the coffee as I brought the mug up to my lips.

"Yes," Dad replied, sipping his own coffee. "Your mother was up and down a bit last night, so I think she's sleeping in this morning. Izzy... well, I'm not sure how late she was up last night, but it was long after I went to bed."

I took another slow sip of the coffee. "Honestly, Dad... how's Mom doing?" I had been worried about her since before I got home and needed to know what was going on for my own peace of mind.

"Honestly?" Dad took another sip and put his mug down. "She's doing a lot better than I thought she would. After the doctor told us about cancer coming back, I was pretty worried. I was preparing myself for the worst, and I thought your Mother would too. Thank God she's stronger than I am with stuff like this. She's approached this fight as tough as the last time, and the new treatment she is on seems to really be helping her. It takes a lot out of her, but she's bouncing back pretty well, and the doctors are hopeful."

"I'm glad to hear that," I said, feeling some relief. "You know if Mom needs anything, you should tell me. I know some people, and with some of the charity work I did in Pittsburgh, we can get her the best help..."

"Wes," Dad interrupted, "I know you can do all those things. Trust me, if we needed the help, I would have asked you already. I think the doctors here are doing fine with her."

"I'm just checking is all, Dad."

"I know, and I appreciate your concern, Wes. Your mother is a lot tougher than you think." Dad put his coffee mug down on the table. "Now on to more important issues. How was your date last night?"

"It went really well," I told him, feeling proud of myself. "We had a nice time and got to know each other a bit. Kristin's fantastic."

"I guess she made quite an impression on you," Dad said to me.

"She sure did. I think I am going to call her today and see if she wants to do something, maybe something with Izzy and me."

"What about you and Izzy?" I heard a groggy voice state. There was Izzy, standing in her pajamas, wiping her eyes.

"What are you doing awake this early?" I asked with surprise.

"I get up before this time every day of the week, Dad," she said to me. "I heard you out here and wanted to come and see you." She came over and gave me a peck on the cheek and then walked to the refrigerator and grabbed the container of orange juice. After pouring herself a glass, she came back over and sat next to me. "So the date with Ms. Arthur went well?" she asked me.

"Yes, it did, honey. We had a very nice time," I answered as I watched Izzy drain her glass of orange juice in one fell swoop.

"So what is it you were talking about for today?" Izzy asked me as she put her glass down.

"I thought maybe you and I and Kristin could do something together. Maybe we can catch a movie or take a ride down to the mall."

"I would love to Dad, I really would," she replied, looking down and taking her phone out of pajama pocket, "but Amy invited me over to her place this morning. A bunch of us are getting together to hang out all day, play music, walk around town, you know, teenager stuff. Is that okay?"

I thought about it for a second before I answered. I wanted to get some time with Izzy, time that we almost never get together, but I also promised her that I wasn't going to disrupt her routine while I was here.

"It's fine, Izzy," I said with a smile. I think she could see I was a little disappointed.

"Let's do something tomorrow, just you and me," Izzy said as she came over and put her arms around my neck.

"Okay, that sounds good. Think about what you might want to do, and we'll do it, your choice," I told Izzy.

"Great! Thanks, Dad! I am going to go take a shower and get dressed. Do you think you could give me a ride down to town? We're all going to meet at the diner for breakfast first."

"Sure," I replied. "Just let me know when you are ready."

Izzy ran off down the hall, and I turned to face Dad.

"That's pretty much how weekends go around here, Wes," Dad said to me. "She's quite the social butterfly this year; it's nice to see that she has a good group of friends. They're all pretty good kids. I just wish one of them would get their license, so I didn't have to drive them all over the place."

Dad got up to pour himself some more coffee and asked if I wanted another cup. I declined.

"So what are you going to do with Ms. Arthur today then?" Dad asked as he poured the coffee.

I thought for a moment, and then an idea came over me.

"I think I just came up with a great idea for today since the weather is supposed to be nice. How's the area around the pond looking right now?"

"It looked pretty good when I was out that way yesterday," Dad said as he sat back down. "The ground is dry, maybe a little firm. That pond water will be ice cold though," he said to me.

"I wasn't thinking about going swimming there, Dad," I said seriously, though when I looked over at him, I could see he was smiling, and I had missed the joke. There was a nice area on the farm where there was a natural pond. Once I had started making some money, we fixed the area up, cleared around it, cleaned it, and worked on the pond to make it a nice area ideal for outdoor parties or just as a secluded place to get away. I thought it would be a great spot to bring Kristin.

I looked at my watch and saw it was still perhaps too early to reach out to Kristin on the weekend, but perhaps by the time I dropped Izzy off, I could have everything in place for a nice afternoon. It wasn't long before Izzy was out of the shower and dressed, her backpack in tow, ready to head out to meet her girlfriends.

"All set?" I said to her as she walked through the door. I could see that she had pulled her long brown hair back and put some makeup on. She was dressed in a simple purple t-shirt with a pair of jeans and had her favorite black sweatshirt tied around her waist. As I looked at her, she suddenly looked very grown up to me, even more than when I had left here just six weeks ago to go to spring training.

"Dad? Are you paying attention?" Izzy said to me. I must have zoned out a bit and shook my head to bring me back to reality.

"I'm fine," I told her as I stood up from the table. "Let's go."

"See you later Grandpa," Izzy said as she headed out the door.

"Have fun Izzy," Dad said, picking up his newspaper. "I'll see you later, Wes."

I waved to Dad as I followed Izzy out the door.

"Where's your car?" Izzy said to me, looking around.

"It's up at the house," I said, pointing up the hill.

"Why didn't you drive down?" she said to me, looking surprised and disappointed.

"Because we live 100 yards away and I wanted the exercise," I told her.

"But now we have to walk up the hill," she whined.

"Or we can run up the hill," I said to her and quickly ran over to her and grabbed her hand, trying to make her run up the hill with me. She got about twenty yards and let go of my hand.

"I'm not running," she said to me.

"Okay," I told her, "but if you beat me up the hill, I'll let you drive the SUV down to the end of the road."

"Really?" she said, suddenly taking an interest. Izzy had been driving Dad's truck around the farm for a year or so for practice, so I knew she could handle it, but I had never let her drive one of my cars before.

"Yep," I said to her. "But I'm pretty confident I won't lose, so don't get your hopes up."

Izzy walked over to me and smiled. She then dropped her backpack on the side of the road and started sprinting up the hill. She was ten yards ahead of me before I could even get started.

Even though I think of myself in really good shape, I was no match for her. Izzy had long, strong legs and a runner's frame, much like my Dad's. Running up the hill was a lot more of a challenge than I thought it would be. I came close to her, but she beat me.

We were both a little out of breath when we reached the car.

"When did you get so fast?" I said to her, still a bit surprised about her ability.

"I forgot to tell you I've been working out too," she said to me. "I'm running spring track this year at school."

"Well if I knew you were cheating..." I said as I caught my breath.

"I didn't cheat!" she shouted. "You're just too old to keep up," she said with a smile. I grinned back at her and tossed her the keys.

"Take it slow," I warned as I got in the passenger's seat.

Izzy excitedly got behind the wheel and dutifully clicked her seatbelt on first. She then adjusted the mirrors so she could see better and pressed the ignition button to start the car. She inched slowly at first to get the car going, and then more confidently began to work down the road. She stopped a bit abruptly so I could reach out and grab her backpack, and then started up once again to complete her drive. We reached the end of the road leading out onto Route 5 when she put the car in park.

"Can I take it down Route 5?" she asked sweetly.

"No way," I said to her.

"Come on, Dad. There's no traffic on the road," she said as she looked around.

"Izzy, it's not happening. You're not sixteen, and you don't even have a permit."

Izzy begrudgingly got out and walked around to the passenger's side of the SUV while I slid over to the driver's seat. She climbed in and closed the door, grinning an accomplished smile. I drove off and could see she was still smiling.

In minutes I pulled up and parked in front of the diner. I could see Izzy's friend Amy standing outside waiting for her along with two other girls that I did not know. There were also two boys in the group waiting for them.

"Whoa," I said to her. "You didn't say anything about boys being here."

"Oh stop Dad," Izzy said to me. "It's Scott and Bradley. They are both in a bunch of my classes. It's no big deal."

"it's a big deal to me," I said, looking out at the boys as they looked back into the SUV, wondering why it was taking Izzy so long to come out.

"Dad, don't embarrass me in front of my friends," Izzy pleaded.

"Fine, go ahead," I said to her. "Do you need any money?"

"Are you offering?" she asked me. I reached into my wallet and took out two twenty dollar bills and handed them to her.

"I thought Grandpa paid you each week to do chores on the farm?" I asked her.

"He does," she said as she gave me a kiss on the cheek and got out of the car. "See you later, Dad!"

After realizing I had been bamboozled twice this morning by a fifteen-year-old, all I could do was smile as I watched Izzy go into the diner with her friends. She was at the back of the group and waited to go in until one of the boys motioned for her to go in just before him. She did and gave him a shy smile as she went in.

One more thing to worry about, I told myself as I sighed.

I took the opportunity while I was parked to pick up my phone and give Kristin a call. I waited nervously as the phone rang a couple of times before she answered.

"Hello?" I heard her soft, Southern voice answer.

"Hi, Kristin. It's Wes. I hope I didn't wake you." I said to her.

"Who is this?" she asked, sounding confused.

"Wes... Wes Martin," I said to her. "We... we had dinner last night."

I heard her start laughing. "I knew it was you, Wes," she said with her laugh. "I was just messing with you."

Great, it must be pick-on-the-old-guy Day today, I thought.

"It's nice to hear from you this morning," Kristin said to me sweetly.

"I... I was just wondering if you wanted to get together today," I said to her.

"Sure," she said to me. "What did you have in mind?"

"Well, it's kind of a surprise," I said to her. "Can you be ready in about an hour?"

"Ooh, a mystery date," she said with some intrigue in her voice. "I like the way that sounds. Yes, I can be ready in an hour," she told me. "Should I meet you somewhere?"

"Nope," I answered. "I'll pick you up; Just make sure you wear something comfortable."

"Comfortable, got it," she said to me. "See you in an hour." I heard her hang up the phone.

I climbed out of the SUV and walked over to Wally's to pick up a few things. I slowly began to map out just what I wanted to get today and how I hoped it would go.

Let's see if you still know how to romance a girl, Wes, I told myself as I set out to do some shopping.

Chapter 16

Wes

I spent the hour I had before I picked up Kristin gathering everything I thought I might need to make the day special. I did some shopping at Wally's and then went over to Fleming's, the lone "department" store we had in town. I don't know that Fleming's qualifies as a department store, but they are the only place in Chandler that has a little bit of everything, and they were likely to have the items I was looking for. I found just the things I wanted without drawing a lot of attention to myself and then headed out to the liquor store before I made a quick stop at the florist.

After I had gathered all my supplies, I made a quick phone call to Dad to see if he could arrange something for me. I let him know about my plan, and he was happy to oblige and said things would be ready when I got home. It was then on to Kristin's place to pick her up.

Since everything in Chandler seems nearby, it was just a short drive over to her apartment to get her. I was ready to walk up to her apartment to greet her, but when I pulled into the parking lot, there she was waiting for me. She had a blue denim jacket on to match the jeans she was wearing, with a simple white tank top on underneath. She didn't see me in my SUV right away, so I got to look at her standing in the sunlight for a moment before she looked my way. Even dressed in a simple outfit, she looked radiant.

I rolled down the window of my SUV and gave her a smile and wave as she headed over to the car. Kristin opened the passenger side door and climbed into the car.

"Good morning," she said to me with a smile as she put her seatbelt on.

"Good morning to you," I said happily. I pulled out of my parking spot and back onto Main Street to head out towards Route 5 and the farm.

"So what are we doing today?" Kristin asked me.

"I have some nice surprises planned," I told her. "You'll just have to wait and see."

"I like surprises," Kristin said with a mischievous grin. We drove along out towards Route 5 as Kristin watched.

"I didn't expect to hear from you this morning," she said to me honestly.

"Why not?" I asked her.

"I thought maybe you would be doing something with your daughter since you just got back home."

"Well, I tried to get her involved in something today, but she had already made plans with her friends. I dropped her off at Harding's this morning, and she said she would be with her friends all day. So it's just you and me, I guess." I looked over at Kristin to see her reaction, and she smiled at me.

"That's okay," she said. "I don't mind some alone time with you."

"Glad to hear it," I said to her as I pulled onto Martin Road. Instead of driving up towards my place or my parent's house, I made the left just onto the road and headed out towards the farm area.

"Where are we going?" Kristin asked, watching the farmland as it went by. The road was more than a little bumpy out this way, and thankfully my SUV was four-wheel drive enough to handle it.

"You'll see in a minute," I told her. I made another left onto another dirt road, and we pulled up to the small parking area before the stables. I turned the car off and hopped out, and then went over and opened the passenger door for Kristin, helping her out.

Kristin took my hand as she stepped out of the SUV.

"How chivalrous," she commented as I closed the door to the car.

We walked towards the rear of the car, where I picked up the bags I had in the trunk, and then we began the short walk over towards the barn. When we reached the barn doors, I slid the large door open to reveal the stable area. George Peters, Dad's right-hand man with the stables, was already in there.

I walked over to George and gave him a hearty handshake. Like my Dad, George had been working around horses his whole life. He was a bit older than Dad, a tad over sixty, but he was in better shape than many of the twenty-something that I would come across each day as a ballplayer. His hands were very strong, and he always had a deep tan, even in the winter months here in Pennsylvania.

"How are you, George?" I said to him, not having seen him in a few months.

"Doing great, Wes," he said to me as he took his work gloves off. "I was sorry to hear that you were home. I was looking forward to seeing you play down at PNC again this year."

I was still getting used to everyone saying how sorry they were that I had been cut.

"Well, we'll see how things work out. I still have some options out there," I told George, reassuring myself as much as him. I turned and looked at Kristin, who had stayed a few paces behind me as she looked around at the stables.

"George," I said to him, "This is Kristin Arthur. She's the librarian in town."

George took his hat off and extended his hand to her. "Pleasure to meet you, Ms. Arthur," he said politely.

"Nice to meet you too, she said, shaking his hand. "Please, call me Kristin."

"Okay, Kristin it is," he said with a smile. George turned to me. "I think I have everything ready for you," George said to me. He looked down at the bags I had in my hands. "You want me to load those up for you?"

"That would be great, thanks, George," I said to him as he took the bags from me. George walked away towards the stables while Kristin walked over to me.

"The barn is beautiful," she said to me as she looked around at the ceiling and the surroundings.

"Dad and George do an amazing job keeping up with everything, and they have a good team of people here helping them all the time."

"How many horses are here now?" Kristin asked as she peered back towards the stables.

"Geez, I'm not even sure right now," I told her. "Somewhere between ten and fifteen, I think. Most of them Dad owns, though he does board a few for some other people."

I gently took Kristin's left hand, and we slowly walked down the stable area where the horses were. I could see the awe on her face as she saw the beautiful animals we had there. There were a couple of the workers milling about in the stables, caring for the horses, but for the most part, it was pretty quiet today.

"The horses are beautiful," she said to me as we walked. Just then, George walked over to us.

"Are you ready?" George asked me.

"Sure are," I said to George as we followed him out the other end of the barn.

"Ready for what?" Kristin asked with anticipation.

We walked outside where George had two of the horses ready for us. Kristin and I walked over to the smaller horse, a chestnut brown filly named Bonnie. Kristin was gently petting her as we walked over to her face.

"This is Bonnie," I told her.

"She's so pretty," Kristin whispered.

"I probably should have asked you this before, but... do you know how to ride?" I said to her, hoping she would say yes.

"It's been a few years," she said to me, "but I did ride with a friend of mine back in Georgia when I was a teenager."

George helped Kristin get into a helmet, and I helped Kristin get mounted on her horse. She seemed to have no trouble getting on and seated properly. When I saw that she was okay and George was there holding Bonnie, I mounted my horse, a dark brown horse named Pops.

It had been a while since I had ridden, but I had been on a horse since I was a toddler and knew exactly what to do.

"All set?" I said to Kristin. She nodded to me with a big smile on her face.

"Thanks, George," I said to him. "I'm not sure how long we'll be out."

"Not a problem," he said to me. "Just shoot me a text when you are on your way back. Either I'll come over and meet you, or one of the hands will be here to help you."

We started slowly down the trail on the farm as Kristin and I both got used to the feeling of having a horse beneath us. Kristin looked a little hesitant at first as she tried to get command of everything, but her previous riding experience seemed to kick in pretty quickly, and she was more at ease with riding in just a few minutes.

We walked along pretty slowly as we took in the gorgeous spring day all around us. Trees and flowers were just beginning to bloom all over, and the clear sounds of the different birds in the area were all you could hear outside of the slow clops of the horses' hooves.

"All this property is yours?" Kristin asked me as we walked along.

"A lot of it belongs to my parents," I said to her. "The initial horse farm wasn't quite this big, but I bought the land adjacent to the farm so Dad could expand out and we wouldn't have to worry about someone developing it into something else."

"This is amazing," she said to me.

After about half a mile or so of riding, we came up a small hill. Once we crested the hill, you could see where the pond area was. The sun glistened beautifully off the water at this time of day, and there was just a hint of a gentle breeze in the air to make the atmosphere perfect. We worked our way down the small hill and brought the horses to a halt in a small grove of trees where there was a hitching area for the horses.

I dismounted my horse and got him hitched and then helped Kristin down from her horse and got Bonnie settled. I then grabbed the saddlebags that were on Pops and carried them with me, taking Kristin's hand as we walked over towards the pond.

About twenty feet or so from the pond we had set up some picnic tables under some trees. The land was pretty flat here and nicely tended to so it looked perfect. Sitting on the picnic table was a large wicker hamper basket that I had asked George to have brought down for us.

I led Kristin over to the picnic table and had her sit down. I stood next to her and reached into the bags I had and took out the small bouquet of flowers I had bought and handed them to her.

"Oh, Wes, thank you," she said to me. She took a quick smell of the arrangement of daisies, tulips, and chrysanthemums. "They are lovely."

"I'm glad you like them," I said to her. "To be honest, it's been a long time since I bought flowers for a woman. I wasn't sure if I had picked out something nice or not."

"It's perfect," Kristin said.

I then took a tablecloth out of the hamper and spread the red plaid cloth over the picnic table.

"I know it's still a little early for lunch," I said to her looking down at my watch, "but I have a few things we can have now." I took out the grapes, apples, cheese and crackers that I had picked up and put them on one of the plates that was packed in the hamper. I then sat next to Kristin as we snacked and looked out over the water.

"This is an amazing spot, Wes," she said to me as she snacked on a red grape.

"It's pretty nice," I said with a sigh. "It's always been my favorite spot on the farm. After we got this all fixed up, I would try to come down here as often as I could. Sometimes we would have parties down here, or I would bring Izzy down here. Many times I would just come down here by myself to enjoy the solitude."

"Did... did your ex-wife like coming here?" Kristin asked with some trepidation. I could see she was a little nervous about bringing her up, but she was probably curious as well.

"Rachel was gone before this place was finished," I told her. "She was never much of the outdoors type anyway. She was more of the indoor, luxury hotel kind of woman."

"I'm sorry," Kristin said to me. "I didn't mean to bring up a sore subject."

"It's fine," I said to her. "Rachel comes from a wealthy family around here. I think she was used to certain things and liked that way of life. I was able to give it to her, but she didn't like the idea of living on a farm in a small town while I was out traveling around to big cities. She had images of a different life than what I wanted. I wanted to play ball, but I would have preferred coming back to the quiet around here than staying at a hotel in a city somewhere."

"Do you talk to her at all?"

"Rachel? Not since the divorce was finalized really," I said to her. "She used to call Izzy now and then, but even that has stopped over the years, at least as far as I know. She's enjoying her life in New York I guess. It's just the two of them, no kids, and I'm sure they go out and travel and do all kinds of fancy things together. If she's happy, then that's fine."

I reached into the saddlebag and pulled out a bottle of wine and a corkscrew. The hamper had a couple of glasses in it so I could pour us some of the red wine to go with our snack.

"Is there anything you don't have in there?" Kristin asked me, half-joking.

"I just wanted to be prepared, so I think there's a little of everything in here," I told her, looking into the bag.

After we finished snacking, we took a walk together down towards the edge of the pond. The water was clear and quiet, and other than the occasional bird swooping down over the water, there wasn't much action going on there. We stood next to each other, holding our glasses of wine, looking out over the water. Kristin reached over with her right hand and took my left hand in hers, holding it. I turned and looked at her and gave her gentle kiss on the lips. We stood on the edge of the water, kissing lightly for a few minutes before she broke the spell.

"So... what else do you have planned for today?" she said to me slyly.

"Well I did pack a lunch," I told her. "Just some sandwiches and chips, and some chocolate for dessert."

"I'm not very hungry right now for lunch," she told me. I watched her as she slowly walked away from me and back up towards the picnic table. She took a look in the hamper and pulled out the two rolled blankets that were packed in there and walked over to the small clearing beyond the table that was shaded by some trees. The clearing was just beyond a small fire pit that we had there.

Kristin spread out one of the blankets, colored to match the tablecloth, on the grass in the clearing, and sat down on it. I walked over next to her and sat down with her and looked into her eyes. She looked at me and placed her left hand on my cheek, cradling it, and then leaned in to kiss me. I kissed her back, deeper than I had before. There was more emotion and feeling behind this kiss, and I felt her move her body close to mine.

I wanted to take cues from her, not moving too fast, but at a pace she was comfortable with. I wrapped my arms around her and kissed her more passionately. I moved my lips from hers and slowly kissed her cheek, sliding my lips down gently to the nape of her neck. As I kissed her, I could feel Kristin shrug out of denim jacket, leaving her neck and shoulders bare to me. I continued to kiss my way down her neck to her right shoulder, planting small kisses along the way, as she held my head there in her hands.

I could feel that her breathing was starting to quicken a bit and the strap of her tank top had slid off her right shoulder as I was kissing her. Kristen moved from me slightly, just enough so that she could lift her cotton tank top slowly over her head. She came close to me again, and I slowly guided her down onto the blanket, kissing down her neck until I reached the top of her breasts. I traced the outline of the tops of her breasts with my index finger, lightly moving my finger back and forth over her as I resumed kissing her. I could see her breathing quicken each time my finger went over her until I slipped my finger down and found the small clasp in the front of her white lacy bra. I deftly undid the clasp with my forefinger and thumb and gently pushed the cups of the bra to the sides of her body.

I caressed her left breast in my hand, placing my palm over it and lightly rubbing, so my palm grazed her nipple over and over as it rose and became erect. I could hear Kristen gasp as her nipple became more and more sensitive in my hand and her back arched up off slightly off the blanket so she could feel a firmer touch on her body. I kept lightly caressing her left breast while I leaned over and began to kiss her right breast, moving over and around it, getting close to her nipple but never touching it, just getting teasingly close with my lips.

My lips hovered just above her right nipple as I kept lightly cupping her left breast. I softly blew on her right nipple, watching her body react as Kristin let out a light moan. I leaned closer and gently drew her nipple into my mouth, causing her to moan louder this time. Kristin pushed her body closer to me again, bringing her breasts tighter against my hand and my lips. I moved my lips over to her left breast then, switching things up, to excite her even more.

I started to kiss my way down her body again, going over her taut stomach until I reached the top of her jeans. I unbuttoned the jeans and slowly eased the zipper down, exposing just the top of the lacy white panties she wore to match her bra. I put a hand on each side of her jeans and eased them down her legs, down to the tops of the sneakers she wore. I quickly pulled her sneakers off and tossed them to the side so I could finish taking off her jeans, which then ended up in a ball off to the side of the blanket.

I worked my way back up her legs, running my fingertips lightly over her calves and up to her thighs. Kristin squirmed lightly on the blanket as my touch sent shivers up and down her body. I was between her legs know, kneeling, moving my fingertips over and over up and down her thighs, tracing along the edges of her panties. My fingers grazed gently over the front of her panties, causing her to gasp again. I held my palm there for a moment and could feel how warm she was, and one finger, and then two, slowly eased their way inside her panties to touch her.

I could feel her wetness right away, and she gasped lightly as one finger slipped barely inside her. I moved my body up to kiss her deeply on the lips as my fingers moved a bit deeper inside her. My kiss stifled her moan once again, and I moved down from her lips to kiss her neck again.

"Wes," Kristin panted softly. I moved my fingers slowly in and out of her, and she moaned again, as I could feel her thighs tighten on my hand.

"Oh God, Wes, please..." Kristin's hands were reaching down, running over my body, practically tearing my shirt open. I was relishing watching her, seeing her react to my touch and how much pleasure it was bringing her, but I also wasn't sure how much longer my body could hold out from wanting her.

I pulled myself away from her body and slowly stood up. I could see Kristin gazing at me through eyes half open as she watched me pull off my shirt. I kicked off my boots and then unbuckled my belt so I could remove my jeans, leaving me in just my black briefs. It was obvious how aroused I was from all the interaction, and I pulled my briefs down to remove them, and then lowered myself back down between Kristen's legs.

My hands immediately went to the waistband of her delicate panties as I pulled them down her legs and tossed them aside. We were both naked now, and Kristin immediately pulled me close to her body. We kissed deeper and more aggressively this time and feeling her soft, bare flesh against mine was almost more than I could take. I went down to kiss her again, this time pulling her close to me so that I could slide myself inside her.

We both groaned at the sensation as I moved into her. Kristin clutched my body tightly, pulling me close to her with her hands on my back. I moved into her slowly at first, but then her body was signaling to me that she wanted to move faster. Within moments we were in a rhythm, moving with and against each other. I felt Kristin wrap her legs around me, pulling me even closer to her if that was possible. Her body then tightened on me, going tense as I felt her start to orgasm.

Her body's response and reaction were more than I could take any more. I groaned as I thrust into her once more and felt my own orgasm overcome me. I held her warm body against mine tightly as we kissed over and over, letting the waves of pleasure roll over us again and again.

I softly rolled to the right, so I was laying next to Kristin. I put my arm around her to pull her closer to me and held her there as we both looked up at the trees creating the shade above us. Sunlight softly filtered through the branches and just budding leaves.

"So is this part of what you planned for today?" Kristin said to me as she caught her breath.

I glanced over at her. "No... I mean I'm glad it did happen, but I never planned for that... I mean..." I was feeling very flustered at the moment, and Kristin leaned in and kissed my neck, nuzzling into me.

"It's okay, Wes," she said to me. "I didn't plan on it either. There was just something about the moment, the mood... and you." I could feel a slight chill run through her as the breeze blew a little, and I grabbed the other blanket and threw it over us for some extra warmth. Kristin's right hand lightly toyed with the hair on my chest as we laid there peacefully.

Within just a few moments, Kristin had drifted off to sleep. Her gentle breathing continued as I held her close to me. I couldn't believe what had just taken place. I had never done something like this before with any woman, but there was something about Kristin that had stirred up feelings in me that I had not experienced for a very long time. I felt drawn and connected to her, even though we had only known each other for a few days. I certainly wouldn't be here with her like this if I didn't feel that way.

This was the first woman in a long time that I felt comfortable and happy with. Kristin was also the first one that didn't care about baseball, how much money I had or anything to do with fame and fortune. I looked at her in my arms and brushed a few locks of her hair out of her face so I could see her clearly and watch her sleep in my arms.

I laid back, putting my left arm behind my head, and closed my eyes to relax. This was the first time in days, maybe weeks, that felt stress-free, without worry, and yes, happy. I could feel myself falling asleep as well.

You could get used to living a life like this, my brain said to me as I drifted off.

Chapter 17

Kristin

The whole experience of the day flooded my dreams as I slept. There I was with Wes, enjoying a day out by the pond, laughing, smiling, getting to know one another. And in the next moment, we were there under the trees with each other, making love, exploring each other's bodies, and becoming intimate for the first time. The pleasantness of both the dreams and of the real experience was enough to make me snuggle closer to Wes' body, to feel him next to me.

As I slowly awoke and my eyes fluttered open, I could see that Wes was asleep under the blanket as well, snoring softly as he lay there next to me. Seeing him there in the dimming light, I could get a closer look at him and see the unique combination of the strength he had physically in his body and the gentleness he had displayed with me before. He had just a hint of stubble on his face, giving him a manly look, and this went perfectly with the strong arm that was wrapped around me as he slept. I took a quick peek again under the blanket and could see that he kept himself in amazing shape and certainly had the body of a well-toned athlete, from his broad shoulders and chest to his strong abs.

I wasn't sure how long we had been there or had been asleep for that matter, but the day seemed like it had gone by quite a bit. I nudged Wes lightly and saw him begin to stir before his eyes opened. He turned and smiled at me, and I gave him a light kiss on the lips.

"I guess we dozed off," I said softly.

"I guess so," Wes answered, rolling over on his side so he could look right at me. I could see that his eyes were an amazing mix of blue and gray. He looked down at his wrist at the watch he was wearing. And sat up.

"Man, it's almost five o'clock. We've been sleeping for a long time."

He looked over at the hitch where the horses were, and they were standing idly by as if they had been waiting for us to finally get up.

I curled under the blanket as I watched Wes reach over and grab his briefs and jeans. He tugged the clothing up his strong legs, and I marveled at his body as he got dressed. He looked down at me and smiled as he reached over and grabbed his shirt and put it on.

"What are you staring at?" he said with a smile.

"I was just enjoying this beautiful view," I said to him wryly.

"We should probably get the horses back," Wes said to me as he sat down on the blanket next to me to put his boots on.

"Rats," I said to him. "I was hoping to enjoy the view some more," I told him playfully as I toyed with his belt. I wrapped my arms around his neck and kissed him, feeling the blanket slip from around me and exposing my bare breasts.

"You make it very tempting," Wes said to me with a sigh. "But I don't want one of the guys to have to stick around late just waiting for us to get back."

"Okay," I said pouting. Wes had neatly piled my clothing together and handed it to me. I couldn't help but notice that he watched me get dressed this time, smiling all along the way.

"What are you looking at?" I said to him as I fastened the front closure of my bra and pulled my tank top on.

"An even more beautiful view," he said to me.

Wes packed up all the items we had brought with us, including the lunch we never really ate and cleaned up the area while I rolled up the blankets and put them back in the wicker hamper on the picnic table. Wes put the saddlebags back on his horse and unhitched the horses so I could get back on Bonnie. I mounted her easily, with a little help from Wes, and the riding started to come back to me more. Wes got on his horse with great ease, and you could tell that he had been both around horses and riding for many years.

We took a walk back on the trail with the horses and got a beautiful view of the sun as it was getting later in the day. The way it peeked through the trees as we got closer to sunset was incredible and could see why Wes loved living on this piece of land. We were quiet as we rode back side by side, giving the occasional glance over at each other. I could see Wes spying me out of the corner of his eye to make sure I was doing okay, and just that look alone made me blush a bit and feel very special at that moment.

We got back to the stable easily, and one of the hands was there to help me dismount. I gave Bonnie a loving pat and a kiss on her nose.

"Thanks for the lovely ride, Bonnie," I said to her as the hand led our horses back into the stable. Wes took my hand in his as we walked slowly back towards his SUV.

"It was an amazing day, Wes," I said to him as I looked up at him as we stood near the front of his car.

"It doesn't have to end now," he said to me. "I never got to give you lunch, so how about we go back to my place for some dinner?"

I was glad that he asked as I didn't want this day to end.

"I could eat some dinner," I said with a smile. Wes looked relieved and opened the car door for me so I could get in. He climbed into the driver's side, and we turned around and went down the short road and then made the left to go up the hill. We drove past his parent's house and came up to the large circular driveway at the top of the hill where the immense house was.

I got out of the car and stood in front of the steps to the house as Wes came around towards me. We walked up the short flight of steps together, and he unlocked the door, moving inside quickly to shut off the alarm system. He flipped the light switch on the wall near the alarm pad, and the large chandelier in the foyer lit up right away, illuminating the area.

Just what I had seen so far of the house was amazing. The entryway had beautiful stone flooring with mixed colors of dark browns and light tans. There was a living room just off to the right with a large sofa and chairs, a beautiful throw rug and a stone fireplace. Wes started walking down the small hallway as I slowly followed him.

We walked into the kitchen, which was an immense area that would be any homeowner's dream. There were granite countertops, top of the line appliances and an island area where there was both a flattop and a grill. Over the island was a large vent that pulled up the heat and smoke. Just to the left was a small set of steps that led down to a dining area with a beautiful mahogany wood table and chairs that looked out over the backyard area.

I felt speechless just looking around the place. "Your home is fantastic Wes," I said to him. I could see he felt a little embarrassed by all that it had.

"It's a bit much really, especially considering the place is empty so often. Even when I am home over the winter, a lot of the time it's just me, with Izzy staying down with my parents. When we had the place built, I think we had different ideas of how it would be used, with a bigger family, more friends, and parties, stuff like that, but it just didn't work out that way. We were young and had too much money to play with I guess."

I was looking around at all that was here before I realized I needed to use the bathroom.

"Wes, where's your bathroom?" I asked him, feeling a bit embarrassed.

"Oh, there's a bunch of them, but the closest one is in my bedroom. The bedroom is just off the kitchen here," Wes said as he pointed, "and the bathroom is on the righthand side of the room."

"Thanks," I said to him as I slowly made my way in that direction. I walked over and into his bedroom, feeling for the light switch so I could turn it on. The bedroom was a very large master suite with a king-size bed right in the center that was nicely made. The room looked immaculate, almost like no one was ever there. I made my way over to the bathroom and turned the lights on in there and was equally as impressed. The bathroom had separate sinks, a sunken tub and a very large shower with glass doors and silver fittings.

I've been in restaurants with smaller bathrooms than this, I thought to myself. After using the facilities and washing up, I walked my way back into the kitchen. Wes was working on getting some things out for dinner.

"I think your bathroom is bigger than my whole apartment," I said to Wes.

He gave an embarrassed chuckle. "Yeah, it's pretty big," he said as I saw him gathering some vegetables. "I don't think I have used it to its full potential."

I walked over to where Wes was at one of the counters. "So what are we having?" I said to him as I leaned over to take a look.

"Well, it's your choice," he said to me. "I have some steaks, chicken, pork chops, seafood, pretty much anything you could want. I just stocked the fridge, so there's plenty around."

I opened up the large double-door refrigerator to look at what was there. Wes wasn't kidding when he said it was stocked. There was a lot of food in there as it was filled with beverages, fresh vegetables, meats and more. I grabbed a package that was labeled shrimp and brought it out to him.

"That's a lot of food for one guy," I said to him as I came back over to the counter.

"I know," Wes said to me. "I didn't know when Izzy would be here, so I think I overordered on the meats, but I eat lots of vegetables and fruits myself to help keep me in shape, so that's the bulk of what you will find in there."

I handed Wes, the package of shrimp. "Let's have this," I said to him with a smile.

"Sounds great," Wes said as he grabbed some garlic and fresh herbs. He pulled a pot down from the rack above the island and grabbed a large saute pan from one of the cabinets.

"Is there anything I can do?" I asked him as I watched him start to peel and devein the shrimp.

He smiled at me and said, "Would you like to put together a salad for us?"

"Sure," I told him excitedly. I gathered some of the greens, a cucumber, some radishes and cherry tomatoes. Wes pointed me to where I could find a cutting board, and he came over with a bamboo salad bowl and a knife to use. I set to work on the salad while Wes got some rice going in a pot and kept working on the shrimp.

It was so much fun to be together in the kitchen cooking with someone. As I was cutting vegetables and getting the greens ready, I spied a Bluetooth speaker on the far counter. "Can we put some music on?" I asked Wes.

"Sounds good to me," he said and took his phone out of his pocket. He selected something to play, and it started to play country music over the speaker. I looked over at Wes and smiled at him as I watched him mouthing the words to the song and dancing along.

He looked up at me and saw me watching him and stopped his lip sync performance. I giggled and went back to making the salad, putting everything together in the bowl and tossing it lightly. By the time I was done, Wes had the shrimp cooking in the saute pan with some butter, garlic, and herbs. He plated everything nicely, along with the rice, and brought it over to the table in the dining area. He then got some plates and bowls and cutlery out of the kitchen and set places for us. He then grabbed a bottle of white wine from the refrigerator and poured us a couple of glasses.

He kept the lights dim in the dining area so that we could see out over the backyard and catch the last of the sun setting off in the distance through the trees. I could see he had an extensive outdoor entertainment area, with a large patio. Beyond that was an in-ground pool and further up the hill behind the house I could see a building there.

"What's that up there?" I asked Wes as I put a forkful of shrimp and rice in my mouth.

"That building?" Wes asked as he pointed. He put his fork down for a moment. "That's my workout area. There's a small gym in there and a batting cage so I can keep in shape."

"Wow," I said to Wes as I ate some salad.

"Wow, what?" he asked as he ate some more.

"I guess I just never met anyone that could afford something like that before. It seems so... decadent."

"I suppose it is, to some people," Wes said casually. "but it is how I make my living. I need to make sure I stay in good shape all the time, and I'm not getting any younger. But the pitchers are," he added, "and they are a lot faster than they used to be."

" I would love to see it sometime," I mentioned while I had another bite.

"I don't think I've ever had anyone else up there before," Wes commented. "You would be the first."

"Ooh, like going to Superman's Fortress of Solitude," I said with a laugh.

We continued eating, making small talk through the meal to find out more about each other. I told Wes about my sister Lucy, and growing up in Augusta and how much fun we had as kids. I let him know about parents, both teachers at the local high school near my home, and how they had been married over twenty-five years now and how happy they were for me to make this move up north.

"I'm sure they're very proud of you," Wes said as he wiped his face with a napkin. Wes stood up and took my empty plate, clearing things off and putting the dishes in the dishwasher. I went to get up and help, but he put his hand on my shoulder to stop me.

"Sit, drink your wine; I got this," he said as he cleaned. I watched him load up the dishwasher and put things away. When he was done, he switched the music over to classical music, something soothing and relaxing, and came back over to the table to sit with me. Wes felt his phone buzz and took a look at it.

"It's a message from Izzy," he said. "She's spending the night at her friend's house. I guess I'll see her tomorrow."

"So I guess you're alone for the night," I said to him. I took another sip of wine while I saw Wes look at me as he went back to cleaning. "You certainly know how to impress a lady," I said to Wes. "Horseback rides, picnics, flowers, cooking dinner, romantic music and... and well, other things," I said with a grin. "You pulled out all the stops today. Thank you for making me feel special."

"It's been my pleasure, truly," Wes said as he smiled at me. He got up from his chair and bent down and kissed me lovingly. I put my left hand on his neck to pull him closer to me. Before I knew it, I found myself standing, kissing him passionately. My knees were feeling weak from his kisses, and his hands went down to my hips, holding me there with him. When we finally broke the kiss, my head was spinning.

"You okay," he said to me.

"Oh yeah," I said to him. "Just feeling a little overwhelmed and lightheaded."

"It must be the wine," Wes told me.

"I don't think that's it," I whispered as I started to kiss him again.

"Maybe you need to lie down for a bit," he offered.

"I think maybe I do," I said to him as I took him by the hand and led him towards his bedroom. I walked into the bedroom and turned around to face Wes. I kicked off my sneakers and laid back on the bed, feeling the soft down of the blanket beneath me. I reached down and opened the button on my jeans and slowly unzipped them. I then wiggled myself out of the jeans, leaving me in my tank top and panties. Wes made a move to reach down to me on the bed when I put a hand up to stop him.

"I think you are overdressed a tad," I said to him. "Maybe you need to take a few things off first." I gazed up at Wes seductively, waiting for him to start to undress.

He stepped back and kicked off his boots first. He then moved on to his shirt, unbuttoning it quickly and tossing it to the floor, revealing his muscular chest and abs. I could feel my breathing begin to get deeper as I watched him take off his jeans, pulling them down his legs so that he was just in his black briefs. The noticeable, telltale sign of the bulge in his briefs told me he was enjoying this just as much as I was.

"How's this," Wes said as he put his hands on his hips, striking a model pose for me. I giggled at the sight and nodded in approval. I pushed myself so I was sitting on the edge of the bed, facing him, and pulled on his hips to bring him closer to me. My hands moved slowly in from his hips to the front of his briefs, giving him a light squeeze. I looked up to see Wes had closed his eyes and I lightly squeezed and massaged him again.

I could feel Wes growing bigger and harder in his briefs with even just the lightest touch. I hooked my fingers inside his briefs and eased them down his legs. Before Wes could take the time to step out of them and get on the bed with me, I reached over and gently grazed him with my fingernails, causing him to shudder. I took him in my left hand, feeling the warm, strong thickness of him, and stroked him up and down, from bottom to top. I loved seeing the look of delight on his face as I continued to touch him. His chest moved in and out more rapidly with each long, slow stroke I took.

"Kristin... I don't how much of this I can take," he whispered to me.

"Does that mean you want me to stop?" I said with a wicked grin, running my index finger up the length of his shaft. I heard a low growl escape from his lips as he picked me up and tossed me further back on the bed and then leaped on the bed next to me. I let out a playful scream and then felt his arms around me as he kissed me hard.

Wes quickly lifted my tank top up and over my head and then undid the front clasp of my bra in one motion. I pulled the bra off and went back to kissing him hungrily. I pushed him down on the bed and positioned myself over him. Standing up on the bed, I grinned as I pulled down my panties and tossed them to him. Wes tossed them aside onto the floor as I knelt down between his legs. I reached down and stroked him again, causing him to stiffen further in my hand. I then slowly crawled up his body, letting his hardness briefly glide between my breasts, before I was in position to take him inside me.

I slowly eased myself down on him, and Wes slid inside me easily. I was more than ready for him and didn't know how long I could hold out myself at this point, but I was loving every minute of it. I moved my hips in slow circles on him, feeling him move inside me, touching me deeply. I could see that he was gripping the blankets tightly in his fists while he tried to hold out. I put my hands on his chest to brace myself as I steadily picked up the pace, feeling his body thrust up off the bed to meet the rhythm I moved at. I could feel my orgasm starting to build as I moaned and tightened all around him. Wes groaned deeply and grabbed my hips, holding me in place as I felt him start to orgasm in me. That feeling inside me was all I needed to feel, and I let myself go to my own orgasm. My body shuddered, and I collapsed onto his chest, holding onto Wes tightly.

When I felt his breathing start to slow down, I lifted my head up off his chest and smiled up at him. I lifted my quivering legs off him and laid in his arms, feeling the sweat on both of our bodies from the experience. I looked over at Wes and saw him still staring up at the ceiling.

"Everything okay?" I said with a grin.

"I think so," Wes said to me as he looked at me and smiled. "That was... I don't even know how to describe it," he said to me with a laugh.

"I'll take that as a compliment," I told him as I snuggled into his arms.

"I don't know that I'll have the energy to drive you home tonight," Wes said to me.

"I think I am okay with that," I told him. Wes got the blanket from beneath us so we could climb under it together. I put my head on his shoulder as we both lay back on the bed, listening to the classical music that was still playing on the speaker in the kitchen. I closed my eyes and sighed, wondering how things could get any better than this.

Chapter 18

Kristin

The sun was peeking through the blinds in the bedroom and it was just enough to rouse me from my sleep. I looked over and saw I was laying close to Wes, who was breathing lightly as he slept. A smile crept across my face as I realized how happy I was here.

I certainly wasn't accustomed to sleeping with someone after knowing them for such a short time. In fact, I wasn't much accustomed to having sex with anyone, let alone spending the night with them. There had been a couple of boyfriends in college that I had been with, but that was pretty much it for me. I was only out of school a short time before I moved to Chandler, and there had been no one else before Wes came along. He had come in and swept me off my feet, quite literally, in a short amount of time, and I was glad about it.

Since Wes was still sleeping soundly, I thought I would get up and make us some coffee and maybe breakfast as a nice surprise. I got out of bed without a stitch of clothing on. I saw my clothes tossed about the room and didn't really feel like putting everything back on. I grabbed my panties off the floor and slid them up my legs. I then walked over to Wes' closet and quietly opened the door. I was bowled over by the immense walk-in closet that was before me and saw it was filled with suits, pants, shirts, shoes and the like. I slowly walked through, touching different things, until I decided to grab one of his light blue dress shirts hanging there. I slid the shirt on, lifting the collar up to my face and getting the faint smell of him on it. Wes was much bigger than I was, so the shirt was easily like wearing a nightshirt for me, coming down pretty far on me to give me coverage. I rolled up the sleeves a bit and slipped out of the bedroom, leaving the door open just a crack.

I stepped out into the kitchen and saw the coffeemaker and poured some water into it. It took me a little bit to track down when the coffee and filters were, but I managed to find everything and got the coffee brewing. As the coffee brewed, I found some bagels in a bag on the counter and thought I would put them in the toaster for us. That was all easy enough to put together for me. As the bagels toasted, I went looking for a couple of coffee mugs.

I found the mugs on a shelf in one of the cabinets above the counter and was stretching to reach them. I could feel the shirt I was wearing riding up a bit in the back as I reached, standing on my tiptoes to grab a mug. I had just gotten the mug around one of my fingers and was pulling it down when I was startled.

"What are you doing here?" the voice said.

I felt the mug slip out of my hand and crash to the counter, shattering it into pieces as I gasped. I turned around and saw Isabelle standing there, obviously surprised to see me in the kitchen wearing her father's shirt and not much else.

"Isabelle," I answered, feeling startled as I tried to gather up the broken pieces of the ceramic mug carefully. "You scared me."

Isabelle walked closer to me, looking confused, hurt, and a little bit upset.

"Why are you here in the morning, and wearing one of my dad's shirts?" she asked in a raised voice.

"Isabelle, please, let me explain," I said to her, trying to think of how I was going to phrase everything to her. I was sure she had a million thoughts running through her head, and none of them were likely very flattering towards me at the moment.

"I don't think there's too much to explain," Isabelle said to me as she was standing in front of me now. She was taller than me under normal circumstances, but with her in her sneakers and me barefoot, it was even more pronounced. I could see that her face was getting a little red as she glared at me. "It's pretty obvious what happened."

I was feeling flustered and had trouble coming up with any way to defend myself right now.

"I know how this must look to you, and I'm sorry for that but..." I said to her.

"But what?" Isabelle shouted.

"What's going on out here?" I looked behind Isabelle and saw Wes standing there in a white bathrobe he had thrown on. Isabelle turned around and saw her father standing there. "Izzy, what are you doing here? I thought I was picking you up at Amy's this morning."

"I guess you didn't read the text I sent you late last night," she said angrily. "I told you Amy's mom was going to drop me off here this morning so we could... spend the day together..." her voice trailed off, sounding as though it had a mix of anger and tears in it, and she turned and looked back at me.

"Izzy," Wes said as he walked towards her, "I'm sorry I didn't see your text."

"Why?" she yelled. "So you could sneak her out early before I got back here?"

"Hey," Wes answered, "that's not fair."

"Really? That's what you would have done, isn't it? So I wouldn't have to walk into the house in the morning to see her strutting around in your shirt?" Isabelle turned and looked at me again. "Are you happy now?" she yelled at me. "You got the chance to fuck a famous rich guy, and now you can brag to your friends about it."

I felt about two inches tall and could feel my own tears welling up inside me. I wanted to fight back, but I thought that would make things worse.

"WHOA!" Wes yelled, coming up to Isabelle and spinning her around to face him. "Don't talk to Kristin that way; don't talk to anyone that way! I don't know what has gotten into you, but I can tell you I don't like it. Now apologize to Kristin and then we can sit down and talk about this."

"I don't think so," Isabelle said to him, wrestling her arm free from Wes. She stormed off, running down the hall.

"Izzy!" Wes yelled at her and followed her, but I heard the front door slam. It opened again quickly, and I could hear Wes yelling again.

I went into the bedroom to quickly gather my things. I grabbed my jeans off the floor and pulled them on quickly. I searched the room for my bra and tank top and tracked them down. I took off Wes' shirt and threw it on the floor as I put my bra on and then pulled the tank top over my head. I sat on the bed, putting my sneakers on as Wes walked in and came over to me.

"Kristin, I am so sorry," he said to me, putting his arms out to me.

"I should go, Wes," I said through my tears. "Maybe this was a mistake." I slipped my other sneaker on and began to look frantically for my jacket. I tried to control my tears, but I was not doing a very good job.

"Kristin, hold on," Wes said to me, trying to stop me. By then I had found my jacket and my purse and was walking out the door. I wasn't even sure what I was going to do. The walk back to my apartment wasn't all that far, and I figured I could make it on my own.

"Wait!" Wes yelled as he got a hold of my arm. I started sobbing harder as he brought me close to him.

"Wes, you need to go talk to Isabelle," I said to him, trying to be rational about everything. "She... she obviously is not ready for you to start seeing someone; certainly not me at least."

"She barely knows you, Kristin," Wes said as he looked down at me. "It's just her gut reaction. She doesn't understand things like this."

"I'm beginning to think I don't either," I said to Wes. I turned and began my walk down the road, away from the house and Wes. I cried with each step, trying to figure out what I did wrong. Wes kept calling out to me, but I picked up my pace and moved faster until I had gone past his parent's house and towards the end of the road.

I raced over onto Route 5 and began my trek back towards Main Street. A moment later I saw a blue pickup truck go by me and then stop about ten feet in front of me. The passenger side door bounced open, and as I slowly walked up to it, I peered inside. There was Wes' father, Wyatt, sitting in the driver's seat.

"Hop in," he said to me gently. "I'll give you a ride home if that's what you want."

I got into the truck and closed the passenger door. Wyatt merged back onto the road and headed into town. We didn't say anything to each other at first, and within moments I found myself crying into my hands. I cried until Wyatt pulled into the parking lot at my apartment.

"Kristin," Wyatt said to me, "Wes was at my house trying to talk to Izzy when I left to find you. You have to know you didn't do anything wrong. I think the whole thing just caught Izzy off guard. She's used to being the only one in Wes' life. I think seeing you at the house just put her on the defensive."

I sniffled a bit from the tears before Wyatt handed me a white handkerchief. I took it wiped my face with it.

"Thank you, Wyatt," I said to him. "I appreciate the hanky, and the ride, and your words. Perhaps things were just moving too fast anyway. We barely know each other, really; I can see why she would be upset. The last thing I want is to come between the two of them."

"Let the two of them hash this out with each other," Wyatt said to me calmly. "They both need time to understand a little more about each other, especially if they are going to be around each other more. Don't jump to any conclusions."

"I'll try not to, but given the circumstances, it's a little difficult," I told Wyatt.

"I know it looks that way," Wyatt said, "but I can tell you one thing for certain. Even though you two have only known each other for a few days, I have never seen Wes like this with anyone. I know you are special to him, and that's not an easy thing to be with him. He doesn't let people in like that. Goodness knows, he needs someone like you in his life."

I tried to crack a small smile at Wyatt as he attempted to make me feel better. I went to hand back the hanky to Wyatt.

"You keep it," he said to me, holding his hand up. "You can give it back to me the next time you see me."

I climbed out of the truck and closed the door, and made my way slowly up the stairs to my apartment door. Wyatt stayed in the parking lot until he saw me open my door and then he pulled away. I got inside the apartment and closed the door, breaking out into tears again. I felt my purse vibrate and opened it and pulled my phone out. There were two missed calls from Wes and then a text message from him:

I'm worried about you. I hope you're okay. Just let me know you're okay.

I sent him a text message back:

I'm home. Your father gave me a ride. I'm okay.

Wes replied immediately:

Okay. Can I call you? Can we talk about this?

I thought about it for a moment and then sent him a reply:

Not now. Talk to Isabelle. She needs you before you can talk to me.

I then turned my phone off so I wouldn't have to deal with more messages. I walked into my bedroom, tossed my purse and phone onto my nightstand, and crawled into my bed, wishing I could roll things back a few hours, or even a day, and do things differently.

Chapter 19

Wes

Everything took a turn for the worse so quickly it was almost difficult for me to react to it. I was sleeping comfortably in bed when I heard the shouting and ruckus develop in the kitchen. At first, it didn't dawn on me just who it was who was fighting, but once I heard the two distinct voices of Kristin and Izzy, I knew something was very wrong. Izzy had apparently come to the house early, seen Kristin there, and had a reaction. I leaped out of bed and grabbed my robe, but by the time I got out there, Izzy was already on a tirade like I had never seen her in before.

I did my best to try to calm the situation, but I think no matter what I said at the moment was going to have little effect. When Izzy said what she said and stormed out, I immediately went after her to stop her. It felt like the right thing for me to do at the time, even if Kristin wasn't going to see it that way. By the time I got to the front door, she was already halfway down the hill to my parent's house, and I thought it was better to let her go and deal with Kristin and then go after Izzy.

I tried to reason with Kristin, to apologize to her and work to figure out what was going on, but she was much too upset to deal with it at the moment. She was down the hill just as quickly as Izzy was before I could try to convince her to stay and talk or at least get in my car with me. I was left standing at the front door in my robe trying to figure out the calamity of the moment.

I raced into the house and put on the first clothing I could find, threw my sneakers on, and hopped in my car. My first stop was going to have to be my parent's house to see what was going on with Izzy. I was down the hill in seconds and swerved into the driveway, kicking up dust and dirt along the way.

When I got inside, my father was standing there with a bewildered look on his face. I could hear my mother trying to talk to Izzy through the door of her bedroom in as calm a manner as possible. I started to walk towards the bedroom, feeling more angry and upset with each passing second. My father grabbed my arm as I was walking by him to stop me.

"Hold on a second, Wes," he said to me as he held me tightly. He began to slowly back me up towards the front door.

"Dad, just let me go to talk to Izzy," I said to him, trying to control myself.

"Barreling in there and yelling at her is not going to help things any right now," Dad told me calmly. "What the hell happened?"

I took a deep breath and exhaled. "I guess Izzy got dropped off at the house this morning, came in, and saw Kristin in the kitchen. She started yelling and screaming, and the next thing I know, she is swearing at Kristin and tearing out of the house. I couldn't stop her from running down here to you guys."

"Okay, well that helps to start to explain things," Dad said to me. "How's Kristin? Where is she?"

"She was upset and left too," I said, my mind racing now. "She got out of the house and down the hill before I could stop her. I got dressed and came here first."

Dad sighed and rubbed his lightly grizzled and gray chin. "You go talk to Izzy," he said to me. "I'll go pick up Kristin, so she's not walking on Route 5." Dad walked to the door and grabbed his keys and headed out while I made my way down the hall to Izzy's room.

Mom was standing by her door, trying to talk through it and soothe Izzy to get her to open the door for her. When I got over there, Mom had a look on her face and shrugged her shoulders. She pulled me lightly to the side.

"I don't know what happened," Mom said to me, "but I've never seen her so upset where she won't even talk to me about it."

I banged on the door loudly. "Isabelle, open the door!" I yelled.

"No!" she shouted back. "Go back home and leave me here!"

I pushed hard on the door with my shoulder, feeling the door was locked.

"Why do you let her have a lock on the door?" I asked Mom in frustration. "Isabelle, open the damn door, or I'm kicking it in!"

"Not the solution, Wesley," my mother said to me sternly. She walked into her bedroom and came back out carrying a small screwdriver and handed it to me. I took the screwdriver and worked it into the doorknob, easily turning the lock and opening the door, so I could go in. I shut the door behind me firmly. I could see Izzy staring up at me as she was laying on her bed, her eyes red and puffy from crying.

"I didn't say you could come in," she said angrily, shocked I would come in uninvited.

"You gave up the right to decency when you started shouting obscenities before," I said to her, trying to contain myself a little.

"What did you expect, Dad? That I run over to her and give her a hug for spending the night with you?" Izzy turned her face away from me.

"Hey, what is going on with you? I don't know where all this is coming from, and if you don't talk to me about it, we can't do anything but keep shouting at each other." I sat down on the edge of her bed near her head and went to touch her hair. She quickly shifted her head away from me.

"If you weren't ready for me to date someone Izzy, you should have said something to me two days ago when it first came up," I said to her.

Izzy turned and looked at me with tears.

"I have no problem with you going out on dates," Izzy said, trying to re-gain her composure. "It's a little different when I walk in and see someone half-dressed in our kitchen. I came home looking to spend the day with you, just us, like we talked about. Instead, I see her in there."

I wasn't sure what I should say to Izzy at this point. I could certainly see why she would be upset, but how was I supposed to change what had already happened?

"Look, Izzy," I said quietly, "I'm sorry that is what happened, and it upset you. I... I don't really know what to say about it."

"There's nothing for you to say, Dad," Izzy replied. "I can't believe you would let yourself be taken in that way. You hardly know her. She's just looking to use you."

I rose from the bed, feeling anger welling in me again.

"How dare you say that," I told Izzy. "You don't know anything about her; you just jumped to conclusions right away. You haven't learned enough about life yet Izzy to say that. And do you honestly think I would do that, or act that way? Just bring someone home and sleep with them just so I could do it? I would hope that you know me better than that to think that was true."

"I barely know you at all!" Izzy shouted back at me. "You've been home three or four months a year for my entire life. How do I know what you are like? What you do, or feel, or anything else? We spend a few weeks together doing things in the winter, but I don't really know you, Dad, just like you don't really know me."

Her statement stung me and caught me off guard. All this time, I had thought we had a good relationship with each other, but clearly, Izzy didn't feel the same way, at least not at this point in her life. I sat back down on the bed next to her, feeling sadder than I had in a very long time.

"I'm sorry you feel that way, Izzy," I said to her. "I know I haven't been the ideal Dad for you, but this is the life I lead, and it allows us to live the way we do and have what we have. I've had to make sacrifices, and so have you. I guess I just didn't consider your sacrifices as much as I should have."

Izzy turned and looked at me. I think she could see that what she had said had hurt me, and maybe that is what she intended at first. She sat up on the bed next to me and put her head on my shoulder.

"It's... it's not all you Dad," she said to me. "I just... I just don't think it's fair I guess. I have spent my whole life having to basically share you with the whole town and half the world because of who you are. And then there's this hope that opens up that maybe I'll get some time to get to know you, and so you get to know me, and someone else steps right in and takes it away. It hurt, Dad. Maybe I didn't react the best way. I'm sorry about that, but it's how I feel."

"I get it, Izzy, and maybe it all happened pretty fast. I have to admit, I was caught by surprise at how I feel about Kristin. It's not something that I planned on when I first got back home. She just... I don't know, I can't really explain it. I think you'll understand it better when you're older, and someone special comes along in your life."

"Do you love her?" Izzy asked me pointedly.

I wasn't sure how to answer that, at least not right at the time. "I think it's a little too soon for me to say that," I answered. "But I can say that I think Kristin could have a place in my life, and in our lives."

"How can you say that, Dad? You're both so different, and you only just met. It seems to me like she's just using you, just like everyone else tries to do, you just can't see it because she's young and pretty." Izzy was having a hard time comprehending it all, and I was having a hard time explaining it.

"Izzy, we have to find a way to work this out," I said, feeling exasperated.

"I don't know how that's going to happen," she said, and laid back on her bed, staring up at the ceiling.

I felt like I had said all I could say for now. We both needed some time to think about each other's feelings on this, and my mind turned back to Kristin and how she was probably feeling right now.

"Think about what I said, please," I told Izzy. "We'll talk more about this later," I said, standing up to go.

"I'm sure we will," she said softly, rolling her eyes and rolling over to her side, so she faced away from me again.

I left the room and walked down the hall to the living room, sitting down so I could text Kristin and see how she was. She gave me some curt answers about her being okay and Dad driving her home, but she didn't want me to call her, not yet anyway.

I felt like I was at my wit's end and slammed my phone down on the coffee table. Mom came walking in from the kitchen when she heard me.

"Don't tell me you're going to start slamming things around here too," she said sarcastically as she sat down next to me on the couch.

"How's Izzy?" Mom asked me.

"Not great," I told her, leaning back on the couch. "She's pretty upset by the whole thing."

"Wes," Mom said to me looking over at me, "it's none of my business what you do in your personal life, and I have always respected that, but..." I interrupted before she could finish.

"Don't you start too Mom," I told her. "Kristin is not some golddigger looking to get her name in the newspaper."

"I'm not saying that she is Wes," Mom replied. "But you've only known her for a few days. Maybe... maybe having her spend the night with you in your house wasn't the right move to make right now, especially with the way things are with you right now with playing, and with Izzy."

"I didn't plan things out like that Mom, it just happened," I told her. "Geez, when did I get the reputation like that? And why are you taking sides with a teenager who has no experience with relationships?"

"I'm not taking anyone's side, Wes, I'm just pointing out to you that when you make decisions like that when you are here, at your home, that you have more to consider than just yourself."

Dad came walking through the door a moment later and tossed his keys on the end table.

"How's Kristin, Dad?" I asked right away.

"I think she'll be okay," he told me. "She's home, but she's upset. I think she feels like she did something wrong here and came between you and Izzy. How's Izzy?"

"Angry, upset, hurt, confused, stubborn, unreasonable, you name it," I said to him. " I don't know how to fix this."

"You want my advice?" Dad asked me.

"Please."

"You're not going to like it," he said to me.

"You may as well say it anyway, Dad," I answered. "I haven't liked anything I have heard all morning so far."

"I think you need to give them both some time to think about it. Izzy needs to sort out her feelings about it, and Kristin needs to sort out her feelings about you and the whole situation."

"You're right, Dad, " I told him as I stood up. "I don't like it." I started walking towards the door.

"Where are you going?" Dad asked me.

"I have to talk to Kristen," I said as I walked out to my car.

I didn't know what I was going to say to her just yet, but I had to talk to her and see what she was feeling and what was going on – good, bad, or otherwise.

Chapter 20

Wes

The entire way over to Kristin's apartment I kept trying to think of what I was going to tell her. I couldn't tell her things had been sorted out with Izzy because they hadn't. I had a feeling she wasn't going to want to hear anything else, but I had to at least try to make things better on one end of this.

I pulled into the parking lot of her apartment and parked the car. I scaled the steps up to the second floor and went to the door she went into after our first date, Apartment 12. It seemed an odd thing to think about at this moment, but my number with the Pirates for all those years was 12. My baseball player's superstition kicked in and hoped this was a good sign.

I knocked lightly on the door and tried to wait patiently, shifting on my feet and looking around. I couldn't even peer into the window of Kristin's apartment since the blinds were closed. I knocked again and saw a neighbor peer out of their apartment door the next one down, giving me a suspicious look. I just nodded and smiled and turned my attention back to the door.

Kristin opened the door and looked up at me. I could see she had been crying and her face was red.

"Are you okay?" I said to her right away.

"Wes," she said to me, "Maybe we shouldn't talk about this right now. You have your daughter to deal with."

"Just... can I come in for a few minutes so we can talk?" I pleaded with her. Kristin relented and stepped aside so I could walk in." She shut the front door and walked over to the couch and sat down. I took the seat next to her.

"First, I'm glad you got home okay," I started saying. "I can't apologize enough for all this. I talked to Izzy and tried to explain things to her, but she didn't really understand what I was trying to say. I think she just needs some time to process it."

"Wes, I don't want to be the cause of problems between you and your daughter," Kristin said bluntly. "If she's not ready for any of this, then maybe we are better off stopping things before... before they get more serious."

"Do you think it's not serious already?" I asked her.

"Wes, we've known each other for three days."

"Kristin, I can tell you that I don't just jump into bed with someone for the sake of having sex. It has to be more serious to me than that. I thought that you felt the same way." I looked over at her and saw her look down into the handkerchief she was holding.

"Despite what Isabelle might think, I wasn't looking to do that," Kristin stated. " I never thought we would end up like that yesterday."

"Are you sorry that we did?" I asked her. "Because I can tell you I'm not sorry at all."

Kristin thought for a second before answering. "I'm not sorry it happened, Wes; it was wonderful. But I am sorry if it is causing a rift between you and your daughter. I am not going to be the woman people in town talk about as a bitch slut homewrecker, and I don't want to have to be around Isabelle if she is going to hate every moment I am there."

We both sat silently for a minute looking at each other. I put my hand on hers and held it.

"There has to be a way to fix this," I said, trying to come up with a solution.

"Go home to your daughter, Wes," Kristin said to me as she stood up. "It's more important that you fix that." She walked over to the front door and opened it for me.

"I want to keep seeing you," I said to her quietly as we stood together by the door.

"I don't see how that can happen," she said, crying lightly. "Not right now."

I walked out the front door and turned to face Kristin, but she gently closed the front door and left me there. I stood for a second, still not believing what happened in just a couple of hours.

I slowly walked down the steps towards my car, feeling dejected.

What the hell just happened? I thought to myself.

Chapter 21

Kristin

After Wes, left, it was hard for me to concentrate on even the smallest tasks. I tried several things to try to take my mind off what had happened this morning, like sorting laundry and straightening up or checking my email, but nothing could shake it from my mind. In my head, I felt like I had done the right thing by telling him to go to his daughter, make that his priority, and move on. My heart, on the other hand, didn't feel the same way. I felt devastated by everything that took place. Even in just the few days that we have known each other, I felt a stronger connection to Wes than I had felt with any man before. He was nothing like I had expected him to be and everything about him was making me happy. Now it was all gone.

I went into the bathroom to take a long shower and hopefully wash some of this out of my system. My mind kept flashing back to the moments we spent with each other at the pond, the time we spent together at the house, and then to when Isabelle came in. I tried to think what I could have done differently, but nothing came to me and every scenario I imagined ended the same way – with Wes and I parting ways and moving on.

When I got out of the shower and put my robe on, I could hear frantic knocking on the door. Part of me wanted to just ignore it. I figured for sure it was Wes, trying to come up with some solution where we could stay together. I tried to ignore it, but the knocking kept up, and at some point, the neighbors were going to think something was wrong and call the police. I marched over to the door, throwing it open and saying "Wes, there's nothing you can say…"

"Where have you been?" Karen shouted at him as she brushed past me and into my apartment. She sat herself down on the couch looking up at me with a frantic look on her face. "I have been calling and texting you all morning, and you're not answering," Karen said to me. She looked up at me and could see that something was wrong on my face. "What's wrong? What happened?" she asked as she came over to me, took my hand, and had me sit next to her on the couch.

I went through the whole story with her – the date with Wes, the picnic, the dinner at the house, our intimate moments, his daughter, everything. By the time I was done explaining the events of the last day, I felt spent and was sobbing again. Karen put her arm around and pulled me close to her.

"Hey," she said to me. "You didn't do anything wrong, Kris. It was just... just bad timing I guess. And there certainly seems to be some issues between Wes and his daughter that go beyond you."

I sat up and looked at her. "I know all that," I told her. "But it doesn't make it any easier to deal with. I really liked him, Karen. He made me feel special, and I think he really cares for me. We were just getting to know each other well, and then it all just fell apart."

"Kris, I don't think it was ever going to be easy for you two," Karen said. "There's a lot to overcome there. His lifestyle, his family, his age – it was all playing against you I think. Maybe that's why he's been alone for so long."

There was some truth to what Karen was telling me, but I didn't want to hear any of that.

"Those just seem like excuses to me," I said to her honestly. "It shouldn't matter how much money he has, what he does for a living, or how much older Wes is than me, Karen. It's supposed to be about how we feel about each other."

"In a perfect world Kris, you are right," Karen responded. "But we don't live in a world like that. Life is messy and complicated and never that easy. It's not like you see in the movies or read in a romance book. Other things get in the way, and we don't always get it worked out perfectly."

I slumped back on the couch. "It doesn't seem fair."

"Love, romance, relationships... none of it is ever fair, Kris."

I looked over at Karen, feeling sad again. I knew she was doing her best to try to cheer me up.

"Why don't you get dressed and let's get out of here for a while," Karen suggested to me.

"I don't want to walk around town, Karen," I told her. "Suppose I run into Wes? Or his daughter? I don't think I could handle it right now."

"We don't have to hang out around here," Karen said to me. "Let's go for a ride. We can head over to the mall, do some window shopping, get some lunch, maybe see a movie. Sitting around here feeling this way isn't good for you." Karen held out her hand to me to pull me up off the couch. I grasped her hand, and she pulled me up. I reached over and gave her a hug as I started crying again. Karen put her arms around me and hugged me tightly.

"I know it hurts right now," Karen said as she stroked my hair, "but it will get better."

"Not soon enough," I whispered back to her. I broke the hug and went into the bedroom to get dressed. After putting on my clothes, I looked at myself in the mirror and saw a pained face looking back at me. I tried to make it better, wiping my eyes with a tissue and taking a deep breath, forcing a smile out, but inside I knew it was forced.

I walked back out into the living room and grabbed my purse and jacket. I picked up my phone off the table and glanced at it, and then decided to leave it off.

"You're not going to turn it on?" Karen asked as we walked out the front door.

"No," I told her as I stuffed the phone into my purse. "I don't see any point. I know Wes has tried to call and text me. It's just going to upset me if I see it and hear it."

We walked down the steps to my car and got in. I started the car and looked over at Karen before I pulled out of the parking lot.

"Thanks, Karen," I told her, giving her a slight smile. "I needed someone today."

"No problem, Kris," she replied. "Now let's get out of here."

I pulled out of the parking lot, heading down Main Street and out towards Route 5 so we could drive the twenty miles or so to where the mall was. As we got onto Route 5, we drove past Martin Road, and I could see Wes' SUV parked at his parent's house. I focused my attention back on the road in front of me as I tried to put the earlier events of the day behind me.

Chapter 22

Wes

The rest of the day seemed like a constant tug-of-war for me. I tried to do my best to connect in some way to Izzy, while at the same time sending messages or trying to call Kristin when I could. I didn't seem to be getting anyplace with either one of them. Izzy would barely talk to me, only giving me passing glances at my parent's house as she moved about. Kristin wasn't answering any of my texts or calls, and it seemed she was resigned to ignoring my efforts to talk to her.

By the time the late afternoon had come around I was getting frustrated. I went out the back door of my parent's house and decided to take a walk. I walked down the path towards the stables, kicking gravel along the way, trying to come up with a scenario where Izzy and Kristin could both be happy. There didn't seem to be any happy medium anywhere.

Part of me felt like Izzy was unreasonable, acting up and acting out like she was a petulant child who just wanted to get what she wanted. The other part of me felt incredible guilt because she felt like I was never there for her through all these years. I always tried to do what was best for her and put her first in my life, whether she realized it or not, but somewhere along the line that became lost on her. Even though she had my parents around to love her and take care of her, I realized that maybe she was feeling like her parents, both her mother and myself, had left her to her own devices.

I had reached the stables and walked inside. There was no one to be seen in the stables area since it was both Sunday and later in the day. I could hear the strands of hay crunch beneath my feet as I walked along, looking at the horses as they seemed to stare back at me. I stopped at the stall for Pops, giving him a friendly pat.

"Life's a lot easier for you I think, Pops," I said to him.

"Oh, I don't think they have it so easy," I heard a voice walking towards me. I looked over and saw Dad walking towards me. "They have to deal with us all day long, waiting for us to tend to them. I'm sure they get just as frustrated with everything as we do."

Dad came over and stood next to me. "Feeling any better?" he asked me as he took a piece of apple out of his jacket and gave it to Pops to munch on. The horse happily took it in his teeth and enjoyed the snack.

"Not really," I told Dad honestly as I turned from the stall and started the slow walk back out of the stables. "I want to understand where Izzy is coming from Dad, I really do. I'm just having a hard time seeing it, where all the anger and resentment is coming from. She's not like that with you and Mom, is she?"

"No, she's not Wes, but we're not her parents. Does she act up and do the typical teenage girl stuff now and then? Of course, she does. If she didn't, I would be worried about her. But you're her father, Wes. The relationship is different, and her expectations of you are different. She tries so hard to do the right thing all the time, to make you proud of her."

"I am proud of her Dad," I said in my defense. "She knows that I am."

"Maybe so, Wes," Dad answered. "But I think there are lots of times in her life where she wishes you were here with her, for good times and bad, so that you can share in her life with her. She's not a kid anymore Wes; you can't just buy her a toy or take her on vacation, and everything is fine. She needs more than that now."

"I'm not going to feel guilty about what I do, Dad," I said to him. "My career has given her opportunities that other kids her age may never have. I know it hasn't always been easy for her, but it's not easy for me either. I've had to watch her grow into a young woman and know that I've missed a big portion of her life."

"I know it hasn't always been easy for you Wes," Dad said as he put his arm around me. "You've made sacrifices for her, for us as a family. Maybe Izzy doesn't understand that, or maybe you need to talk to her about it to explain that to her."

The two of us walked along the path back towards the house. As we walked in the back door and into the kitchen, Mom was there getting dinner together. Izzy was in the kitchen with her, peeling some potatoes. I smiled over at her, and she quickly looked away, going back to her task. I opened the fridge and grabbed a cold bottle of water and left the kitchen quietly.

Dad was sitting in the living room now, in his recliner, flipping channels on the TV. I sat down on the couch next to him, hoping some mindless TV could take my mind off everything else that happened today. Dad had settled on the sports channel, and I could see a game was coming on. It was then that it dawned on me that it was Opening Night for baseball. The season was starting, and I wasn't part of it.

The graphics flashed on the screen, and I could see that the game was taking place at Great American Ball Park in Cincinnati. Of course, with my luck lately, the Reds were playing the Pirates tonight.

Dad looked over at me. "I can turn it off if you don't want to watch it," he said to me, pointing the remote at the TV.

"It's fine, Dad," I said resignedly. Part of me was curious to see the team and how they would fare tonight. It was odd for me to watch the game from this perspective for the first time in a very long time. I would normally be out in the field or on the bench, watching the action right in front of me, hearing the sounds of the ballpark, the smell of the grass or the leather of my glove. Instead, I was sitting on the couch, smelling the pork chops Mom was cooking in the kitchen.

I took a glance at the lineup for the Pirates and saw that Bill Thomas was playing first base and batting fourth, my usual spot. I had nothing personal against Bill. In fact, I had helped him last year in spring training and this year, giving him advice about playing first base, helping him with defensive positioning, and giving him tips about reading certain pitchers and what to expect in situations. He seemed like a good kid, all of twenty-one, and I was in the same boat he is in now years ago, taking over a position from an older player.

The Pirates went down quickly in the top of the first before it was the Reds turn to hit. John Stephenson was pitching for the Pirates, a pitcher that had been with the team a few years now and I got to know. He had good stuff and had been the best pitcher on the staff the last couple of seasons, earning him the Opening Day start. Unfortunately for John, he got off to a rocky start, walking the first two batters and then giving up a ringing double to left-center to drive in a run. The Reds quickly followed that up with a single, another double and another walk to load the bases. It wasn't going well for the Bucs tonight, with the bases loaded already and no one out.

The Reds first baseman, Bob Irving, who like me was an older player on a team of youngsters, was next up. Bob was a big, strong guy that had seen his numbers taper off in recent years, pushing him down to batting seventh in the lineup. The first two pitches to him from Stephenson were well out of the strike zone. I thought this was the point where I would normally walk over to the mound to calm my pitcher down, help him regain focus, and may give him a kick in the butt to get someone out, but Bill Thomas didn't move off his position.

Rookie mistake, I thought to myself.

Instead, the Pirate pitching coach, Pete Starling, jumped out of the dugout for a mound visit to try to settle Stephenson down. Stephenson simply nodded at him a few times as he spoke, likely agreeing that he had been lousy so far and needed to change the course of the game.

After the mound meeting, Stephenson focused in on the catcher, nodded, and proceeded to throw a fastball in on the hands of Bob Irving, ricocheting off him and down the third base line. Irving immediately dropped his bat, shook his wrist, and squatted down, clearly in pain. The umpire signaled a hit batter and waved him to first, forcing another run home, but I could tell by the look on Irving's face that he was hurt. The trainers came out while Reds' fans rained boos down on Stephenson for hitting their player.

The close-up replays they show on TV today showed a clear view of the ball hitting Irving square on the wrist. It certainly didn't look good watching it on TV that way. When something like that happens during the game, when you are that close you can almost hear the ball striking bone and breaking it, and I can imagine Bob Irving let out quite a yell and a bunch of expletives as it happened to him.

It wasn't long after the hit batter that Mom was calling Dad and me in for dinner. We sat around the table, and I looked down at the meal set.

"Looks great Mom," I said to her as I placed a pork chop on my plate and passed the platter over to Dad.

"Thank you," she said nicely. "I don't have the energy to cook much anymore, but I felt good today. Izzy helped me quite a bit actually; she's usually the real cook around here."

I looked over and smiled at Izzy as she put some roasted potatoes on her plate. She glanced at me and then looked right down to her plate. She didn't show any signs of breaking the silent treatment just yet.

Dinner passed quietly, with Dad offering up some small talk about the schedule for the horses this week, and Mom mentioning that she had some doctor's visits this week to take care of. Other than that, the conversation was limited as everyone seemed afraid of saying the wrong thing.

I helped to start to clean up and went to take Izzy's plate. She didn't even look up and looked right at my mother.

"Is it okay if I skip cleanup tonight, Grandma? I have some stuff to get ready for school tomorrow." Mom gave me a look to see what I thought, but I just picked up the plate and turned towards the sink.

"Sure honey," Mom said to her. "That's fine."

Izzy got up from the table and walked out towards her room. I loaded items in the dishwasher as Mom passed them to me.

"How long do you think this will go on?" I said to Mom.

"Hard to say," Mom said as she passed me another dirty dish. "She's a teenage girl and has the stubbornness of her father, so I am guessing it could be a while," Mom said with a smile.

By the time I was done with cleaning the kitchen, the ballgame had pretty much gotten out of control. The Reds scored a few more times while we ate, and by the time we got back to the game it was the seventh inning and the Reds were winning 8-0. Things looked bad for the Pirates. It got worse when the Reds had a man on second and a groundball to short occurred. The shortstop made the easy toss to first, but Bill Thomas whiffed the ball and missed it completely, leading to another run scoring.

"This is ugly," Dad griped to me. "Are you done with this?" he said to me in frustration, anxious to turn the TV off.

"I was done a while ago," I told him. I could smell that Mom had put the coffee on in the kitchen and walked in to see her cutting a few slices of a pound cake and sprinkling some blueberries on it.

"Nice looking cake," I said to her as I poured some coffee.

"Izzy made it," Mom said. "I think she was doing anything she could today to take her mind off things. Want some?"

"No thanks, Mom," I said to her. "Coffee is good for me."

"I'll have some cake," Dad chimed in, as he took one of the plates and sat at the table. Mom cut herself a slice and poured coffee for her and Dad, and the three of us sat down at the table.

Mom smiled over at me as I sipped my coffee. "What are you smiling about?" I asked her.

"This is nice," she said to me. "The three of us haven't sat at a table like this in a very long time."

"It is nice Mom," I said to her, returning her smile. I stared off as I took another sip of coffee.

"But you think it could be better," she said to me.

"I'm sorry," I said to her. "It's just hard to get it all out of my head."

"You'll work it out Wes," Mom said to me. "I know everything will work out as it's supposed to."

"And how do you know that?" I asked, sitting back in the chair.

"Oh, a mother just knows these things, Wesley, trust me."

I took another sip of coffee and then felt my phone vibrate and heard it ring. I looked directly at Mom and froze for a moment before I answered it. Mom just smiled at me again.

I grabbed my phone and stood hope, hopeful it was Kristin. Instead, I saw it was Randy calling me.

"It's just Randy," I told my parents, sounding disappointed. I pressed the phone and answered.

"Hey Randy," I said to him as I walked around the kitchen.

"Wes, how's it going?" Randy said to me, sounding like he was out of breath.

"Okay, I guess," I answered. "Why do you sound like you just ran a marathon?"

"Sorry, I was on the treadmill working out, and then my phone rang, and well... it doesn't matter. Did you see the game tonight?" he asked me.

"I watched some of it before it got really ugly."

"Well, the game sucked for the Pirates, but I just got off the phone with Felix Burton, the Reds' GM. Turns out Bob Irving broke his wrist. He's going to be out for a few months. They wanted to know if you were interested in signing with them," he said excitedly.

I was feeling a bit of shock. I had been hoping for a phone call from someone, anyone, so I could get back to playing, but with everything else going on, I hadn't really thought much about playing again at all.

"Wes? You there?" Randy yelled into the phone.

"Yeah, I'm here," I told him. "I guess I'm just surprised is all. I feel bad for Bob; that's a lousy thing to happen the first game."

"Rough for him, good for you," Randy said hurriedly. "Think about it, Wes. This is the perfect script. Your comeback against the team you have been with for years. The team wants you there tomorrow for the afternoon game in Cincinnati. I can fax the paperwork to you. I can get you on a flight out tonight if you want, or there's one tomorrow morning first thing."

"There's nothing later?" I asked Randy. He paused for a second before answering.

"Well the game is at 1, Wes; how much later do you want it to be? It's less than an hour flight non-stop. The best I can do is have you fly out by 10."

"How about I just drive there?" I responded. "It's only a four-hour drive from here."

"What's going on with you? You should be more excited about this. This what you wanted, right?"

I looked around the room at Mom and Dad, both staring at me, wondering what was going on.

"Can I call you right back Randy?" I asked.

"Sure, Wes, but I need to hear from you right away so we can make arrangements and get contracts going, so call me, okay?"

"No problem, I told him. "I'll get back to you in 5 minutes." I hung up the phone.

"Randy has an offer for you?" Dad asked me.

"Yeah, the Reds want me to come in and start tomorrow," I told him and Mom.

"That's great," Mom said quietly. "Congratulations, Wes."

"I just don't know if it's the right time to do this," I said to both of them. "Leaving right now, with the way things are with Izzy... and with..." my voice trailed off as they both knew where I was going with this.

Dad walked over to me and stood in front of me.

"Wes, we'll stand behind you whatever you want to do, you know that," he said. "If you want to wait a little while and see if something else comes along, that's fine. You want to retire, that's fine too. But don't do something that you might regret. You don't know if you'll get asked by another team or not. This might be your last chance."

"I have to talk to Izzy," I said as I walked down the hall to her room. I tapped lightly on the door and heard a soft voice say, "come in."

I walked in and saw Izzy's face, looking surprised that it was me.

"I... I thought it was Grandma," she said, turning her attention back to her laptop.

"Izzy, I need to talk to you," I said as I sat down on the bed near her.

"Dad, I don't want to get into this again, not now. I have to study and get ready for school tomorrow."

"It's not about... all this stuff," I said to her. "Randy just called me. The Reds want me to play for them. I would have to be there tomorrow."

Izzy looked over at me, looking at surprised at first, and then a look of resignation on her face. "Are you going?" she asked me.

"Not if you don't want me to," I said to her. "I can't leave here knowing that there's this wall between us Izzy. I wouldn't feel comfortable with it, and I would be miserable. If you want me to stay, I'll stay."

I could see she was thinking about it for a moment. "I can't ask you to do that Dad," she said to me. "It wouldn't be fair to you. You should go."

"Are you sure, Izzy? I need you to be okay with this."

Izzy looked at me and smiled a little. "I am, really," she said to me. She then lunged towards me and gave me a big hug. "I'm sorry Dad," she said to me, crying as I held her. "I didn't mean to be so mean to you. I think I was just jealous, jealous that Ms. Arthur was able to get so close to you so fast and be important to you, while I... I was on the outside..."

"You were never on the outside, Izzy, ever," I told her as I hugged her tightly. "And you never will be. You need to know that."

"I do," she said through her tears. We broke our embrace and smiled at each other.

"I need to go pack," I said to her. "I have to leave tonight and drive to Cincinnati. I'll give you a call tomorrow. It probably won't be until after the game." I got up to leave, and Izzy got up with me, taking my hand. We walked out into the living room together where Mom and Dad were sitting.

"Okay," I said to everyone. "I need to get my stuff and get on the road to Cincinnati if I want to be able to get there and get some sleep tonight before going to the stadium in the morning." I walked over and gave Mom a hug.

"Have a safe drive, Wes" she said to me as she hugged me back.

"Thanks, Mom." I looked over at Dad and went and gave him a hug too.

"Good luck," Dad said to me.

"Thanks for everything, Dad," I whispered to him.

"It's what father's do," Dad said to me with a smile. "Send me a text when you get to Cincy."

"Me too," Izzy chimed in, coming over and giving me another hug.

"I will, I promise," I told both of them.

"I love you Dad," Izzy said softly to me.

"I love you too, sweetie," I said, feeling choked up.

I walked out to my car and drove it up the hill to the house. All my baseball gear was still in the trunk of my car, so all I needed was some clothing to have to help me get started on the road. I could always send for my things once I got settled somewhere. As I packed my last suitcase, I gave Randy a call.

"That was more than five minutes," Randy said to me with an edge to his voice. "What's going on?"

"I just had to talk things over with Izzy first," I told him. "I'm just finishing packing now. I'll be on the road in a little bit." I looked at my watch and saw it was a bit past eight. "Can you book me a hotel for the night? I should be there around 1 AM?"

"I'll get right on it, pal," Randy said happily. "I'll make sure the contracts are there for you at the stadium in the morning, so you can take your physical and get right into uniform. Call me if you need anything else. Congrats, Wes; you're back!"

Randy hung up with me as I zipped closed the small bag I had for my toiletries. I grabbed my two suitcases and a garment bag and left the house, making sure to turn the alarm system on before I went. I put the bags in the trunk of my car, set my GPS for the Renaissance Hotel in Cincinnati near the ballpark and got ready to go.

I reached the end of our road and thought for a second before I made the turn to head out towards I-70 to get to Cincinnati. I went towards Main Street instead, knowing I had one stop to make before I left town.

Chapter 23

Kristin

The time I spent with Karen was just what I needed to get my mind off everything with Wes. Karen and I spent the day walking around the mall, doing more window shopping than actual shopping, and just laughing and having a good time. We got plenty of stares and looks everywhere we went, with everyone from teenage girls to older couples looking at us like we were crazy. Karen convinced me to go with her into different stores to try on dresses and clothes that we had no intention of buying, just to see what it was like to wear $500 dress or a ridiculous pair of heels that I would fall in at the library.

After shopping we went to lunch at one of those casual restaurant places where you can get five-dollar frozen drinks and cheesecakes the size of your head. We were giddy with excitement with each drink that came and probably made our waiter a little uncomfortable with the not-so-subtle flirting that Karen did with him. I made sure to leave him a good tip to make up for our silliness, including Karen leaving her cell phone number written on one of the napkins at our table for the waiter, "or anyone else," which she said loudly.

We thought about going to a movie but decided to do some laser tag instead. I couldn't remember the last time I did anything like that, but there we were, strapped into our laser vests, rolling around and hiding from the preteen boys trying to shoot us. Neither one of us could do anything because as soon as we tried to shoot there were five twelve-year-old sharpshooters there to take us down. Even with our loss, I still had the time of my life.

By the time we left the mall, it was already evening, closing in on seven o'clock, and we decided to call it a day since we both had work tomorrow. We giggled our way back to my car and piled in, making sure not to forget the extra helpings of cheesecake we ordered to go so we had a snack for later tonight.

We were on the road for just a few minutes when Karen flipped on the radio to listen to some music. Naturally, we sang along with every song that came on the whole way, singing at the top of our lungs and even opening the car windows so cars passing us could hear our voices. When we got closer to Chandler, and it got closer to eight, the news came on at the top of the hour. Normally, I don't pay much attention to it as the news is never good, but when they went over the sports section and mentioned that the Reds had thumped the Pirates, they also threw in a brief news blurb about how the Reds first baseman broke his wrist, and they wouldn't be surprised if Wes Martin were their first choice to replace him.

Karen looked over at me after she heard the news report. I had managed to get through the whole day with focusing on Wes, and here it was being dragged back in front of me. Only now, it seemed like he was going to be leaving town quickly.

"Well, I guess that answers any questions for me," I said to Karen as I turned off the radio.

"Kris, that story doesn't mean anything," Karen told me. "Just because they're thinking about him doesn't mean the team will make it happen."

"Maybe it's better this way," I said as we made our way down past Martin Way on Route 5. I looked over at the lit driveway outside Wes' parent's house and didn't see his SUV parked there. "If he was going to leave anyway, I didn't want to get wrapped up in a relationship, right?" I think I was saying it more to convince myself than anything else.

"Sure," Karen said, not sounding as certain about it as I wanted her to be. "He could be gone for six months. There's no telling what could happen in that time."

"Right," I said, not sounding so sure anymore. I drove the few blocks past my apartment to drop Karen off at her place. Before she hopped out, I leaned over and gave her a hug.

"Thanks for today, Karen," I said to her, trying not to get all mushy and weepy again. "I had so much fun."

"I'm glad I could help," she told me as she picked up the bag of cheesecake. "Now to finish off my night right," she said as she ogled the cheesecake bag. "I'll see you in the morning."

I watched her walk into her home, and then took the short drive back over to my apartment. I was just getting out of my car, bag in hand, when a pair of headlights came barreling into the parking lot, briefly blinding me. The car came to a stop right behind mine in the lot. Once I could focus, I could see the familiar outline of the SUV and Wes as he got out of the car.

I closed the door to my car and took a deep breath as Wes walked over to me.

"Kristin, I know you said you didn't want to see me, but I had to talk to you, and you're not answering your phone or returning texts, so here I am."

"I shut my phone off, Wes," I said to him as I tried to walk past him. "I just needed some time to clear my head of... of everything."

"Kristin, please," Wes said as he held my arm. "Look I know everything got messed up, and you have no idea how sorry I am about all that. I'm leaving town. Now. I have to go to Cincinnati."

So it was true, I thought to myself.

"I... I heard that on the radio a little bit ago that you might be going there. Congratulations. I hope you do well there." I tried to keep walking again, but Wes stood in front of me.

"I don't want to leave like this," Wes said to me. "I can't leave like this."

"What do you want from me, Wes?" I said raising my voice. "You have too many obstacles in your life right now. I just don't see where I fit into all of this."

"Come with me," Wes said to me. "Come to Cincinnati with me and stay with me. Maybe if we just had some time away from all this, we can work things out. You'll get a chance to see... to see how much you mean to me."

I was stunned that he had asked me to go with him. I never expected him to say that at all, and I stood there for a moment unable to answer him.

"Kristin?" Wes said softly. He took my hand in his and held it.

I shook my head to clear the cobwebs. "Wes, I can't just pack up and leave," I said to him. "I have a job, an apartment, and responsibilities here."

"You don't have to worry about any of that," he said to me. "I can take care of all that stuff for you."

I let go of Wes' hand. "But this is my life, Wes. Just throwing some money at it doesn't change the fact that I would have to give up what I love doing... and to do what? Follow you around like a lovesick teenager from city to city with no one around me and nothing to do? I can't do that. And what about Isabelle?

Nothing has changed with her, has it? You think she's upset now. Imagine how she would be when she finds out I ran off to Cincinnati to be with you while she is home. You can't ask me to live my life that way."

Wes stared down at me. I think he was shocked that I had said no to him. Part of me wanted to just jump in the car with him and go, just to see what would happen. The realistic part of my brain knew nothing good could come of that.

"I don't understand," Wes said to me, trying not to let me go.

"It's better this way, Wes," I said to him, bringing my hand up to his face. I could feel tears building up, starting all the way down in the pit of my stomach until they came up and out, stinging my eyes. "Go to Cincinnati and keep your career going. In a few weeks, you'll have forgotten about me."

"That's not going to happen," Wes said, a hint of desperation in his voice now.

"It has to happen, Wes. Let me forget about you." I reached up and gave him a light kiss on the lips and then ran towards the steps, up and into my apartment and closing the door quickly. I didn't even want to look out the window to see if he was still there or not. I was sobbing again, and it was more than I could take. I even resisted the temptation to turn my phone on again.

After a minute or two, I heard a car door slam, and the sound of a vehicle leaving the parking lot. When I looked out the window into the night, I could see that Wes' SUV was gone.

You did the right thing, I told myself repeatedly.

"So why doesn't it feel like it?" I said out loud as I sat on the couch, feeling hurt again.

Chapter 24

Wes

The ride to Cincinnati was, to put it plainly, miserable. A four-hour ride anywhere is not usually a pleasant thing, and after the long ride back to Pennsylvania from Florida just a few days ago, I don't know what I was thinking by believing the drive now would be okay. If anything, I had even more to think about now than on the way back from Florida.

I was absolutely excited for the opportunity to get back into playing ball. I felt like I still had a lot I could contribute to a team. I knew I could have an impact, and I was anxious to show it. Starting over with a new team was going to be odd for me. I had spent my whole adult life in the Pittsburgh organization, and now everything was going to be new. It wasn't going to be like when I was starting out as a rookie since I had a track record to fall back on, but it was still going to take some adjustment.

Everything that happened with Kristin was weighing heavily on my mind as well. I was so sure she would be willing to come with me, to give us time to sort everything out together, be with each other, and hopefully grow closer. When she said no to me, it was crushing. I felt like all the good feelings I had about going to Cincinnati were torn out from under me. I could see that she had a life she was establishing in Chandler, but it was all still new to her, and she was young. Isn't that the time to do things like this? To take risks?

Maybe Kristin was right. Maybe I needed this time to forget about her, focus on my career again and my family. I spent so many years playing and trying to build my career, I had obviously let my family life slip away from me. First, it was Rachel that went away, and now Isabelle was falling away from me as well, right before my eyes. I couldn't let that happen, and I had to make a concerted effort to do things differently and show her I can be the father she wants me to be, and I need to be for her, even if I was hundreds or thousands of miles away.

At one point during the road trip, I thought about turning around, going back to Chandler, and just calling it quits. Maybe it was time to spend my life caring for Izzy, helping my parents, making sure Mom was okay, and that Dad had help with the farm... just living a quiet life for a change. After focusing on all of that, then I could pay more attention to my personal life, and maybe, if Kristin were still around, she would want to be part of that. Life might fall into place better that way.

It was then I realized that doing that might make me happy for the moment, but I would still feel like my life was unfinished. I had to see if I could still do this and make my mark. I didn't want to be remembered as the guy who hit .150 in spring training and just disappeared.

And so, I pressed on to Cincinnati. I got a glimpse of the stadium as I drove past it on my way to the hotel and got the same old feeling of excitement I always got when near the place we were playing. I arrived at the hotel at about 1 AM and got myself checked in, getting into my room comfortably. There was a nice welcome note from the Reds in the room, along with instructions to get to the stadium at around 9 AM for a physical and then to sign a contract.

I sat down on the bed and took my phone out, looking to see if there were any messages from anyone. I had a few texts from old teammates saying congratulations. Word travels around fast, even if it is just rumored, so I wasn't surprised to see the texts. I sent a quick text to Randy to let him know I was in Cincinnati and then texted Dad to let him know I arrived safely. He sent a brief note of thanks back to me and said he would talk to me tomorrow after the game.

I sent another message to Izzy to let her know I was okay and that I loved her. I expected her to be sleeping, but she sent back a smiling emoji to me almost immediately. I texted back, telling her to go to sleep.

I thought about trying to send one more text to Kristin, but I knew it wasn't likely she would answer me. I didn't know what else I could say to her anyway. I felt at a loss when it came to her. Maybe the next move I make is to do just what she wanted – give her the time and space to forget about me.

Exhaustion started to get the better of me. I set my phone alarm for 8 AM, and I crawled further up on the bed and put my head down to get some sleep. Sleep came quickly to me as the day had taken a lot out of me and I was ready to turn the page and move on to other things in my life.

The alarm sound went off, and 8 AM came a lot quicker than I had expected it to. I was grateful that the weather looked nice when I glanced out my hotel window, and a mix of nervousness and excitement filled me as I got ready to start the day. I took a shower and put a suit on, wanting to at least look good when I got to the ballpark. I grabbed the two bags with my gear and headed out of the hotel.

On any other day, I would have walked the few blocks over to the stadium. The weather was perfect, with abundant sunshine and the weather already in the fifties, with it expected to go higher for game time this afternoon. However, I had too much stuff to carry with me, and the concierge at the hotel kindly arranged for a car to pick me up and take me over.

I got to the stadium, went through security and headed up to the offices for the team and take care of paperwork. Felix Burton, the team GM, greeted me happily. He was a young man, not much older than me, short and stocky, with thinning brown hair. He gave me a firm handshake and brought me into his office.

"I'm glad you could get here so quickly Wes," Felix told me as he sat down. "We were in a real bind with Bob's injury. I think you can be a big help to us. How are you feeling?"

"I feel great," I told him, which was only a white lie. Physically, I was in great shape. Mentally, I wasn't sure if I was there.

"Perfect," he said as he got his paperwork together. "I just need you to sign these contracts, and we'll be good to go, right after your physical."

I took a brief look at the contract, and it seemed standard to me. I assumed Randy had read all the small print since that was his job. The Reds were only on the hook for $535,000 of my contract for this year. Pittsburgh was still picking up the bulk of the 15 million dollars I was owed for this season. I signed on the dotted line and handed everything back to Felix.

"Great," Felix said, standing up. "Let's get you downstairs for the physical and once that's done, we have a brief PR thing scheduled with the press about the signing. Is that okay with you?"

"Sounds good," I replied. "Thank you for the opportunity." I shook Felix' hand again, and we left the office, taking the elevator down to the clubhouse area.

Walking back into the locker room was a great thrill for me. Many of the players and coaching staff were already there, getting ready for the game. I saw a few familiar faces of guys I had played against over the years, and even a few I had played with in Pittsburgh in the past, making me feel a bit more comfortable. Felix dropped me off in the training room as he went in to speak to the team manager, Pete Doyle.

I never liked taking team physicals, but it was a necessary evil of the job to make sure we were in shape. The doctors looked closely over all my medical files and records, checking everything and asking about every treatment, illness or anything else that I have had in my life. They spent a lot of time checking out my left knee, asking about the surgeries, and checking to make sure it was sound. I went through the battery of tests on every inch of my body, had blood drawn and gave a urine sample, and got poked and prodded in ways and in places no one enjoys.

When the doctor was done having his fun, I got dressed and was led down to Pete Doyle's office. I had met Pete casually over the years when our teams played each other, but neither one of us knew each other very well. Pete was the typical grizzled baseball manager, with his gray hair and beard and gruff attitude towards everyone – players, coaches, the press, umpires and anyone else who got in his way. He stood up from his desk and gave me a firm handshake when I came in.

"Wes, it's great to have you here," He said as he sat back down. "Welcome to the team. Call me Pete."

"Thanks, Pete," I said as I kept standing, anxious to get on with everything since the game was just a few hours away.

"I've got you in the lineup today, hitting sixth," he said to me. "I know you're used to hitting fourth, but we've got that covered by Anton Rogers. I hope that's okay."

"I don't care where I'm hitting Pete, as long as I'm playing." Felix came back into the office, shuffling his papers."

"Okay Wes, we'll make this quick. Just get into uniform, and I'll be over by your locker with a few press guys for some questions."

I walked out of Pete's office and into the locker room. Felix led me over to a locker that already had my nameplate on it. I saw the Reds jersey hanging there, the crisp white jersey with the red trim and the classic logo. There was my name on the back, with my number 12 on it. A smile crept across my face as I held the jersey in my hands.

I worked fast to get myself dressed in my uniform, impressed that they had everything that fit so well right off the bat.

Those clubhouse guys know their business, I thought as I tucked my jersey in, tightened my belt, and put my cap on.

Felix walked over with about six or seven press guys, several of whom I knew from the past. The TV camera lights lit up, and I was asked questions about what it was like to play for a new team, was I anxious to play the Pirates, was I in game shape, and so on. I gave all the obligatory answers about being glad to get the chance to play, how I looked forward to getting on the field, and all the things you expect to hear. The conference was over as fast as it started, and I grabbed my bat and glove and headed out to the field.

I took some groundballs at first and fielded throws for about ten minutes, getting back into the groove of moving and stretching to field the position. It all felt natural right away, and I was glad that I seemed to be moving well.

Maybe those few days off were what you needed, I told myself.

I was nervous about taking batting practice because I hadn't swung a bat in days and thought I might be rusty. The first few swings were fouled off and slow groundballs on the infield, but once I got into a groove I felt better and was seeing the ball better. I found myself grooving more than a few over the right field and centerfield walls, catching the attention of players, the press and the fans in the stand.

Once batting practice was over, it was back to the locker room to get some introductions to other guys on the team. Most were cordial, saying they were glad I was here and wishing me luck. After that, I kept to myself, prepping myself for the game, getting my glove ready, checking my sunglasses and trying to get my head ready for action.

I did a quick check of my phone before I put it away. There were more messages from lots of people now that the signing was official, including a good luck message from Dad. I scanned down further, hoping against hope for something from Kristen, but there was nothing. I turned the phone off and stored it in the locker.

Pete Doyle came out and did a pep talk to the team before we went out to the dugout, and then it was game time. We walked through the tunnel out to the dugout, and I could feel the electricity now from the crowd. The murmur got louder as I went down the tunnel, and once in the dugout, you could hear the loud mixture of the crowd and the music in the stadium. I looked up at the scoreboard and saw my name listed on the screen, and a feeling of pride came over me.

We were announced onto the field, and I trotted out to my position at first base. Hector Martinez, the Pirates' first base coach, was in the box there and gave me a friendly pat on the back when he saw me. I concentrated on the throws from my new teammates for practice, and once we were ready for play, everything fell back into place for me, and it was like I had never been off the field.

The first two batters went easily for the Pirates, one pop fly to left and the other a strikeout. The third batter, Glenn Hopkins, the Pirates catcher, rapped a groundball down to me that I fielded easily on two hops and jogged to the base for the out. I flipped the ball to Glenn, who was not the fastest of runners, as he came back towards the base as I was leaving the field.

The next inning went routinely, with each team going down in order. I was due up now in the bottom of the second. Anton Rogers, the slugging behemoth of a right fielder, lined a single to right. Our third baseman, Brett Thompson, followed that up with a single of his own. I heard my name announced and slowly walked to the plate, amid a good reception from the crowd. I could see that some Pirates fans that had made the trip also stood up and clapped for me. I took a few practice swings, stepped in the box, and got ready for the first pitch.

The Pirates pitcher today was Freddy Gutierrez. I didn't know Freddy that well as he came up to the team in September last year and pitched a few meaningless games for us as the season ended. He had a nasty curveball, but I knew he relied heavily on that, so I went in looking to see it. As I got ready to hit, Glenn Hopkins peered up at me.

"Nice to see you could hobble to the plate, Grandpa," Glenn said to me. We had been teammates for years, and this was typical Glenn to try to rile the batters.

"Careful Glenn," I told him. "I may have forgotten which way to swing and crack you in your thick head."

I looked out at Gutierrez and saw him peer in for the sign and nod his head. I was guessing curve; he came in with a fastball over the plate for a strike. It had good speed on it, better than I remembered he had.

"Nice hack, Gramps," Glenn remarked.

I ground my right foot in and got ready for the next one. I knew the curve was coming this time; he couldn't resist trying to loop one past me. Sure enough, I saw it spinning right out of his hand and heading for the middle of the plate. My swing swooshed through the zone, and I heard that cracking sound that I loved to hear.

You know when you've hit one well; it makes a much different sound than the dull thud the sound of the ball makes when you don't get it. This sound is the prettiest one you can hear as a batter, a unique crack that comes and goes quickly. I looked up and saw the ball soaring deep and was deposited into the right-field seats.

The crowd erupted loudly as I circled the bases and savored every moment of my jog. I slapped hands with my teammates when I crossed the plate and gave Glenn Hopkins a wry smile and saw him smile back at me. The team in the dugout greeted me with high-fives all around.

The next two innings went by well for us as we tacked on another run to go up 4-0. When I came up again in the fifth, Anton had gotten on base ahead of me with another single. Gutierrez was still in the game, but he was clearly rattled and running out of gas. I could tell he wasn't happy when I stepped in, and I knew he was going to try to slip another fastball by me and stay away from the curve this time. The pitch came in, hanging fat down the middle, and I crushed it, driving it to deep center and well over the wall.

Hitting a home run is great; hitting two in a game is even better. I had done it a few times in the past, but this one felt sweeter since it was my first game with a new team. The crowd felt even louder than before, and the smiles in the dugout were even bigger.

By the time I came up again in the seventh, we were up 6-1. The new pitcher, Aaron Lake, was the mop-up guy for the Pirates who came in when things were going poorly. He threw mostly junk, lots of off-speed stuff and a fastball. No one was on base this time, and the game was pretty much in hand. Lake had that look on his face that meant he wanted to try to get out of here as fast as possible and get to the post-game buffet. He threw two pitches in the dirt to me before coming in with an expected fastball that had nothing on it. Boom! Like magic, this one carried over the right-field fence as well.

I felt like I was running on clouds as I went around the bases again. Glenn Hopkins wasn't even looking at me anymore, disgusted by his pitch selection and the results each time. The crowd was going crazy, screaming, jumping up and down, and chanting "Wes" over and over until Anton Rogers came over and said, "You better give them a wave, dude." I peeked out of the dugout and doffed my hat to the crowd in thanks.

Needless to say, we won the game easily, 8-1. I had reporters swamping me after the game, asking about my performance, how it felt, was it especially sweet against my old team and more. I dutifully answered the questions, saying it was great to get a win and it felt good to be on the field. The furor eventually died down, and I got changed back into my street clothes. Teammates slapped me on the back and invited me out for drinks and dinner, but I declined, just wanting to get back to the hotel.

I checked my cell phone. There were voicemails from Randy, screaming into the phone saying how awesome this all was. He sent me a text as well, with nothing but dollar signs showing, saying he was already getting calls about endorsement deals. There were other messages too, from former teammates, asking me where that all came from.

I walked out of the locker room and up and out to the street, getting thanks and congratulations from the staff at the stadium along the way. Once I was out on the street, there were a few people there looking for autographs, so I signed a few for some of them. One young guy came up to me, saying he had caught the ball from my last homer and asked if I would sign it for him. I did and took a picture with him as well, that I was sure was going to show up on social media somewhere.

The walk back to the hotel was invigorating. I felt spent after the game, and the adrenaline rush of playing was wearing off. The anonymity you get when you are a ballplayer in street clothes in a new town is awesome, and I could walk back to the hotel casually without anyone even knowing who I was. I walked into the hotel and went right up to my room. It was after six, so I ordered some room service for dinner and then called home.

Dad answered on the first ring. "Hell of a game today, Wes," Dad said. "I wish it didn't come against the Pirates though."

"Sorry, Dad," I told him. "I sure didn't plan it that way, but it felt pretty good. Is Izzy around?" I asked hopefully.

I heard Dad call out for Izzy and she was on the phone right away.

"Hey, Dad," she said to me excitedly. "How are you?"

"I'm doing great, how about you?" We went on to have a real conversation, one we hadn't had in a while. Izzy told me about her day at school, how things went at track practice, how she cooked dinner tonight, and more. She was genuinely glad to talk to me and happy for how my day went.

"Dad?" she asked, taking that tone where I knew she was about to ask me something I knew I might not like.

"What's up?" I answered, expecting the worst.

"Well, there's this dance at school on Friday night that all my friends are going to, and I was wondering if it would be okay if I went." The phone was silent as she waited for an answer, and I waited for the other shoe to drop.

"That's it?" I asked her.

"Not really..." she said with some hesitation. "You see, Bradley asked if I would go with him. Dad, I really want to go so please..."

I interrupted her. "Izzy, you know how I feel about you dating. I thought we agreed when you were sixteen."

"It's just a month away Dad," she pleaded. "This dance is in four days."

I considered what she was saying and how things had been lately.

"Do you like this boy?" I asked her sincerely.

"I do," she said quietly.

"Do your grandparents know him?"

"Grandpa does because he works at the diner after school and on weekends," she said. I could tell she was feeling anxious about where this was going.

"Okay," I said to her and then heard her squeal into the phone.

"Thanks, Dad! Thank you, thank you!" Izzy yelled. "I have to go call Amy. I love you! Go Reds!"

I heard the phone drop, and then Dad was on again.

"I guess she's done," Dad said with a laugh.

"You know this boy, Dad?" I said, asking seriously.

"I do, Wes," he told me. "He's a good kid. He's Clyde Stuart's grandson. Works at the diner. He's quiet, polite, and respectful. Don't worry, he's nothing like Clyde."

"Well that's a relief," I said. "Does he drive? How are they getting to the dance? What time does it end?"

"Wes, relax," Dad said to me. "I don't have the whole itinerary for the evening yet. When I get the details, I will let you know. Trust me, she will be fine. Your mother and I will make sure of it. What are you going to do with yourself tomorrow? It's an off day you know."

"I hadn't even thought about it yet," I told him. "I'm sure I'll find something."

"Okay, well get a good night's sleep, Wes. I'll talk to you later. I'm proud of you," Dad said to me.

It made me feel good to hear that from him.

"Thanks, Dad. Tell Mom hi for me. Have a good night."

I hung up the phone and placed it on the nightstand. There was a knock at my door, and it was room service with my dinner. The man brought in the tray of food and placed it on the table. I signed the slip to have it charged to the room, and the man smiled up at me, showing a big smile.

"Great game today, Mr. Martin," he told me.

"Thanks," I said as I handed him a five-dollar tip. He thanked me graciously and left the room happily.

I sat down at the table, lifting the silver cloche off the steak and french fries I had ordered. It looked and smelled delicious, but I just wasn't ready to eat yet. I kept thinking that this was such a great day, so much better than the day before, and I just wish I had someone to share it with, to share the night with. I picked up my phone again and found Kristin's contact information. I was going to call, but I didn't think she would pick up knowing it was me. I sent a text to her instead, the safer way out:

I had a good day today. I wish you were here to share it with me, but I get why you aren't. Just know I am thinking of you.

I pressed send and waited to see if I would get a reply. After about thirty seconds, when I hadn't heard anything, I figured she wasn't going to reply, and

I didn't really blame her. If she really wanted to move on, this was how she had to do it.

I started cutting into my steak, flipping the sports channel on to see highlights of the game and interviews with me looking awkward on camera.

"It's a new start for me, and this is a great way to do it," I saw myself say in response to one of the reporter's questions after the game.

Maybe great for you, I thought to myself as I took another bite of dinner.

Chapter 25

Kristin

Monday mornings are not often a joy, but this one seemed even worse than others. Waking up in the morning was a chore as I groaned when the alarm went off and bade me to wake up. Instinct had me reaching for my phone right away, and it was then I remembered that it was off, and for a good reason. After spending the day yesterday with Karen trying to forget about Wes, coming home and seeing him there, asking me to go with him to Cincinnati, was more than I could take.

I sat up in bed, flipped my phone on, and decided today was going to be a better day no matter what. I was determined to move on, take control of my life again, and get back to the way things were before Wes Martin came in and disrupted everything for me. It was the only way I was going to be able to move on.

I spent some extra time in the mirror after my shower this morning, doing my hair and makeup, things that I didn't often pay close attention to before I went to the library. I needed to feel good in every way today, and this was as good a place as any to start. I even dressed in prettier clothes than usual, putting on a linen floral dress that I had hanging in the closet, unworn since I moved here. Since the weather was predicted to be nice today, this seemed like the perfect opportunity to wear it.

I left the apartment and made my usual walk to the library, walking past Harding's Diner and the men's morning meeting in the window. I didn't quite know what to expect in regards to a reaction from people in town. Small towns are notorious for gossip and news spreading fast, and I am sure the word about my whirlwind dating with Wes Martin was already making its way around town... and perhaps even our falling out was news to some people as well. I walked down the street, going by the front window, and saw Clyde Stuart and his crew smile at me and wave as I went by. Wyatt Martin was there as well and lifted his cup of coffee to me and smiled as I went by. I gave a small wave and smile back and tried to move on as quickly as I could.

I reached the library door and Karen, as usual, was waiting for me.

"Well don't you look nice this morning," Karen commented, gazing up and down at the dress I was wearing.

"I just felt like something pretty today," I told her as I unlocked the door. "The nice spring weather must have brought it out in me."

"Okay," Karen said, following me in, probably wondering why I was going to great lengths to defend my selection of clothes.

We both went about our morning routine of getting things set up for the library. When Karen was done with her tasks, she brought two cups of coffee into my office and sat down across from me.

"I know you probably don't want to talk about this," Karen started, "but did you see the news this morning about Wes Martin? They confirmed he got picked up by the Reds."

I sat back from my computer and looked at Karen and sighed.

"I know," I told her. "Wes came by my apartment last night before he left."

"He did? What did he say? Why didn't you call me?" Karen said as she sat closer to me.

"He was only there for a few minutes," I told Karen. "Wes showed up right after I dropped you at home. He told me he was leaving for Cincinnati and he asked me to go with him."

"Wow," Karen replied with a look of shock. "I guess since you're here this morning you told him no."

"Karen, I couldn't go with him. Besides everything that was going on between the two of us and with his daughter, I wasn't going to run off to Cincinnati and just leave town like that. That's not me."

"Don't get me wrong Kris," Karen stated. "I'm glad you stayed; I like having you here. You're one of the few things in this town that make living here worth it. And I know you don't really know him that well, but from what you told me, the last few days with him were intense for both of you. It would be tough to not go and at least see what happens."

"Karen, I've only been here for a couple of months," I replied. "I'm just getting my feet under myself here in Chandler and with my job. I like my life here right now, and I don't want to just give that up in the hopes that something might work out with Wes. What if I went and then two months from now he decided he wanted someone else? Where does that leave me? It's too much risk. I need some stability in my life right now."

"I respect your choice," Karen said, raising her cup of coffee to me, "it couldn't have been an easy thing to do."

"It wasn't," I said honestly. "I know it was only a few days, but... I have very strong feelings for Wes. To see that fall apart like it did hurts. His offer was tempting, for a second, but then I realized it was best for both of us if went separate ways. He has other things he needs to focus on, and I have my life that I need to focus on. I have to start thinking about life beyond Wes Martin."

We could hear some people moving about in the library, so Karen got up to see what was going on and if anyone needed help. I went back to my computer, checking and answering my emails, and then reading the news. I could see that one of the top stories was Wes going to Cincinnati, with a picture of him and a brief story questioning whether or not he was the answer for the team. I quickly moved down the page to get the rest of the news, instead of getting caught up in the story about Wes.

The rest of the morning went along normally, with the usual events going on at the library – helping patrons find books, ordering books from other libraries, coordinating events, and the like. I went out for lunch at around one, choosing to avoid the diner and instead going to the Chinese food place down the street to pick up some wonton soup and an egg roll for lunch. It was nice enough to sit outside today, so I sat at one of the tables placed on the lawn area outside the library and enjoyed the spring sun and breeze.

After I finished eating, I went inside to get back to work. Karen was there at the front counter listening to something, and when I walked in, she turned the volume down.

I walked up to the desk smiling. "Were you listening to one of those romance books on audio again? I told you to be careful; you never know who might walk in."

"No, I wasn't," Karen said with a smirk. "I... I was listening to the ballgame. Pirates and Reds."

I looked at Karen and quickly composed myself. "You don't have to hide it, Karen," I told her. "There's nothing wrong with listening to the game."

"Okay," she said, turning the volume up slightly. "Just so you know, Wes hit a home run his first time up."

"Good for him," I commented, trying not to show any interest. I walked back to my office and went back to work, going through messages on the phone and email, and tried not to pay attention to the ballgame.

A little while later, Karen peeked her head into my office. "He just hit another one," she said quietly. I just nodded, not even looking up from the paperwork I was doing. A little while later I heard Karen exclaim "Holy crap!" I ran out from behind my desk to see what was wrong.

"What is it?" I said, panicking over what I might find.

"Sorry, Kris," Karen said to me as I came out looking frantic. "It was just the ballgame. Wes... well, Wes hit another home run. That's three in one game. It's pretty amazing."

I sighed and looked at her. "Great," I said to her and walked back to my office. I knew it was good that Wes was doing so well, but part of me didn't want to know he was doing great in Cincinnati, moving on with his career and making a big splash. A little part of me was jealous that he could move on so easily.

By the time five came around, and it was time to close, the game was over. The Reds had won, and Wes was a hero in Cincinnati, at least from what Karen told me. She could tell I really didn't want to hear any more about it as we were cleaning up and locking up for the day. When we walked out and locked the door, Karen turned to me and looked me right in the eye.

"I'm sorry this is so rough on you Kris," she said sincerely.

"It's okay," I said to her. "I think it's just going to take some time. It doesn't make it easier that we live in a town where Wes is a hero and I will hear his name or see his picture all the time."

Karen decided to walk with me back to my apartment. We strolled along Main Street, watching as some of the shops started closing for the day. The diner was just up ahead of us on the street.

"You want to grab something to eat?" Karen suggested as we got closer to the diner.

I thought about it as a possibility. It would be better than going home and sulking and wallowing in pity in my apartment right now. Before I could answer, I looked up as we got close to the door. Coming out the front door was Isabelle dressed in the school track uniform of a tank top and green shorts, holding hands with a young boy with a white apron wrapped around his waist. We stopped and stared at each other for a moment.

"Hi, Isabelle," I said politely, trying to smile at her and put on a good face.

She looked down at the ground and quickly let go of the boy's hand. She gave me a brief glance and said: "Hello, Ms. Arthur." Isabelle turned to the boy and said, "I'll talk to you later Bradley," and then ran past us up the sidewalk and down the street.

Bradley stood there holding the door open for us, waiting for us to enter. I decided to keep walking and went by the diner and towards my apartment. Karen hustled to catch up with me.

"You okay?" she said, worried about me.

"I'm fine," I replied. "I just don't feel like eating out tonight."

We walked on quietly for a few paces before Karen tried to resume the conversation.

"That went better than I thought it would," Karen remarked. "It's not like she jumped over and tried to punch you or anything."

I gave her a sideways glance and could see she was smiling at me.

"Who's the boy?" Karen asked me.

"I have no idea," I said curtly, wondering if Wes had any idea that Isabelle had a boy in her life. I kept walking on silently until we reached my apartment building.

"Well, thanks for the stimulating talk," Karen told me. I looked over at her before I went up the stairs to my apartment.

"I'm sorry I wasn't such great company today," I said to her. "I do appreciate you trying to cheer me up, really. Hopefully, tomorrow will be a better day."

"If you need anything or want to talk, just give me a call," Karen stated. "I'm only a few blocks away. You can even come over if you want. I don't have much to offer – maybe some leftover pizza – but you'd have some company at least."

"I'll keep that in mind." I walked up the steps to my apartment door and went in. I put my purse down and went to the fridge to see what was there. I had some leftover spaghetti and meatballs that I tossed in the microwave to have for dinner. When the microwave dinged, I pulled out the steaming bowl and slowly walked around the apartment. Finally, I settled on sitting on my bed to watch some TV while I ate.

If my parents could see me eating spaghetti in bed, I thought to myself and gave a little smile.

Nothing interesting was on the TV, and as I was passing the sports channel, I saw highlights of Wes hitting his home runs. There was a brief clip of an interview he gave after the game. He was talking about how it was a new start for him, and it was great to get off to a good one. I quickly grabbed the remote and turned to watch something else, anything else, and settled on some reality show that I paid little attention to. I heard a faint beep come from my phone, which made me realize I had turned my phone on. I got off the bed and walked over to my purse and grabbed the device. I saw there was a recent message from Wes, along with a bunch that I hadn't read from previous days. The one from today was just from a few minutes ago, stating how he had a good day and wished I was there with him and that he was thinking of me.

I held the phone in my hand for a minute, started to type two or three times, and then deleted each message I came up with before I sent anything. Wes was not making it easy to forget him, near or far.

I carried my phone back into the bedroom with me and put it on my nightstand. I concentrated on the reality show, watching the antics of people trying to renovate their house, hoping to get lost in what they were doing, to get lost in anything that wasn't Wes Martin.

Chapter 26

Wes

Some people might see waking up in hotels as a glamorous, decadent thing. When you do it all the time, it starts to lose its luster, even if you are staying at a nice hotel. There are constant reminders that you are just a visitor here, and nothing about it makes it feel like its home for you. That was how I felt this morning when I woke up to the sound of my alarm at 8 AM.

I had set my alarm early because I needed to get myself back into the routine I kept during the season. Sleeping right, getting in workouts, eating right – it was all part of what kept me in good shape, kept me strong, and allowed me to play for as long as I had. Even though today was an off day on the schedule, I still wanted to dive back into my routine.

I got dressed in just a pair of jeans and a t-shirt, packed a small bag with some of my exercise clothes, and decided to head over to the stadium to work out. Today was a good day to walk over there, and to walk like I meant it, not take a casual stroll that one might take when enjoying a day off in the city. The streets were a bit busy as people got themselves into their offices for the day, but I was still able to make it over the stadium relatively quickly.

I got in my usual workout, exercising for about two hours. I stretched, did some cardio and a little bit of work with weights until I had worked up a good sweat. I then went over to the indoor batting cages and hit against the machine for a while, just trying to keep my eyes and pitch recognition sharp. Once I was done, I went and showered, got back to my locker and changed back into my street clothes. A few guys were hanging around the locker room, reading mail or getting ready for workouts. I picked up my things and left the clubhouse, starting the walk down the corridor to go outside the stadium when I heard a voice calling to me from behind me.

"Wes!" the voice yelled. "I turned around to see Bill Thomas standing there. He had just come out of the Pirates locker room and began walking towards me. I stood there and waited for him to come up to me. He wasn't the guy I really wanted to spend time talking to right now.

"Hey, Wes," he said, extending his hand to me. I shook it, reluctantly and politely. He had a strong grip, and maybe he tightened it a bit just to show me how strong he was.

"How are you, Bill?" I said to him, as I started to move towards the door again.

"Good, good," he said as he walked next to me. "You had some game yesterday."

"It's one to remember," I told him as I pushed the door open, hoping once we were outside he would go his own way. Instead, he kept walking next to me.

"I wish I had gotten off to a better start," he said to me. Bill was without a hit in the first two games, striking out five times, leaving guys on base, and making an error along the way.

"You'll get it. Everyone has ups and downs."

"It's a little tougher than I thought it would be," he said honestly. "It was always so easy in the minors. I'm sure it will happen."

We walked along the street for a few minutes and for some reason he was still with me.

"What are you doing today?" he asked me.

"Just going back to the hotel to relax I guess," I told him, hoping he would take the hint.

"Oh, where you are staying? I'm at the Renaissance," he told me.

"I thought the team always stayed at the Westin," I asked him quizzically. I can't imagine that they would spring for all those rooms at the Renaissance.

"They are," Bill said with a smile. "I felt like living it up a little, you know. Spend some of that extra cash."

A typical rookie who makes too much money and doesn't know how to take care of it, I thought to myself. I've seen it so many times, where I guy comes up, makes money he never saw before, blows through it and then is out of baseball in a year or two with nothing to do or fall back on.

"Is Tim okay with that?" I asked him, knowing there was no way Tim would okay that as manager of the team.

"I didn't tell him," Bill said. "They think I'm there with the team. I mean, what's the big deal, right? Who cares where I stay?"

"Whatever you say, Bill," I said as we reached the front of the hotel.

"Hey, come with me and grab lunch," Bill said. "It's the least I could do to pay you back for the help you gave me."

"I don't know, Bill," I said, not really wanting to get involved with him. It was bad enough he took my job with the team; now he was trying to be friends.

"Come on," he said, dragging me along. "There's this great place down the street. They have good burgers, great beer, it will be fun."

As much as I didn't want to go along with him, I found myself caught up with it and followed him. We walked into the restaurant, which had a pretty good crowd in it for lunch already. Bill pushed his way up to the hostess counter, bragging that we were two ballplayers - loud enough for anyone to hear what he was saying - so that he could get the booth that he wanted. The hostess relented while Bill ogled her up and down, and I followed along two paces behind, wondering why I was doing this.

A young lady came over to our table right away and introduced herself as Lisa, our server. She looked young, not more than her early twenties, with blonde, curly hair, a big smile and an outfit that seemed just a little too tight and short. It became obvious that this was a typical sports bar place, where the waitresses dressed to impress the guys in the hopes of getting them to buy more beer and food.

"What can I get you guys," she asked us with a smile, leaning over the table a tad too far and giving Bill a view down her shirt. Bill smiled at her right away and ordered a beer. I asked her for an iced tea, and she went off to get the drinks.

"Iced tea?" Bill said to me, shocked I didn't get a drink. "Come on, man; it's a day off. Relax a little."

"I'm trying to stay in good shape Bill," I said to him. "You might want to think about it too. Those beers and eating out all the time starts to catch up with you."

"Yeah, yeah," Bill said, waving off my suggestion. Lisa returned quickly with our drinks and took our order. Bill ordered the most expensive thing on the menu, of course – a ribeye steak with all the trimmings. I kept it modest and got a chicken sandwich.

"Here's to being pro ball players," Bill said loudly as he held up his beer mug. He quickly downed most of the beer and called out to Lisa, who was taking care of the people at the table next to us, for another one. I could see the direction this lunch was going to take from a mile away and already wished I had turned down the invitation.

Bill kept checking his phone, taking selfies of himself and posting them on social media. It wasn't long before a couple of women came over to the table, knowing who he was, to moon over him a bit. They both looked to be about Bill's age, in their early twenties as well, and both were dressed in short skirts and revealing blouses. They introduced themselves as Tina and Beverly, college girls who were in the city for the day. Bill immediately invited them to sit down with us in the booth and snuck his arm around Tina as she cozied in next to him. Beverly sat closely to me, and I inched over as much as I could to give her more room, but she kept getting closer.

"You ladies know who this is right?" Bill said as he pointed to me and then drank another beer, ordered another one and drinks for the girls.

The girls looked over at me, not recognizing me, which I was completely fine with.

"This is Wes Martin," he said to them. "All-Star first baseman?"

"You're the guy who hit the home runs yesterday!" Beverly said to me. I just nodded in agreement, hoping this would end soon. She got closer to me, bringing her head right next to my shoulder and feeling my arm. "Boy, you've got some serious muscles," she said to me.

"Thanks," I said quietly as I drank my iced tea.

Bill kept up the show, doing what he could to impress anyone he could, ordering more drinks whenever the mood hit him. It was taking forever for the food to arrive, and I was starting to feel claustrophobic with Beverly pressing her body against me and with Bill on the other side of me, his hands all over Tina. Finally, I had enough.

"I need to use the men's room," I said, asking Beverly to get out of the booth so I could get up. Beverly slid out of the booth, making her skirt hike up even more as she did. She stood up, giving me room to get out while she straightened and pulled her skirt back down, smiling at me. I walked over to the men's room, which was down a small hallway to the side of the bar area. I walked into the restroom, washed my hands, and looked in the mirror and wondered what the heck I was doing here.

I turned and walked out of the men's room, and Beverly was standing there, right outside the door as if she was waiting for me.

"Hey," she said to me, with a glint in her eye.

"Hi," I said, starting to walk back towards the booth. She stepped in front of me to stop me.

"I think Bill and Tina wanted to be alone for a second," she said to me.

"In a booth in a crowded restaurant?" I asked her.

"I guess," she said, putting her arms upon my shoulders. "Tina's not very shy." With that she kissed me, trying to push her tongue into my mouth as she did. I pushed her back down, and she looked at me and giggled. "I'm not really shy either," she said slyly.

"I gathered that," I told her. "Look, Beverly, you seem like a sweet girl, but I think I'm heading out," I said to her as I started to walk past her.

"What the hell?" she said to me loudly. Beverly followed me as I walked over to the booth. There was Bill, brazenly kissing Tina in the booth, with his hands all over her.

"Bill, I'm out of here," I said to him. He looked up at me, finally noticing I was there.

"What do you mean? The party is just starting," he said with a laugh, looking at Tina. Beverly was now pushing past me so she could slide back into the booth.

"The party's over for me," I told him. "Nice to meet you ladies," I said to the girls.

"You don't know what you're missing out on," Beverly said to me with a huff.

"I'm pretty sure I do," I told her. I started walking out and saw Lisa, our waitress, walking towards the table with another round of drinks. I stopped her, reached into my wallet, and handed her a fifty-dollar bill.

"Here, Lisa," I said to her. "This should more than cover my drinks and lunch; the rest is for you. Thanks for your help."

"Thanks!" she yelled to me as I walked to get outside. I gave her a smile and wave and got out of there as fast as I could.

Just walking outside, I felt the anxiety leave me, and I could breathe better. I walked up the block to get back to the hotel and went inside and straight up to my room. Once in my room, put the Do Not Disturb sign on the door, and went to the bed.

There was a time, many years ago, when I might have stayed and had lunch, had some drinks, and maybe stayed to see how things played out, but that life gets old. Nothing good comes of it besides a hangover and feelings of regret the next day. It was not a part of the lifestyle I relished or wanted to be part of anymore. At some point, Bill Thomas hopefully would realize that as well, at least if he wanted to have a long career.

I looked at the clock on the nightstand and saw it was still early afternoon. Izzy wouldn't be home from school yet, so I couldn't even call her to see how her day was. Dad would be out on the farm, Mom was probably resting, and Kristin... well, Kristin was at the library, working, trying to forget about me. Kristin hadn't answered any of my text messages, and I foolishly checked my phone again to see if I had heard from her. As expected, there was nothing there.

I turned the TV on to see what was on, hoping to find something to pass the time. There was Humphrey Bogart on the screen, in one of his detective roles where he grilled the bad guys, solved the crime, and got the pretty girl in the end.

"If only real life were that easy, Bogie," I said to the screen as I put another pillow behind my head and watched.

Chapter 27

Kristin

Tuesday went by a little better than I thought it would. I focused hard on getting work done, not letting anything distract me along the way that might bring my mind back to Wes. I worked on setting up more spring programs for the library, booking some different readings and crafts programs for kids and adults that might bring some more people around to see what we were all about. I also started working on applying for some grant money and seeing what we could do about getting some extra funding or a budget increase so we could make some changes – add more computers, upgrade our technology, add some more space. It was a long shot, but I was determined to see it through and petition the library board at the next meeting.

Karen could tell things were different for me on today. She left me to my own devices, only coming into the office if she had a question or issue I needed to address. Other than that, I didn't see her much all day, from morning until closing time. The day roared by, and I felt good by the time I turned my computer off and was ready to head home for the night.

We both locked up and headed out, moving out into the waning sunlight and into the cool air that still lingered around in early April. The cool air felt good on my face, and I felt invigorated for the day.

"Boy, you really went at it today," Karen said to me as we walked along. "You must have gotten a lot done."

"I did," I said proudly. "I think I came up with some good ideas for programs, and I was getting everything together for the board meeting in a few weeks to see if we can hit them up with expanding the budget a bit for next year so we can do some more things."

"Like get a raise for dedicated employees?" Karen chimed in with a hopeful smile.

"You bet!" I said enthusiastically.

"Awesome," Karen answered as we got close to the diner.

"Want to grab some dinner?" I asked her. "I never left the office today, and all I had was yogurt. I'm famished."

"I would love to Kris, I really would," Karen said to me. "But... I have a date tonight."

I stopped walking, and Karen kept moving a few steps ahead of me before she stopped and turned around, smiling.

"You have a date?" I said to her. "Why didn't you say something earlier? Who is the date with?"

"I didn't want to bother you, you were working so hard. It seemed like a silly thing to interrupt you with, and... and well I felt guilty about it because of everything that has happened lately." Karen looked down at the sidewalk before glancing back up at me.

"Karen," I said to her, "You weren't going to bother me. And you shouldn't feel guilty about getting to do something fun. I'm happy for you! So, who is it with? That cute guy who works the seafood department at Wally's who's always flirting with you?"

"No, it's not Gene, though that would have been nice too," she said with a smile. "Do you remember our waiter when we went to the restaurant on Sunday? "Brian?"

"The waiter you left your phone number for on the table called you?"

"Yes!" she said with a giddy scream. "Completely out of the blue, he called me last night. He was so cute, acting all bashful. He asked me to drive over and meet him tonight so we can go out for dinner over that way." Karen looked at me and then said, "But I don't have to go. If you want some company tonight, I can cancel."

"Don't be ridiculous Karen," I told her walking up towards the diner again. "Go on your date and have a great time. I'm a big girl; I can eat dinner by myself."

"Oh good," she said, giving me a hug. "I didn't really want to cancel with him. I'll tell you all about it tomorrow. See ya!" Karen then picked up the pace to head home and get ready for her date.

I'll admit I was a little sad and jealous of her, and I almost decided to head for home, put on my pajamas and just eat ice cream for dinner while I watched a movie. However, I decided then and there that I was not going to be that girl. I walked over to the diner door, took a deep breath, and went inside.

The diner wasn't too busy at this time of day, and even the usual cronies who held court with Clyde Stuart at the table in the window weren't there tonight. One of the waitresses looked up at me as I entered, smiled, and told me I could sit anywhere; so I slid into one of the booths just inside the door and picked up the menu that was on the table.

The waitress came over, an older woman with brown and gray hair, to see what I wanted to drink and gave me a glass of water and some silverware. I ordered a diet soda and went back to reading the menu. There was more to choose from than I had imagined, including the daily specials, so I took my time reading over everything. My reading was interrupted by a deep voice standing next to me.

"Mind if I join you?"

I was surprised and put the menu down and looked over. There was Wyatt Martin, standing there smiling at me.

"Hello, Wyatt," I said with a hint of nervousness. "Please, sit." Wyatt slid into the bench seat across from me, placing his customary cowboy hat on the seat next to him.

"What are you doing here?" I asked. "Aren't you only here in the mornings for Clyde's court?"

"I come down on Tuesday nights too," Wyatt told me, picking up the menu. "Izzy and Jenny always have girls' night on Tuesday. It's usually a healthy dinner, a movie, or reading, or sometimes a board game, and then dessert. I am invited not to be home when it happens, and I'm okay with that," he said with a smile.

I let out a laugh and smiled back at him. "Well, I'm grateful for the company," I told him.

"Nice to see you smiling," Wyatt said as he leafed through the menu as if he didn't know every item listed on the pages already. Our waitress came over with my soda and saw Wyatt sitting there.

"Wyatt are you bothering this nice girl?" she said to him, winking at me. "Just say the word honey, and I'll toss him out of here."

"Now Rita," Wyatt said to her, "I was just keeping her company, you know, to keep the vultures away."

"Clyde's having dinner with his daughter tonight, so there's no danger of that," Rita said to me. Coffee for you, Wyatt? And your usual Tuesday night special for dinner?"

"You know me too well, Rita," Wyatt told her. "You're going to scare poor Kristin away, thinking I'm here all the time."

Rita gave a laugh and turned back to me. "What can I get you, honey?"

"I'll have the Tuesday special as well," I told her, putting the menu away.

"You got it," Rita said as she walked away.

"Wyatt," I said to him, "What's the Tuesday special? Will I like it?"

Wyatt laughed at my remark. "Meatloaf, mashed potatoes with gravy, and green beans," he said to me. "And you get a choice of dessert too."

"Sounds perfect," I said to him. "I don't get full meals like that too often when I'm cooking just for one."

Rita brought Wyatt's coffee over, and he took a sip right away. We sat quietly for a few seconds, and I could feel my feet fidgeting under the table as I looked around at the decorations on the wall of the diner.

"It's okay if you ask about him, you know," Wyatt said to me as he sipped his coffee.

I blushed and took a sip of my soda through the straw. "I... I was trying not to bring it up," I told him.

"Not a problem," Wyatt said to me. "We can talk about something else if you want."

We sat silently for what seemed like hours, but was probably about twenty seconds before I said: "Have you talked to him recently?" I said quietly.

"Wes calls every day," Wyatt replied. "He's good that way. To be honest, he probably calls too much. We're used to getting along fine when he's not here, even if he doesn't want to believe that's true. I just talked to him before I came in here."

"Oh," I said trying not to show too much interest. "So... how is Wes? I saw he did well that first game."

"He sure did," Wyatt said proudly. "Unfortunately, it was against the Pirates. It will be tough rooting against them after all these years. Anyway, he's doing okay. He's pretty lonely though."

I looked over at Wyatt. "Is he? Well, I'm sure he would love to have Izzy there with him if it were the right time of year."

"Yeah, I guess he would, but he's never taken her on the road with him. He always thought she was too young. I think he was hoping for someone else."

"Wyatt," I said to him seriously, "it wouldn't have been right for me to go with him. Not with the way things were... or are. And why does everyone think I should have just gone off with him? What about me and my life?" People were turning around and staring at us as I realized I was getting louder.

"Easy, Kristin," Wyatt said, trying to calm me down. "I think you did the right thing. It was unreasonable of Wes to think that you would leave like that."

"Thank you," I said, bringing the volume down.

"That being said, he misses you... a lot. I know he's tried to send you messages. He's getting frustrated with that, I think."

"I can't, Wyatt," I told him, feeling myself getting choked up. "I miss him, too; but I can't answer those messages. It's just going to open things up again, and I don't want to get hurt like that over and over. Or get hope for something that isn't going to be there."

Wyatt just nodded at me. "I get it," he told me.

"Can we talk about something else now?" I asked him nicely.

Rita appeared with our plates of food, big platters of meatloaf and potatoes smothered in brown gravy and onions, and a nice side of fresh green beans on the side. She also gave us a little basket of bread in case there weren't enough carbs on the table.

We both started eating without saying another word. The food was great, and I looked over at Wyatt occasionally as he dug into his meal. I must have been very hungry, and wanted to avoid more talk about Wes, so I ate dinner with fervor. Wyatt looked over, with his meal about three-quarters done, and saw my plate was empty.

Rita appeared to give us refills of soda and coffee. "I guess you liked it," she said with a smile as she took my empty plate.

"It was fantastic, thank you," I told her. Wyatt passed his plate over to Rita.

"I'm done Rita," he said, patting his stomach.

"No room for dessert?" Rita said to him.

"Of course there's room," Wyatt said defiantly. "That's why I left most of those green beans on the plate. You have room for dessert, Kristin?" Wyatt asked me.

"Sure," I said with a smile.

"Rita, two slices of cherry pie, and don't skimp on the whipped cream," Wyatt stated.

Rita laughed and went off to get the pie.

"Mary Harding makes the best pies," Wyatt assured me.

Rita quickly came back with two big slices of pie with generous sides of whipped cream on the plate.

"I don't want to hear from Jenny when your blood pressure is through the roof Wyatt," Rita scolded.

"She won't even know about it," Wyatt said as he dove into the pie.

I picked at the flaky crust of the pie and tasted it. It had been a while since I had a homemade pie, and this brought back great memories of the fresh pies my Mom would make back in Georgia. As I picked at the pie, I tried to change the conversation.

"Wyatt, how is your wife?" I asked casually as I took a bite of pie.

Wyatt looked over at me, seeming surprised I would ask about her.

"I don't mean to pry," I said, feeling embarrassed about asking now.

"No, no it's fine," Wyatt said as he kept eating. "I get people around town asking me all the time. Jenny was always a people person and has a lot of friends around here that worry about her. She's doing okay. The new treatments take their toll, but so far, she's responding well. I think she's hoping for the day when the treatments are done, and she has more energy to get out and about and do things again. She hates having to coop herself up in the house like that. But she does love to read, always has. Nowadays she goes through a book a day, so it's hard to keep up with her and get things new."

"Well I'd be happy to recommend some books for her if you want," I told him.

"That would be nice," Wyatt answered. Wyatt scooped up what was left of his crust with his fingers and popped it into his mouth. "You know, you could always bring some books out to her, as part of your delivery service." He smiled over at me.

"I don't know Wyatt," I told him. "I don't want anyone to feel uncomfortable."

"Izzy's in school until two, sometimes later when she has track practice. You could come by any time before then. Shit, it's my house; even if she's there, you can still come by." Wyatt realized he had sworn and blushed a little. "Pardon my language."

I laughed out loud, a strong laugh that felt good and made people turn around and look at me again.

Rita came over with the check, and I reached for it. She pulled it back away from me.

"No way honey," Rita said to me and handed the check to Wyatt. "Mr. Moneybags here can pay the check. Don't skimp on the tip either, Wyatt. You have a nice night, dear," she said to me with a smile before walking away.

Wyatt laughed and looked at the check.

"I can get it, Wyatt," I said to him, reaching for it before he pulled it away.

"No ma'am," he said in his courteous cowboy voice. "I can't let a young lady treat me to dinner. Besides, if word got around that I let you pay I would never be able to show my face in here again."

Wyatt left money on the table for the check, and we walked out of the diner. Darkness was starting to settle in over Chandler, and most of the stores had closed for the night. Wyatt put his cowboy hat back on and looked at me.

"Thank you for dinner, Wyatt," I said to him.

"My pleasure," he said to me, tipping his hat. "Think you can find your way home from here?" He asked with a smile.

"I think I can manage," I said to him with a laugh. "But now I see where your son gets his manners and suave demeanor from."

"Hmph," Wyatt grunted. "Wes is about as smooth as a gravel driveway. He was never very good at the dating thing. Now his manners, well Jenny mashed that into his head years ago. He better know how to treat a woman right. If she ever found out otherwise, he wouldn't see a baseball straight again."

"Well, he was nothing but kind to me," I said honestly.

"It's always nice to hear that about your child, even if when they are older," Wyatt told me. "I better get going. The girls will be finishing up their dessert about now and wondering where I am. Have a nice night, Kristin."

"You too, Wyatt," I told him as I watched him walk over to his pickup truck. I turned and walked off towards my apartment. I had a full belly and was feeling good about myself again. I got into my apartment, flipped the lights on and dropped my purse on the table, taking out my phone. I glanced at it and saw I didn't have any messages from Wes today. I read the last message from him again, where he said he was thinking about me. I typed out a message on my phone:

I was reminded today of what a kind person you are and where it comes from. Thinking about you too. Good luck tomorrow.

I quickly hit send before I lost my nerve to send the message, then shut off my phone so I wouldn't sit around all night obsessing about whether I got a reply.

Chapter 28

Kristin

E ach day seemed to get a little better. At first, I thought the dinner with Wyatt last night would be bad for me, stressing me out and having me think about Wes all night long, and getting depressed in the process. Quite the opposite came of it for me, though. I felt better about myself after dinner with him, and I think it changed my outlook about Wes as well. I realized that there didn't have to be this whirlwind romance there for me to be happy with him. I thought there was still a possibility there for us, and maybe we both just had to give it time and work at it slowly to make it happen.

I went to the library that Wednesday morning ready to take on the day, and anxious to see how Karen made out with her date with Brain, the waiter. I was a little surprised when Karen wasn't there to greet me as I opened and turned the lights on, but within minutes she was running through the door, out of breath. She looked up at me smiled as she walked by me behind the counter and placed her sweater on the back of the chair there. She sat down at her desk, humming to herself, fixing her lipstick.

"Well?" I said to her, waiting to hear something from her. "How was the date?"

"Oh, the date?" she said casually. "I forgot that was last night, wasn't it?" She looked at herself in her compact, put in back in her purse, then picked up her phone and started scrolling through it like no one had asked her anything.

"Karen!" I shouted at her, putting my hand on the screen of her phone. "Are you going to tell me anything about it?"

She looked at me and laughed, and then took my hand. "It was awesome," she said to me in a whisper. "He was so nice. I met him at the mall, outside the restaurant. He came out all dressed nicely and met me, and we went in his car to a little place not far from the mall. He had flowers for me at the table, and we had a nice dinner. He is very shy, so I thought the conversation might be tough, but eventually, I think I wore him down. We had a great time. He drove me back to the mall to my car, and I think he was too bashful to try to kiss me goodnight, so I grabbed him and planted one on him. He got all red and flustered and said he'd call me so we could go out again this weekend."

"That sounds so sweet," I said to Karen. I could see that she was happy about it, even if she was making a bit of fun of the date along the way. "I'm glad you had such a good time."

"What did you do last night?" Karen asked me as she organized the front desk.

"I went to the diner for dinner," I told her. "It was nice. Wyatt Martin came in and joined me."

Karen looked up at me, surprised. "Really? And how was that?"

"We had a nice dinner and talked about different things. I think it opened my eyes to some things that I needed to see."

"And just what does that mean?" Karen asked, taking a greater interest now.

"Well, Wyatt made me realize that I had to do what was best for me, no matter what other people say or think. And I saw that Wes has a lot of the same great qualities that his father has, and that I like being around someone that is like that. So, I sent Wes a text message last night."

"What did you tell him?" Karen said, spinning around to face me as I walked towards my office.

"I just told him that I saw what a kind person he was and that I was thinking of him. I didn't want to get into more than that. I think if we just take things slow, maybe we can work things out."

"And what did he say?"

"Nothing," I said, looking dejected. "I haven't gotten a call or message from him since Monday. I'm not sure what to make of that. Maybe he got tired of not hearing from me. Maybe he's busy and doesn't have time. I don't know. Wyatt says he calls them every day, so I'm sure he's using the phone. He's just not using it to get in touch with me."

"It could be he's just not sure what he wants to do, Kris," Karen reassured me. "I mean he is far away, and who knows when he's coming back this way. If he's trying to give you space, like you wanted, that's what he's doing."

"I know. It's just all very confusing, and I'm sure Wes sees it that way too. Or he just thinks I'm a crazy person and he's better off not getting involved. I'm hoping I hear from him before the game tonight."

I walked into my office and sat at my desk. Karen followed me in.

"So now you know the game schedule?" Karen said with a smirk.

"I'm taking a passing interest, yes," I replied with a smile. "I don't know if I'll hear from Wes today or not. If the game starts at seven, it might not end until 11 so it will be late by the time he gets out of there. Who knows when he looks at his phone. Who knows."

I turned on my computer and went to work, hoping that the day would go by quickly and that I wouldn't get obsessed with checking my phone to see if Wes got back to me. I had to concentrate on my work and let the rest of life take care of itself in its own time. If Wes Martin wanted to get in touch with me, the ball was in his court now. Or in his baseball glove. Or some other sports metaphor.

I was determined not to let the day drag on, look at my phone constantly, or look at the clock. I took my phone and put it in my desk drawer and left it there.

Out of sight, out of mind, I told myself as I closed the desk drawer. If Wes did send me a message or call, he would have to wait for an answer. Better he didn't think I was just waiting to hear from him. I really did have a life to lead outside of him.

We had a senior program at the library that morning, with a guest coming in to talk about exercising as you got older. I was happy with the attendance, and it was enough of a turnout that all the chairs were taken. Even Clyde Stuart came down, making sure to give me a smile and hold my hand as he talked to me about how he walks back and forth to the diner every day for his exercise. The program broke up just around noon and Karen decided to go to lunch, leaving me to man the front desk until she got back. I decided I would rather hang out in the library than sit by my computer, so I went around, straightening up, putting books back where they belong and checking items back in.

I glanced out the window and could see it was getting overcast outside. Soon, there were a few drops that I could hear hitting the windows and the roof as the rain picked up. I went over to the far corner of the library, where there was a notorious small leak in the ceiling whenever it rained and checked to see how it was doing. Sure enough, it was starting to drip, so I grabbed a bucket from the back room and placed it to catch the water.

Sitting in the front, the only sounds I could hear were the rain pattering against the windows, and the steady drum of the drops hitting the bottom of the pail. I heard the door to the library opened and looked over to see who it was. Dave Dryer, the owner of the flower shop, came walking in, shaking off the raindrops on the floor mat before he walked carefully on the slick flooring in the library. He was gingerly carrying a nice arrangement of flowers in a vase.

"Hi Kristin," Dave said to me. Dave had been generous enough to help us with getting some flowers planted outside the library to spruce the place up, and he had even given a few instructional classes for us at the library about flowers and flower arrangement. He walked up to the front desk and put the flowers down as my eyes widen.

"Hi Dave," I said, excited to see the arrangement of roses.

"I've got some flowers for Karen," Dave told me as he smiled. I felt some disappointment when I heard they weren't for me. "Who's Brian?" he asked me.

"Someone she just started seeing," I told him, handing out gossip that I was sure would spread around town by the end of the day. "She's at lunch, but she'll be back in a bit. I'm sure she will be thrilled to see them."

"Well I guess he likes her," Dave said, "Based on what he spent for the arrangement. Not many guys around here going all out for the roses."

I gazed at the arrangement and thought back to the flowers Wes had given me the afternoon of the picnic, right before we were together for the first time. Even though it was less than a week ago, it seemed like the distant past, and it made me long to go back to that moment when everything seemed so perfect.

"Kristin, you okay?" Dave said as he could see I was daydreaming.

"I'm fine, Dave," I said to him as I got my focus back. "Yeah, Karen seems taken with him, so I'm glad he's a nice guy."

"Okay," Dave said as he pulled up the hood of his jacket. "I've got other deliveries in the truck. Have a good one," he told me as he waved goodbye.

"Thanks, Dave," I shouted to him.

I spun the vase around to get a good look at the red roses with baby's breath sprinkled in the arrangement. I then moved the vase off to the side of the counter so Karen could enjoy it without anyone knocking it over.

Looking for something to do, I went back into my office and sat at my desk. I avoided the temptation of checking my phone, and instead read my email. I saw a message there that had the subject of 'Book Request'. I opened the message and read it:

Kristin,

I was wondering if you had any copies of Little Women available? It was always one of Jenny's favorite books, and I think she might enjoy revisiting it when she's looking for something to read. Let me know if you have it and I could swing down and get it from you, or you could always bring it by if you happen to be out this way. Thanks for your help.

Sincerely,

Wyatt Martin

"Even in his emails, he sounds like a gentleman cowboy," I said with a laugh.

I knew we had Little Women and probably had several copies of it. I doubted any of them were out as it did not seem like something that people were clamoring for right now, but I remember enjoying the book thoroughly when I was a young girl and could see why Jenny would like it.

I walked out to the fiction section and found the book on the shelf. I picked it up and brought it over to scan it and check it out myself and placed it down next to me as I heard the door open again. In walked Karen this time, a little drenched from the rain.

"Yikes, it's crazy rain out there right now," Karen said to me as she tried to shake some of the rain off. She glanced up and noticed the roses on the counter. "Ooh, we got flowers! Who are they from? Did Wes send them to you?"

"Nope," I said to her. "They came for you."

"Get out," she said as she walked over and looked for the card in the flowers. She read the message and smiled, tucking it into her pocket. "That boy is so sweet," she said to me, bending over to smell the flowers. Karen looked back over to me and did her best to make her smile go away.

"I'm sorry," Karen said, feeling bad about the flowers.

"Stop with the sorry stuff, Karen," I told her. "I'm glad you got flowers from Brian, and it's okay that I didn't get any from Wes. I wasn't expecting to get any."

"I know, it just seems like bad timing for everything is all," Karen replied.

"Enjoy your flowers," I told her, going into my office and grabbing my windbreaker off the back of the door. "I am going to go grab some lunch." I started to walk towards the door when Karen called to me.

"Hey, who's Little Women for?" Karen asked as she held up the book.

I walked back over and took it out of her hands. "I almost forgot about it," I said to her as I took it, the plastic covering crinkling in my hands. "Special delivery," I told her and walked out the door.

Lunch will have to wait, I told myself as I put my hood up and raced back towards my apartment so I could get my car.

Chapter 29

Wes

I had pretty much ignored my phone the rest of Tuesday, choosing to just be by myself for the day, other than when I called Dad to check in. He was on his way down to Harding's as Mom and Izzy were getting ready for their regular Tuesday night, girls-only time. I was glad Izzy got to spend some quality time alone with Mom since she was the only female role model Izzy had in her life right now. Mom had become the one person Izzy could open up to, and maybe the time they spent together could ease some of the icy moments that were going on between Izzy and me.

As Tuesday night was ending and I was in bed, watching a ballgame on TV, I saw my phone buzz with a text message. I expected it to be from Izzy or even Randy, and I was stunned when I saw it was from Kristin. I was almost a little nervous to read it, wondering what she could have to say after ignoring my messages for days. The message from her was nice and simple, saying that she was thinking of me and wishing me good luck.

I wasn't sure how to respond. Kristin had made it clear that she wanted some space between from the few moments of conversation we did have, and she had not answered any messages from me up until now. Even this one was a late reply, so I had to wonder what prompted it. In any case, I didn't want to read too much into it or jump at it, thinking that it was a sign that she wanted more interaction right away. I decided to treat it the way she wanted me to and just take it for what it was. I put the phone back down and decided not to respond to it. Instead, I turned the TV off and tried to get some sleep so I would be rested for the game the next day.

Wednesday morning started to feel more like the game days I had experienced for the last thirteen years. I got up at a decent time, ate some breakfast, and even got in a workout at the hotel in the morning. I tried to relax and not think too much about Kristin, though the urge to write back to her was certainly there. I threw myself into work instead and decided to go to the stadium early as a distraction. I could at least get in some batting practice and do some other things there until game time.

I didn't want to chance running into Bill Thomas again, so I made sure that I got out of the hotel and got a cab to take me the short distance over to the stadium. The sky was a bit overcast today, and there was a forecast for rain in the afternoon, but it should clear up by game time. The cab took me over to the stadium, and I walked in and went straight to the clubhouse.

There were more people around today since it was a game day and approaching early afternoon by the time I got there. A few of the players came over to get more familiar with me since we were new teammates. It felt good to be accepted and getting off to a good start the game before this one probably made things easier for people to want to come up to me. We talked for a bit, and then I decided to hit the exercise bike for a bit and listen to music to take my mind off things.

The bike gave me both a good workout and time to get lost in the music, and out of my head, for a little while. I listened to a mix of country and some older rock to get me going, and it was good to help block out the louder music that pervaded the speakers most of the time in locker rooms today. I went to work, using one of the programs on the bike so that it would go up and down in intensity and give me a good workout. By the time I was done, my legs were tired, and I was sweating a lot.

One of the younger players on the team, Albert Morris, saw me walking back to my locker covered in sweat.

"Take it easy there old man," he said with a smile. "We don't want you keeling over before the game starts."

"Don't worry about me," I told him. "Just make sure you get on base for us tonight." Albert got a mad look on his face, but Anton Rogers came over, laughing, and slapped him on the back.

"He's right, Morris," Anton told him. "If you had gotten on a couple of times maybe I would have had some RBI instead of Wes here."

Albert went on his way, and Anton sat down next to me at his locker.

"Damn kids in the game today don't know it takes hard work to stay here, Wes," Anton said to me.

"How long you been playing now Anton?" I asked him as I wiped the sweat from my brow.

"Six years," he told me. "This is my walk year, so I want to put up some big numbers, maybe get a nice contract like you got last time," he said with a laugh. "With you hitting behind me, maybe I'll see some good pitches for a change."

"I'll do my best, Anton," I told him as I headed towards the showers. I had forgotten that game days often turned into two or three shower days for me.

After a quick shower, I put on a t-shirt and shorts and headed over to the indoor batting cage. There were a couple of guys there already, along with the hitting coach, Ken Abernathy. Ken and I had played together early in my career as his was coming to an end. He was still a big guy, easily three or four inches taller than me, and he still had the thick arms and legs he had during his playing days. He moved away from the cage when he saw me.

"Wes, sure you want to hit? I don't want to jinx what you did Monday," he told me.

"I need my swings, Ken," I told him. "Besides, I think Monday was all adrenaline, but I sure was seeing the ball well."

"Whatever it was, keep it going." Ken patted me on the shoulder and went back to watching one of the other guys hit, giving some advice about his swing.

When it came to my turn, I only spent a few minutes taking swings. Everything felt so good that maybe Ken was right and I didn't want to jinx anything. I went back inside and saw a bunch of the guys gathered around the TV, laughing at something on the screen. I walked over just as the story was ending and saw Anton walking away from the TV, muttering the word "asshole."

"Anton, what was that?" I asked as I sat at my locker.

"News story on Bill Thomas," Anton said. "Pirates suspended him today. Seems he went out, got drunk yesterday, was staying at some hotel with two girls with him messing around with them, and he trashed the place. Police came and busted him."

"Word to the wise, rookies," Anton yelled from his locker, getting the attention of others in the room. "You can fuck up your career real fast by being stupid. Pay attention to what you do. Look at Martin here. Man's been in the league thirteen years; keeps his nose clean, stays in great shape, people respect him. See where it can get you," he said glaring at the young guys in the room.

Anton turned back to me. "They're going to learn a lot from you and me this year Wes, whether they like it or not." He broke out into a big smile again as Pete Doyle came in the room.

"Let's go, guys! Suit up. Infield practice and batting practice in twenty minutes," he said, clapping his hands and walking out of the clubhouse.

I took one last look at my phone before turning it off and storing it for the night. I re-read Kristin's message to me. It made me feel good knowing she was thinking about me because I sure was thinking about her. I turned off the phone without doing anything and put it in my locker.

Put your game face on Wes, I told myself. I knew that if Kristin was in my head all night I wouldn't play well. I had to do something for a distraction. I grabbed my white wristbands and held them in my hand.

"Anton, you got a Sharpie?" I asked him.

"Yeah," he said tossing me a black one from his locker he used to sign baseball cards. I took the pen and carefully put a "KA" on each one.

"What's KA?" Anton said as I handed the pen back to him.

"Somebody special I want with me tonight," I told him.

"You know they can fine you for that," Anton said.

"I can afford it," I said to him with a smile as I started getting dressed for the game.

Chapter 30

Kristin

R ain continued to fall as got into my car and then made my way down Main Street. People were scattering into the storefronts or hiding out under canopies as they waited for the spring storm to pass, but it didn't seem like this was going to be rain that went away easily. I eased my way onto Route 5 and then made the quick turn onto Martin Way and up to Wes' parent's house. I could see Wes' home looming up on top of the hill, all dark with no one there, and I tried not to think about the last time I was up this way. Instead, I pulled into his parents' driveway and parked next to Wyatt's familiar pickup truck.

I tucked the book into my purse so it wouldn't get wet from the rain, tugged my hood over my head, and made my way to the porch. I knocked on the door and glanced up at the camera that I now knew was there, pulling my hood back off so that I could be recognized. The front door quickly opened, and there was Wyatt inside, greeting me with a smile.

"Wow, I didn't expect you to come by so quickly," Wyatt said to me with surprise.

"It was my lunchtime anyway, so I figured I would just bring it over," I said to Wyatt, putting the book out in front of me for him to take.

"Why don't you take it in to Jenny?" Wyatt said to me. "I'm sure she would like to meet you after hearing about you."

I was a little nervous about meeting Jenny, particularly because the circumstances lately may not have been ideal. I nodded to Wyatt and took my wet windbreaker off. Wyatt took my coat and hung it on one of the hooks by the door, and then took the lead as he walked through the living room and down the hall. I followed a few paces behind, trying to keep my composure.

Wyatt knocked on the bedroom door, and I heard a voice say, "Come in." He swung the door open and went in, and then waved me over to follow him. I walked into the room and saw Jenny Martin for the first time. She sat there on the bed, blanket pulled up to her over her lap. I could see the oxygen machine she was using sitting on the nightstand next to her and hear it as it was working. Jenny looked over at me and smiled and then looked at Wyatt.

"Wyatt, why didn't you tell me we had a guest over? I would have gotten more presentable. I look a mess," she said, trying to straighten her hair.

"Don't be ridiculous Jenny," Wyatt said, moving to the foot of the bed. "You look fine. This is Kristin Arthur, the librarian."

Jenny looked up at me and smiled. "It's nice to meet you, Kristin," she said to me with a smile. "I've heard a lot about you around here," she said as she looked at Wyatt.

"It's nice to meet you as well, Mrs. Martin," I said to her, giving a nervous smile.

"Please, call me Jenny," she said to me. "What brings you out in this horrible weather today?"

"Oh, well Wyatt had sent me a message about a book he thought you might be interested in," I said as I held out the book to her. Jenny reached over, her thin hand taking hold of the book and bringing to her lap.

"Wyatt, you made this poor girl come all the way out here in the rain for this?" she said to him, scolding him.

"I just sent her a message," Wyatt said in his defense.

"I came out on my own, really," I said to her.

"That was very sweet of you," Jenny said. "It is one of my favorite books. I've probably read it a dozen times, but it has been a while since I read it. And I don't think Izzy has read this one yet either so it will be good for both of us. Thank you, Kristin."

"You're very welcome, Mrs. Martin," I said as she glanced at me, reminding me not to call her that. "I mean, Jenny," I said with a smile.

I stood nervously for a minute as Jenny leafed through the book and Wyatt smiled at her. Jenny then looked up at me and then at Wyatt.

"Wyatt, why don't you get some tea for Kristin and me?" Jenny said to him. Wyatt arose from the bed.

"Sure thing; I'll be back in a few minutes," Wyatt said as he went to go to the kitchen.

"Oh, no, you don't have to do that," I replied. "I should probably get back to the library and leave you to rest."

"Nonsense," she said to me. She reached over and patted the chair positioned next to her side of the bed. "Come and have a seat."

I walked over to the chair and sat closet to her. I could see close up that she looked a bit weary and a little thinner than I had expected, but she had the same fire and spirit in her eyes that I saw in Wes. I sat and put my hands in my lap, nervously fiddling with my skirt as I sat there.

"I'm sorry if Wyatt pushed you into coming out here," Jenny said to me quietly. "I know it probably wasn't easy for you to come out here with all the turmoil that went on."

"He didn't push me, honestly," I said to her. "I was happy to do it. Actually, I was glad for the opportunity to meet you after all I had heard about you from Wyatt and... and Wes."

"I'm surprised they had nice things to say about me," she said with a laugh. "I run a pretty tight ship out here. All three of them can tell you that."

We sat silently for a moment as Jenny adjusted the oxygen cannula in her nose to make it sit more comfortably. "This thing is a royal pain," she said to me.

Wyatt appeared with two cups of tea, passing one to me and then one to his wife.

"Thank you," I said softly, placing the cup and saucer in my lap while Wyatt placed a bed tray on the bed for Jenny to use.

"If you ladies don't mind," Wyatt started, "I need to run down to the stables for a minute. George was having an issue with a delivery. I won't be gone too long."

I felt nervous about staying with Jenny, but she chimed right in. "Go ahead Wyatt," Jenny told him. "But you better not be running down to the diner to tell Clyde Stuart that you got this pretty girl to come to your house."

I blushed when she said this, and Wyatt cracked a smile.

"Well, I was going to tell him I had two pretty girls here, but now you've gone and spoiled it," he said as he leaned over the bed and gave Jenny a kiss.

"Be back in a bit," Wyatt said as he waved.

Jenny turned and looked at me. "So, what shall we talk about?" she said as she smiled at me.

I felt like a schoolgirl before the principal. "Um, I'm not really sure," I answered. "What would you like to talk about?"

"How do you like being the librarian here in Chandler?" Jenny asked me.

"I love it," I told her. "Being a librarian is something I always wanted to do, and to get the chance to share my love of books with everyone else is a real treat for me. I think we can do some great things with the library if we get the chance."

"Well if you can pry some money out of Marion Harris and the rest of the board, I'm sure you will," Jenny said to me. "I used to be on the board before I got sick," she said to me. "But, I was missing too much of the going ons and thought it would be better to leave it to someone that could devote more time to it, but I do miss it. And I know how tough it can be to deal with them. But from what I have heard about you, it seems like you can handle yourself well. They're the ones that should be worried," Jenny said with a laugh.

I laughed along with her. "Thank you for the vote of confidence," I told her. "I try to stand up for myself as best I can."

"That brings me to another topic," Jenny said. "My granddaughter, Isabelle." I was little worried this was going to come up and could feel myself feeling uncomfortable.

"I am sorry for all that unpleasantness," Jenny said to me, stretching her hand out to put it on top of mine. "I'm afraid Wes, Wyatt and I didn't do such a great job preparing her for something like that. We never talked much about Wes dating and seeing people because it was never around us. I think she was taken by surprise by it and by how she reacted to the situation."

"You don't have to apologize to me, Jenny," I told her quietly. "I understand that there were special circumstances. If I were in her shoes, I might have reacted the same way."

"Don't defend the way she spoke to you," Jenny said strongly. "She had no right to speak to you that way. I gave her a good lecture about all that. She let her emotions get the better of her and acted badly, and rudely, and she knows it."

"It may have been for the best anyway," I told Jenny. "If Wes was going to be leaving, I'm sure he didn't want to get tied down into a long-distance relationship. It would just be a difficult distraction for him."

"I think you underestimate him a bit, Kristin," Jenny said. "I know my son pretty well, even if he doesn't want to admit it. I could see it in his face when he talks about you. You may not have known each other very long, but you mean a great deal to him. It hurt him deeply the way things played out, and I think he would do whatever he could to try to make it work for you."

"He is special to me too," I told her softly. "I just don't want to be a complication in his life, and that's what it seemed like to me. It was very hard for me to just give up that easily."

"Then don't give up," Jenny said to me. "You don't have to give up your life and your dreams to accommodate Wes' lifestyle. What you do, and think, and believe is just as important as him swinging that baseball bat. Will it take compromise? Absolutely. But if you both really want it, then there's no reason why you can't have a relationship."

"But what about Isabelle?" I said to her. "I don't want her to think that I am trying to take her place or push her out. I don't want her to hate me or seem like some kind of threat to her relationship with her father."

"There's only one way that is going to resolve itself, Kristin," Jenny sat up against the pillows on her bed. "You and Izzy are going to have to talk about it so you can let her know how you feel."

I sat back in the chair. Jenny was right of course but having that conversation didn't seem like it would be an easy thing for either of us.

I heard the front door open and close and footsteps coming down the hallway. I figured it was Wyatt coming back from the stables, but then I heard "Grandma, I'm home. Track practice got canceled because of the rain, so I thought..."

Isabelle walked into the bedroom and saw me sitting there next to Jenny. We were both taken a bit by surprise, and I could see that she was as unsure as I was about what to do.

"I should go," I said to Jenny, putting my teacup down on the nightstand and going to stand up.

"Kristin, you sit," Jenny said to me. Isabelle went to back out of the bedroom. "Isabelle, come over, please." It was not as much a request as a command. Isabelle walked gingerly into the room and sat on the bed near to Jenny's waist.

"Now I know this may not be exactly as the two of you wanted your day to go, but this is as good a time as any to hash things out. Isabelle," Jenny said, looking at her, "I know you have something to say to Kristin to start with, for sure."

Isabelle blushed and looked down at first. She looked over at her grandmother, who gave her a bit of a glare.

"I'm sorry, Ms. Arthur," Isabelle said to me. "I should not have spoken disrespectfully to you."

I could tell it was very tough for her to have to say that to me, but I was glad to hear it.

"Thank you, Isabelle," I said to her. She looked up at me, and I could see that she was turning red and feeling choked up.

"Izzy, I know this has been difficult for you to deal with," Jenny said to her, turning her attention to her and taking her hand with her left while still holding mine with her right. "It was far from the ideal circumstances for your first exposure to your father having a relationship with someone. I know your Dad and Kristin both feel that way. You need to take a step back from the emotion you felt right away and look at it from the other side. It has been a long time since your father has felt close to someone and let them into his life like this. It hasn't happened since your mother; he wouldn't let it happen because he was trying to do what was best for you. You're a young woman now Izzy, not a little girl anymore. In time, when you start to have romantic interests and boyfriends, you may understand the whole thing a little better."

I saw Isabelle look over at me when Jenny mentioned boyfriends. I am sure she was worried about what I had seen down at the diner.

The three of us sat there silently for a moment. Jenny slid herself over to the side of the bed where my chair was and put her feet on the floor. She grabbed her oxygen concentrator and slung the bag over her shoulder and stood up from the bed, shakily at first. I grabbed her hand so she could brace herself and she looked at me and smiled.

Jenny leaned down and whispered into my ear. "Talk to her," she said to me as she shuffled around the bed, gave Isabelle a kiss on the forehead, and walked out of the room, closing the door.

I wasn't sure what I should do. I had a wave of nerves run through my body as I tried to figure out what to say. I looked over at Isabelle and saw she was looking down at the bed, tracing the outline of the quilting with her index finger. She probably wasn't any surer about what to say than I was.

"Did you," Isabelle said nervously, "Did you say anything about what you saw?" she asked.

"No," I told her. "That's your business. It's not my place to say anything."

"Thank you," she said quietly. "I know Dad would freak out about it. He's already all tense about me going to the dance on Friday; this would just make it worse."

"There's a dance this week?" I said to her.

"Yes, it's the big spring dance, and the first one I got asked to go to. I'm pretty excited," Isabelle told me, relaxing a little bit.

"I remember my first dance," I said to her, leaning forward in my chair.

"Did you go with a boy?" she said, scooting closer to me as she stayed on the bed.

"I did," I said with a smile. "Charlie Everson. He was captain of the basketball team. I was so excited to get asked, and he was very sweet."

"How was it? Were you nervous?" Isabelle was showing greater interest in the conversation now.

"I was very nervous," I told her honestly. "It was my first date. Thankfully my older sister was there to help me out and get ready. She drove me to the dance since I couldn't drive yet, and neither could Charlie. Once we met there, we had a good time. We danced, we laughed and had a good time with our friends. It was fun."

"Did he... did he kiss you goodnight?"

I smiled at her. "He did. It was... it was special."

Isabelle looked at me and smiled. "Bradley hasn't kissed me yet," she said sounding disappointed. "I think he's nervous about it."

"Boys usually are," I told her. "When the time is right, he will, I'm sure, and you'll remember it forever."

"I wish I had a sister to help me like you did," Isabelle told me. "Grandma means well, and she tries, but it's not quite the same thing."

"If... if you want to, I'd be happy to help you get ready Friday night," I told her. I didn't want her to feel like I was imposing myself on her or anything. I could see her eyes light up a bit after I told her.

"That would be nice," Isabelle said to me. "I would like that a lot."

I looked down at my watch and saw it was almost two-thirty. I jumped up out of my chair.

"Oh geez, I need to get back to the library," I said to her in a panic. I walked around the bed, and Isabelle got up and opened the door for me. I smiled at her as we walked out of the bedroom.

Jenny was sitting in the living room, and Wyatt was there with her. They both looked over at the two of us as we entered the room and saw we were both smiling.

"I need to get back to work," I said to Jenny and Wyatt.

"Thank you so much for bringing the book out," Jenny said to me. I came over and stood in front of her, and she smiled and took my hand again.

"It was wonderful to get to meet you," Jenny said to me.

"Same here," I said to her softly. "Thank you."

I turned and looked at Isabelle and smiled at her and she gave me a little wave.

"Say, Kristin," Wyatt said to me as he handed me my windbreaker. "The three of us will be watching the ball game tonight. We'd love for you to join us if you want."

I put my jacket on and looked at Isabelle, who was looking hopeful like she wanted me to say yes.

"That would be nice," I said to Wyatt. "I would be happy to join you."

"Well then come over after work," Jenny said to me. "We can have some dinner and then watch the game together."

"Great," I said. "I will see you then."

Wyatt held the front door open for me and then followed me out to the porch. The rain had let up quite a bit, but it was still drizzling slightly.

I smiled and looked at Wyatt as I zipped my jacket.

"Did you know this would happen when you invited me out?" I said to him.

"Did I know?" Wyatt said with a laugh. "Heck, when it comes to women I learned a long time ago that I don't really know much of anything. I sure hoped everything would work out though, and I know Jenny well enough to know she could steer things the right way. She has that effect on people."

I leaned over and gave Wyatt a peck on the cheek. I could see he turned red from it.

"Thank you, Wyatt," I said to him. I turned and walked out to my car, not caring if the raindrops got me a little wet, or if I got rain on the seat of my car. For the first time in days, I felt like life in Chandler was going pretty good for me.

Chapter 31

Wes

Waiting around for the game to start can seem to take forever at times, and today was one of those days. The overcast skies made everyone worry that there would be a rain delay or even a postponement. Rain delays are the worst, especially after you have gotten yourself ready for the game mentally and physically and then you must wait and wait and wait some more. Luckily for us, the rain had held off and it looked like the game would start on time.

Pete Doyle had moved me up to bat fifth tonight, hitting behind Anton in the hopes he might see some better pitches than the night before. I was far from expecting to have anything close to the night I had before and just wanted to make sure I got good swings so as not to embarrass myself and make people think the first game was just a fluke. As we got ready to take the field, I glanced down at my wristbands, adjusting them, so the KA I wrote on them was turned out to the sides. It made me feel like Kristin was with me to give me some extra motivation.

Our pitcher tonight, Colby Dalton, was another of the young players that were on the Reds this year. He had just a few games of experience last year, and this was a big chance for him to prove himself. He took the mound in the first and promptly walked the first two batters he faced on eight pitches. He heard some light boos from a restless crowd, and after the second walk, I went over to talk to him.

"Decent crowd tonight," I said to him as I looked around the stadium.

"I guess," he said to me, looking around nervously as he felt the ball in his hand.

"You got anyone here tonight?" I asked him.

"My parents, and my girlfriend," he said, adjusting the bill of his cap.

"My parents used to come to my games in Pittsburgh all the time," I told him. "It freaked me out the first few times. I would try like hell to do good to impress them and always ended up sucking. Play your game, Colby. You got these guys. Slow it down, throw at your pace. Have fun."

"Thanks," he said, exhaling. I patted him on the back and moved back to first base. Frank Vincent, the Pirates second baseman who was on first base now, chatted with me.

"What did you tell him, Wes?" Frank said with a smile.

"I told him you guys don't have a chance tonight and that he should go ahead pick you off, Frank."

Colby went on to strikeout the next batter on three pitches. Two pitches into the fourth hitter, I saw him looking over to me. He could tell Vincent had a decent lead, even with a man on second. Colby fired the ball to me, I blocked the base with my right foot and slapped the tag on Frank for the out.

"See you later, Frank," I said to him as I smiled and fired the ball back to Colby. Colby went on to strike out the hitter to get out of the inning. He smiled at me as we walked off the field.

We got off to a quick start again with our leadoff hitter getting on. Then, with two batters out, Anton singled to left field. I came to the plate, getting a good ovation from the crowd. Hank Swan was pitching tonight for the Pirates, and I tipped my helmet to him as I got into the batter's box. If anyone knew me well on the Pirates, it was Hank since we had played so long together. But I also knew what his tendencies were, so we were on a level playing field. We went back and forth with strikes and balls, and even when the count went to 3-and-2, I fouled off six pitches in a row after that. Finally, on the twelfth pitch and with my arms feeling tired from swinging, Hank hung a slider right over the middle of the plate. I wasted no time and drove it over the right centerfield wall for a home run. Hank looked at me as I rounded third, with a mix of a heated glare and a smile, knowing he had been beaten that time.

Going up 3-0 early made Colby even more comfortable, and he settled in quickly and mowed through the Pirate batters in the second, third and fourth. Hank settled down himself, getting us in order in the second and third, and with two outs in the fourth, he walked Anton ahead of me. Hank had already thrown a lot of pitches by the fourth inning, pushing eighty, and I could see it was wearing on him in his first start of the season. He had a habit of dropping down when he got tired that always got him in trouble, and sure enough, he threw one that was meant to be down but just kept rising for me until it was in the sweet zone. I flicked the bat quickly, and the ball exploded off the bat. It was high into the night, and I lost sight of it as it crossed paths with the bright lights in the outfield. The only sign to me was the crowd yelling and the umpiring circling his finger in the air like he was spinning a plate, signaling home run.

It was stuff out of a fairy tale, or things you dream about when you are playing ball in your backyard as a kid. No one hits five home runs in two games, let alone five in a row. When I got back to the dugout, the guys were going nuts. Ken Abernathy came over and sat next to me on the bench.

"That ties a record, you know," Ken said to me quietly. Sure enough, they flashed on the scoreboard that I had tied a record for most home runs in consecutive games. I glanced over at the scoreboard and smiled back at Ken.

"Neat," I said to him and went over to grab a drink of water.

Colby Dalton made into the sixth before running into trouble but only gave up one run to keep us ahead 5-1. Unfortunately, in seventh, our relief pitchers let us down and gave up four runs, so the Pirates tied it up. We came up in the seventh with Hank Swan out of the game and Vic Williams on in relief. Vic was big, strong, and nasty, and not just nasty in what he threw but in how he played. Luckily, we got one man on thanks to an error. Anton then muscled a hit down the left field line for a double, putting men on second and third for me. The crowd was on their feet now when I came up, giving me an incredible rush of adrenaline. I peered out at Williams, not sure what to expect from him. I should have known what to expect when his first pitch was a fastball coming right at me. I quickly turned, and the ball hit me square between the shoulder blades, just where you want to hit someone when you want to send a message. I crumpled to the ground, feeling a searing pain in my shoulder and back. The crowd rained harsh boos down on Vic, and I could hear Anton shouting expletives at him from second base, taunting him and trying to draw him into a fight.

The Reds trainer, Phil Dawkins, trotted out to see if I was okay.

"Where'd he get you, Wes?" Phil said as I sat up.

"In the back," I said as I started to get to my feet. Phil gave me a hand as I got up and dusted myself off. "I'm good," I told him as I jogged down to first, eyeballing Vic as he smiled at me.

Our next batter, Brett Thompson, hitting behind me today, lined a single to center to drive in a run to put us ahead. Vic slammed the ball into his mitt, angry with himself for giving up the hit. He went to get two strikeouts and a pop up to end the inning, but we were ahead. I walked slowly back to the dugout and watched Anton cross in front of Williams on the way back, making sure to let him know he was watching him.

My back was sore, but I played on, even as the Pirates tacked on two runs in the eighth to go back in front of us, 7-6. Our lineup went out meekly in the eighth, and we held them in the ninth, so we were still down a run. The Pirates brought in their closer, Pat Stringer, to close things out. Pat was an All-Star closer, one of the bright spots on the Pirate staff. He was tough on everyone and threw lights out stuff from all different angles. Our manager, Pete Doyle, tried to remain upbeat.

"We can do this," he said, clapping his hands roughly. "We got Anton, Wes, and Brett this inning. We can do this."

Anton was out watching Stringer warm up while I went out to the on-deck circle to watch.

"Got any tips?" Anton asked me as we watched him throw.

"He's only got two pitches, Anton," I told him. "Fastball and cutter, and he always throw the cutter first. Take it and look for the fastball."

"Got it," Anton said as he strode to the plate. I watched, taking some practice hacks, and sure enough, the first pitch was a cutter that ran low and away. Anton pumped himself after that pitch, bearing down with his back foot in the batter's box. The fastball came, and out it went, deep into left field and over the wall. The crowd erupted as Anton tied the game. I slapped his hand as he crossed the plate and saw he had a big smile on his face.

I stepped in and looked out at Stringer. The catcher, Glenn Hopkins, had been surprisingly quiet to me all night. He looked up as I stepped in and grunted. I figured after Anton's home run, there was no way Stringer was throwing a fastball at all this at-bat, so I had to hack at whatever looked good. I quickly stepped out, adjusting my batting gloves and then took a fast look at my wristbands. The KA was still there on each one, though a little faded on the left after hitting the ground last time. I smiled and got back to the plate.

Stringer threw the cutter, and it was coming in fast, but it didn't cut like it normally does. This one stayed up a fraction longer, and it was just enough for me. I knew I hit it well; it was just a question of whether it was fair or not. I saw it carrying down the line high and watched it as I moved slowly down the line. When I got close to first base, I heard the ball clang of the foul pole for a home run. I was never one for showing emotion on the field, but I pumped my fist as I rounded first base and made my way around the bases. The whole team was waiting for me at home, jumping up and down with excitement as I stepped on the plate. Fans were screaming like I never heard before.

Anton grabbed me and hugged me.

"I thought you said take the cutter?" he yelled to me over the shouts of the crowd.

"Yeah... for you," I told him with a laugh as we headed into the clubhouse with a walk-off win.

For me, this was the World Series moment I had imagined over my thirteen years. It was the kind of thing you dream about, hitting home runs like that and then one to win the game. Reporters were all over me, asking me questions left and right. After a string of questions about how good it feels, one TV reporter looked at me and said, "What's the KA on your wrists for?"

I looked down at the wristband on my right wrist and smiled, and then held it up for the cameras to see.

"That's someone special I was thinking about tonight," I said to the reporter. "She knows who she is." I didn't say anything more about it.

The reporters finally thinned out so I could shower and dress. Anton was sitting at his locker dressed in his suit.

"Hell of a way to open the season," Anton said to me. "It will make the flight to St. Louis that much sweeter tonight."

I finished getting into my suit while the clubhouse guys scrambled around, gathering gear for the road trip. I snatched up the two wristbands from the game and looked down at them as I sat at my locker. I stood up and put the wristbands down on my chair.

"You bet Anton," I told him. I grabbed my phone and took a picture of the wristbands and sent the picture to Kristin with just the text:

For you.

Chapter 32

Kristin

A day ago, I would have been nervous about going to Wes' parent's house to see everyone. Now I couldn't wait for the evening to come so I could go there for dinner and watch the game. When I got back to the library, Karen wanted all the details about where I went and what happened, and I explained to her how nice Jenny was, how great it was to talk with her, and how I feel like I was making a connection with Isabelle. It all gave me a much better outlook about the potential of a relationship with Wes and where things could go down the road. At least, for the time being, it seemed like there was some potential there.

I hustled Karen out the door at five so I could be sure to get to Wyatt and Jenny's for dinner before the game started.

"I can't believe you're rushing me out to go watch a baseball game," Karen told me as I locked the door behind us. "A week ago, you didn't even know who the Pirates and Reds were."

"Like you wanted to hang around and work anyway," I said to Karen. "I'm sure Brian will be calling you anyway."

"Actually," she said with a smile, "I'm driving up to meet him tonight. I may be in a little bit late tomorrow morning. Is that okay?" Karen asked.

"Oh, really?" I replied. "And why would you be late?"

"Well, we're going to have dinner together after he gets off work at ten, so I may get in late. Or I may stick around and see if I could work the shy out of him." She let out a laugh as she started walking away. "Have fun watching the game!" she yelled back to me.

I walked over to my car and drove the now familiar drive over to Martin Way. I pulled into the driveway and parked and walked over to the front door, ringing the bell. Wyatt came and answered wearing a Pirates jersey.

"Come on in," he said to me with a smile.

"A Pirates jersey?" I said to Wyatt.

"I don't have a Reds jersey for Wes yet," he said apologetically. "Besides, I have been rooting for the Pirates for over fifty years. It's a hard habit to break, even when your son plays for the other team."

I walked in and could smell a wonderful aroma wafting from the kitchen. I followed Wes into the kitchen and saw Isabelle and Jenny hard at work by the stove. I could see Jenny manning a hot cast iron pan bubbling with oil while Isabelle was hard at work mashing potatoes. Jenny looked over and smiled while Isabelle waved to me.

"I hope fried chicken is okay with you," Jenny said to me as she flipped a piece of chicken in the pan.

"Okay?" I said to her with delight. "I'm a Southern girl; my blood is part oil from frying chicken."

"Great," Jenny replied. "It was Izzy's idea; she thought you would like it."

"Can I help with anything?" I asked.

"Perhaps you could set the table for me please since I can't seem to pry Wyatt away from the TV watching the pregame stuff," she said loud enough for Wyatt to hear in the living room.

"Thanks, Kristin," Wyatt shouted back.

I just laughed and grabbed the stack of plates and set the table. Moments after I was done, Jenny came over with a big platter of fried chicken pieces. Isabelle had a bowl of mashed potatoes and then went back for some green beans. I went into the kitchen with her and grabbed the basket of biscuits there and brought them out as well.

"You made biscuits too?" I asked, feeling pangs for home.

"Izzy made those," Jenny said. "She's quite the cook."

"You'll have to come over to my place to cook," I said to her as we sat down.

"Wyatt!" Jenny yelled into the living room to get his attention. Wyatt trotted in and sat at the head of the table. We passed around the food, and I filled my plate with all my favorites.

"They said Wes is batting fifth tonight," Wyatt said as he bit into a piece of chicken.

"Wyatt Martin, not with your mouth full, please," Jenny scolded. "You'd think you were the fifteen-year-old around here."

Wyatt just smiled as he kept eating. I savored each bite that I took, from the crispy crunch of the chicken leg to the warm biscuits with just the right touch of honey in them. It was just like being back home in Georgia.

"This meal is amazing," I said as I wiped my mouth with my napkin.

Jenny and Isabelle both smiled, happy with their accomplishments. I went back for seconds of everything and ate much more than I probably should have eaten until I was completely stuffed.

"Ladies, that may have been the best meal yet," Wyatt said to them as he polished off the last of his biscuit.

"Thanks, Grandpa," Isabelle told him as she started to clear the table. I got up to help, and Jenny tried to stop me.

"Jenny, if I don't clear the dishes I will probably get a call from mother tonight about it. Somehow, she will know I wasn't contributing," I told her as I picked up some plates.

"Well thank you," she said. Wyatt came over and helped her up to bring her into the living room so they could sit down and watch the game. Isabelle and I went about loading the dishwasher and then she washed while I dried the pots and pans.

"I have a couple of ideas for dresses for the dance Friday," Isabelle said to me as I dried the frying pan. "They are dresses I haven't had a chance to wear yet. Maybe you could look at them and let me know what you think?"

"I'd love too," I said to her.

"This is going to be so much fun!" I Isabelle said with delight as she washed another pot.

By the time the dishes were done, and everything was put away, the game was just about to start. Wyatt was seated in the recliner and Jenny was in an easy chair on the other side of the couch from the recliner. I sat down on the couch while Isabelle took a seat on the floor. I was excited to watch even though I didn't really know that much about what I was watching.

When the Reds took the field, Isabelle pointed towards first base. "There's Dad!" she said excitedly. Wes was all decked out in a crisp white uniform with red trim, wearing the number twelve on the back. It was exciting to see him for a few reasons. I had missed seeing him, and this was the first time I had ever seen him while he was playing. I had to admit, he looked very good in his uniform, and you could clearly see his big, strong forearms in the short sleeve jersey he wore.

The Reds pitcher seemed to struggle at the start, and Wes walked over to talk to him after two batters. After that, he fell into a good groove and got everyone out. The Reds came to bat, and two men got on base before Wes came up. The announcers talked about his last game and how great it was to start out that way. The at-bat went on and on, with Wes fouling off pitch after pitch until he finally hit one, hitting it deep and out of the park. The family erupted in a cheer, and I had to admit I got caught up in the excitement of seeing him do well. I looked and saw smiles on all their faces and could tell how happy they were for him.

The game went on, with the Reds leading. I had a hard time keeping up with everything, and Wyatt and Isabelle would explain things to me about the game, so I had a better idea of what was going on. I felt embarrassed that I didn't know more about baseball, but it wasn't until now that I found anything worth watching about it. When the Reds were batting again, one man had gotten on before Wes came up. This time, Wes went after the first pitch and hit it again. We watched as it soared over the fence, the crowd in the stadium yelling and screaming and Wyatt and Isabelle yelling as well as Jenny calmly sat in her chair and smiled at them. I gave Wyatt and Isabelle high-fives.

"You know that ties a record," Wyatt said excitedly. "No one hits home runs like this in back-to-back games."

The game then swung a bit, with the Pirates scoring to tie the game up before Wes was due up again. Jenny got up out of her chair and yawned.

"That's it for me, folks," she said as she stretched. "Isabelle, not too late; you have school tomorrow. Wyatt, get Kristin a piece of pound cake for dessert." After she gave her instructions, Jenny came over and put her hand gently on my face.

"Thank you for coming back tonight," she said to me with a smile.

"Thanks for having me," I said to her, placing my hand over hers on my face.

I watched as she walked down the hall towards her bedroom, and then the yelling of Isabelle and Wyatt grabbed my attention. The Reds had two men on base as Wes was coming up again. The man pitching for the Pirates had a mean look on his face. He had big, bushy, black hair and a long mustache and beard. Wes stood up to face him, and the man threw the pitch, with the ball hitting Wes right away. I heard myself gasp and Isabelle gasped too as Wes hit the ground. He lay on dirt for a few seconds before sitting up. The team trainer came running out to him, and you could hear the fans booing.

"Son of a bitch Williams. That guy has always been a bastard," Wyatt grumbled as Isabelle and I looked over at him. "Pardon my language ladies, but it's the truth," he spat out. We waited and watched closely as Wes stood up and jogged down to the base, indicating he was okay. The next batter for the Reds got a hit to score a run, and the Reds were ahead.

The lead was short-lived as the Pirates scored again to take the lead back, 7-6. The game was tense as it went to the bottom of the ninth inning.

"How do you watch this all the time?" I said to Wyatt. "This is nerve-racking." I could feel a knot in my stomach.

"You get used to it," Wyatt said with a smile. "Izzy, you should go to bed."

"Come on Grandpa," she answered. "It's the last inning, and Dad comes up. Just let me watch him."

"Okay, but don't tell your grandmother."

The first batter for the Reds came up, and after one pitch, he hit the next one over the wall for a home run to tie the game. That brought Wes up again. Wyatt was sitting on the edge of his seat now, watching the game intently. All three of us sat there silently and watched the Pirates pitcher throw the pitch. Wes hit it, and the camera followed it across the screen, going higher and higher until it hit the yellow pole out by the fence. Isabelle and Wyatt both jumped up and screamed as the fans in the stadium and the announcers both yelled loudly.

"What happened?" I asked.

"It hit the foul pole," Wyatt said happily.

"And that's a good thing?"

"If you hit it, then it's a home run," Isabelle shrieked. "Dad won the game!" She came over and gave me a hug, surprising me. I hugged her back, getting caught up in the excitement. I looked at the screen and saw the players on the Reds mobbing Wes.

I was so happy for him. This was obviously a big accomplishment for him, and he had proved to everyone, especially in Pittsburgh, that he was far from done playing. The field emptied as the game ended and Wyatt turned to Isabelle.

"Izzy, you should go to bed," he told her.

"You know they are going to interview Dad," she said. "Can I watch it just for a minute, please?" she said, batting her eyes at him.

"She's good," I said to Wyatt with a laugh.

"Too good," he said to me. "Go get us some cake. You can watch him, and then that's it."

Izzy ran into the kitchen and came back quickly with three pieces of pound cake. I was probably too full for it, but I had some anyway and enjoyed every bite. It wasn't long before the cameras were interviewing Wes in the locker room, asking him about the game and the home runs. He had a smile on his face and was covered in sweat, but he answered each question humbly, saying it was a great team win and it was a good bunch of guys to play with. It was then a reporter asked him about something on his wristbands that they had noticed. He held the wristbands up to the camera, and I could see clearly in marker he had written KA on them.

Wes looked into the camera and said "That's someone special I was thinking about tonight. She knows who she is."

Isabelle and Wyatt both looked over at me. I was stunned, and I felt like my heart would explode. I could feel tears welling up in my eyes as I looked at Wes' face on the screen before they cut away to something else.

"Bedtime now, Izzy," Wyatt said to her. Isabelle came over to me and took my hand and asked me to walk with her down to her bedroom. We walked into her room, and she stood, facing me.

"I know it was wrong to say the things I did to you like that. I'm sorry that I was so mean, and it hurt you, and Dad. I see that you are important to him and that he wants you to be part of his life... and I want that too." I could see she had tears in her eyes, and now I did too. She gave me a hug and held it tightly.

"Thank you, Isabelle," I said through the tears.

"Can you come by tomorrow, so we can talk about dresses and hair for Friday?" Isabelle asked me, wiping away her tears.

"Of course," I said. "I'll see you tomorrow. Have a good night."

"Good night, Ms. Arthur," she said to me politely.

"Please call me Kristin," I said to her.

"Only if you call me Izzy," she said with a smile. "Only Grandma calls me Isabelle, or Dad when he's mad at me."

"Okay, Izzy. Good night."

I walked back down the hall to see Wyatt turning the TV off and cleaning up.

"Thank you so much for having me over Wyatt," I said to him as I grabbed my jacket. "I had a great time."

"Our pleasure," he said to me. "It was a heck of a game."

"It's the first one I've ever watched," I said to him honestly.

"Well you picked a good one to start with," He said with a laugh.

I gave him a hug before I left. "You have a wonderful family, Wyatt."

"Why thank you," he said, "I think they're pretty good. And I think we'll be seeing you around a bit more, which will be nice, too."

"Yes, it will," I told him as I stepped on the porch. "Have a good night."

I walked out to my car and drove home, though I felt like I could have floated there and don't remember anything about the drive. I pulled in and went up to my apartment and heard my phone ding with a message. I figured it was going to be Karen if she had seen any of the game. Instead, it was from Wes. There was a picture of the wristbands with my initials on them and the brief message of "For you" following the picture. I smiled and hugged my phone, flopping back on the bed.

I pressed the phone number of the text and tried to call him, but the phone went right to voicemail. He probably had lots of calls he was receiving or making, so I wasn't surprised. I decided to send him a text message instead:

I told you once that you know how to woo a girl, and I meant it. I'm falling hard for you. Missing you and hoping you have a good night.

I just lay back on the bed, relishing the entire day, and wondering when I would hear from him again.

Chapter 33

Kristin

I had felt like I was on a roller coaster for the last week. Ever since I met Wes my life has been turned every which way, with more highs and lows than I had ever thought possible. After last night, I was convinced it was going to all be worth it. The connections I had made with Wes' family, especially with Izzy, were so important to me and gave me hope that Wes and I could have some future together. Then, when I saw Wes' gesture on TV after the game, I was certain I was making the right decision by seeking a relationship with him, even if it meant that we might be apart for months at a time.

My only concern was that I had not heard from him since he sent me the picture of the wristbands he wore with my initials on them. He had sent me the text, and I responded to him right after I got it, but I didn't hear back from him at all. I tried calling him a few times, but the phone went right to voicemail. I left a message one time, letting him know I was thinking about him and wanted to talk to him, but I still had heard nothing back.

I knew the team was flying to St. Louis after the game last night for their next series, so I assumed that meant he was traveling all night, getting to the hotel late. He was probably still asleep at the hour I woke up to get ready for work, but I was still worried.

I guess I need to get used to this kind of life and relationship, I told myself to make myself feel better.

While I showered and got ready for work, I did get a text from Karen. All she told me was that she would be in late this morning, or even early afternoon if that was okay. She volunteered to take my late shift at the library for me instead since it was Thursday and we were open late tonight. I replied to her that it was fine, and she sent me a smiling face back to say thanks. I was glad she and Brian were hitting it off so well.

After yesterday's rain, today was sunny and nice, and the temperature was even a bit warmer, making my walk to work seem more pleasant. There was just a bit of a breeze along the street, enough to give some bounce to the skirt of the light olive cotton dress I was wearing. As I sauntered past the diner, there was Clyde and friends to wave hello to me, with more of them taking an avid interest in me than usual. Clyde even rapped on the window to get my attention, and I turned to look to see what he wanted. He held up a copy of the local newspaper in his hands, which had a big picture of Wes on the back cover, holding up his wristband for the camera for the world to see. I looked up at Clyde and smiled, shrugged my shoulders at him playfully, and walked away with the smile still on my face.

I picked up the copies of the newspaper outside the library that we made available to patrons and brought them in with me as I opened. I laid the paper out on the front counter to look at the story. It talked about how Wes had won the game and set a record by hitting six home runs in two games, and in six successive at-bats. It also questioned who the "mysterious" KA was that his home runs were dedicated to and wondered who he was thinking about that had him so motivated these days. The paper even sought comment from his parents, but Wyatt Martin was quoted as saying "I don't know who he's talking about."

Good old Wyatt, I thought with a smile. I reminded myself to pick a copy or two of the newspaper today on my way home as a keepsake.

It wasn't long before I got another text from Karen. Apparently, she had just seen on social media the video of Wes. Her message to me was:

Holy shit, Kris!

I just sent back a blushing face emoji to her and left it at that.

I was convinced there was nothing that was going to bring down my mood today. I floated through the library, humming to myself, putting books back on the shelves, straightening up the tables, vacuuming the rugs, and every other chore and task that came along. I smiled and greeted everyone happily that came in all morning, no matter how grumpy they might have been. I did get an email from Marion, reminding me to have my proposals for next week's board meeting ready, and I didn't panic or stress about it at all. It didn't even bother me that I had forgotten to pack myself a lunch for today and munched on one of the cereal bars I kept in my desk for emergencies while I drank my coffee.

After a while, I was looking for things to do to occupy my time. There were a few patrons in the library, sitting at the tables reading, but other than that, it was a quiet afternoon. I decided to clean out some of the areas underneath the counter, pulling out boxes of supplies and junk and sorting through them. I was down on my hands and knees pulling a box out when I heard a voice at the front counter clear his throat.

"I'll be with you in one second," I said cheerfully as I was trying to reach the far corner underneath the side counter.

"Take your time," the voice said, sounding muffled since most of me was under the counter. "I'm enjoying the view anyway."

It was then I realized that my backside was sticking out while I cleaned. It was a bit embarrassing, but I thought it was a bit forward and rude of whoever said that to me out there, and I scurried out from underneath the cabinet to give them a piece of my mind.

"Excuse me?" I began with as I got up and brushed myself off since I was covered in dust. "I'm happy to help you, but there's no need to be..." I stopped in my tracks as I looked up.

Wes was standing there, holding a bouquet of roses for me. Shock ran through my body as I dropped the duster in my hand.

"What are you doing here?" I said to him, still unable to believe he was here.

"I was in town and thought I would stop by the library," he said with a smile. "I'm curious as to how you were going to finish that sentence."

I walked around the counter and stood in front of him.

"I was going to say there's no need to be rude," I said softly and smiled at him.

"Well I do apologize for that," Wes said. "I hope these make up for it." He handed me the flowers. I took them in my shaking hand and immediately placed them on the counter. I reached up and pulled him to me, giving him a long kiss. When we finally broke the kiss slowly, I could hear some light applause coming from the tables from the people sitting there, now watching us instead of reading.

I blushed and giggled a bit as I buried my face in Wes' chest. I could feel tears coming to my eyes.

"Aren't you supposed to be in St. Louis?" I said to him.

Wes took my hand, leading me into my office so we could have some more privacy.

"Yes, I was supposed to be in St. Louis," he started to tell me. "After the game, we were all packed and dressed and ready to go. I had just had this amazing run of two days playing... better than I had in my entire career. It was satisfying, but it wasn't making me happy. You know why? Because you weren't there to share it with me. We were walking to the bus to head to the airport, and I couldn't do it. I told the manager that this was it, I was done. There was no better way for me to go out. I felt bad leaving my teammates that way, but I've spent the last fifteen years of my life putting what should be most important to me on hold. I didn't want to do it any longer, to miss out on what was going to make me happy no matter what."

I looked up at Wes, feeling overwhelmed by what he was telling me. He smiled at me and continued speaking.

"I was nervous about it, and after I got my stuff from my locker and back to the hotel I went to call Dad, and that's when I saw your message. It made me happy to know you felt that way. Then when I talked to Dad, and he told me about last night... About how you were there, and talked to my Mom and to Izzy, and said how things were... I knew I was doing the right thing. I got in my car and drove all night to get back here. I got home early this morning, saw Mom and Dad, sent Izzy a message to let her know, and then I came here to see you. That's it."

I took Wes' hand in mind and held it tightly.

"Wes, I just want you to be sure this is right for you," I said to him. "I'm perfectly okay with you playing and being on the road, and we can make this work that way. I'm convinced of it."

"If I weren't completely convinced this was right for me, I wouldn't be standing in front of you right now," he said to me.

"What about your contract? All that money," I said to him.

"Kris, I never played for the money," Wes told me. "Hell, the money is great; I'm not denying that. But I've taken good care of what I have earned. I played because I loved to be out there playing, because it's where it felt right for me to be. Now it's right for me to be here... with Izzy, and Mom and Dad... and with you... if you'll have me."

Tears were streaming down my face now and I could them falling on our hands as we held them together.

"Yes..." I said quietly. "Of course, I'll have you. I've never wanted anything else more."

We kissed again, just as passionately as before, and were only interrupted by a cough from outside my office.

I looked over and saw Karen standing there, smiling and holding a cup of coffee she brought with her.

Wes and I broke our embrace and stood looking at Karen.

"Karen," I said to her, feeling flustered, "You made it in. Great. Karen, this is Wes Martin. Wes, this is Karen. She works with me here in the library."

Wes held out his hand to Karen and shook it.

"I know who he is," Karen said as she shook his hand. "I'm a big fan. It's nice to meet you."

"Thanks," Wes said humbly. He turned to me and said, "I should let you get back to work." I felt disappointed he would be leaving after he just got here.

"Kris can go with you," Karen said, jumping in. "She covered for me this morning, so I could be off and now work the rest of the day." Karen pulled me out of the office to be next to Wes. She reached in and grabbed my purse, handing it to me.

I mouthed a "thank you" to her as I stood next to Wes, taking his hand again. I saw Brian, the guy Karen has been seeing, standing on the other side of the counter. He was staring at Wes, somewhat star struck that he was there, right in front of him.

I took my flowers off the counter to bring with me.

"I'll see you tomorrow," I told Karen. She was still beaming at me as she leaned on the counter. I saw Brian lean closer to her and whisper "That's Wes Martin!" Karen playfully slapped his arm, telling him to be quiet.

Wes and I walked out the door, with all eyes on us as we left. We went straight to his SUV, and in moments we were on the road, going back to his house. As we pulled onto the road and headed up the hill past his parents' house, I took a smell of the flowers and looked over at Wes. I just grinned at him, feeling like my heart was overflowing.

Wes parked the car and came around and opened the door for me. We walked into his house and towards the kitchen, when he grasped my hand, took my flowers and tossed them on the kitchen counter, and pulled me over towards his bedroom door.

We started kissing immediately, giving short kisses to each other as we began to quickly undress. Our hands could barely be kept off one another, and more than once I found myself giggling as we fumbled with zippers, buttons, and clasps until we were each rid of our clothing.

Wes guided me down onto his bed, slowly kissing my neck, while he lay on top of me. The heat and excitement coursing through my body seemed almost unbearable, and I wanted my hands all over him and his all over me. I was already excited, and Wes clearly was as well, but I could tell he wanted this experience to last. He was very deliberate with me and my body, exploring it closely and tenderly with his fingers and his mouth. I felt him kissing his way down my body, down my breasts, and across my stomach. I could feel my body almost involuntarily lift my hips up to meet his lips as he kept going lower, planting slow, lingering kisses on me until I felt his tongue gently slip between the folds of my flesh and inside me. I gasped deeply with pleasure, trying to contain what was building up inside me so quickly. His kisses and licks were more intense than anything I had felt before, and when he found my clitoris with the tip of his tongue, my body couldn't take much more. He kept bringing me right to the edge with his mouth, teasing my body until I was crying out for him.

Wes smiled down at me as he saw my heavy breathing starting to subside. I peered up at him as he lowered my legs back down to the bed. Wes laid next to me, tracing my body lightly with his fingers. I was so keyed up now that even the slightest touch like this was sending jolts through me, and I felt myself quiver as his fingers glided over the side of my left breast. I quickly turned to my side to kiss him deeply, our tongues mingling in mouths, and soon enough our bodies were pressed tightly against each other again.

Wes broke our kiss and ran his right hand through my hair as he raised himself up over me. He looked deeply into my eyes as I could feel him slide into me so easily. I was so ready for him to be in my body was aching for it, and I felt myself wrap my legs tightly around him, holding him there, pulling him deeper and deeper inside me. His thrusts were calm, kind and deliberate, and I closed my eyes tightly and held on to him, pressing my chest against his, kissing his shoulder, and hearing the moans from my body matching the deep breaths he was taking.

My legs were shaking as I held onto him, and when I felt him hold me tightly and surge forward, his orgasm pushed me over the edge once again. We just held each other as close as our bodies would allow. I am sure Wes could feel me trembling in his arms as he continued to hold me. He rolled to my side, keeping his arm around my shoulders to bring me closer to him.

Wes looked over at me and kissed me softly on my lips.

"God, you are so beautiful," he said to me brushing the hair from my face so he could see my flushed cheeks. I could feel tears falling from my eyes again, and he gently wiped them away with his finger.

"Why are you crying?" Wes asked, giving me a gentle smile as he kissed me again.

"I've never been so happy," I whispered to him, leaning over to kiss him again.

"Well I hope I can keep you feeling this way," Wes whispered back, pulling me into his arms.

My head was resting against his chest.

"I know you will," I answered, closing my eyes, feeling safe, happy, and loved.

Chapter 34

Wes

Laying there, holding Kristin in my arms while she slept gently, gave me a chance to reflect on the last day or so. I think I knew the moment I put my suit on to go to the team bus that I was never getting on that bus to go to the airport. There was too much of a pull to bring me back to Chandler. I had done everything I thought I could do in baseball by this point. Even though I had never been to a World Series, I felt like I had accomplished everything I could, and there might not ever be a better way to go out than this. When I reached the team bus, I pulled Pete Doyle aside to let him know about my decision. Pete didn't take it as well as I had hoped he would. He ranted, raged, and cursed about abandoning the team, letting them down, and how I owed it to them and the fans to keep playing. The other players were watching and listening as all this went on, and I calmly stood there and let Pete have his say.

Anton Rogers lumbered out and told Pete to get on the bus. He and I walked a few steps away from the bus as I explained to him that I was retiring.

"Why now, man?" Anton asked.

"I've got too much going on at home to keep traveling like this Anton. I have a teenage daughter that needs me, a mother who is sick and... and someone that I care about deeply that I need with me. The time is right for me."

"People are going to say you're a quitter, Wes," Anton said honestly.

"Let them say what they have to," I told him. "I can take it. I'm sorry if I'm leaving you guys short, and I'm sorry if I let you down, Anton, but I have to do this."

"You're not letting me down, Wes," Anton said, putting his hand on my shoulder. "You do what's right for you and your family. It's a game, man. People forget about that and take it way too seriously. I'll be fine, the team will be fine. They'll bring some kid up to play, and I'll work him into shape like the rest of them. You go home, take of your daughter, and take care of that girl, KA. She must be someone pretty special."

"She is," I answered. We shook hands, and Anton leaned in and gave me a hug.

"You bring those girls down to Pittsburgh when we're in town Wes," Anton said to me. "I need to meet them."

"You got it."

Anton turned and walked back to the bus. "Let's get this bus moving!" he yelled as he boarded. I watched the bus pull out before I went back and gathered my things from my locker. I walked out of the stadium and back to my hotel to check out and gather my car. Before I started the car up, I checked my phone and saw the message from Kristin about how she was falling for me. I smiled and started the car, and then called Dad to let him know I was coming home, again.

I explained my decision to him, and he was silent for a moment before answering.

"Wes, if you know this is right for you, then you know we'll stand behind you. If it's time, it's time," Dad told me.

Dad then went on to explain to me how Kristin had come over that day and night, and what had transpired between Mom, Izzy and Kristin, and how Kristin had stayed to watch the game with them. I was elated, to say the least.

"Everything you said to me just confirms that I made the right choice Dad," I said to him.

"I thought it might," he said with a laugh. "You drive safely now. If you get tired, stop somewhere and come home tomorrow."

"I don't think anything could stop me from driving all the way back now," I replied. "I'll see you in the morning. Thanks, Dad."

I hung up with Dad and knew I had one more call to make, and it would be a tough one. It wouldn't be long before word got out that I wasn't with the team on the way to St. Louis. There were reporters on the plane, and they would be looking for me. Someone was bound to say something to them. I needed to give Randy a heads up about what happened.

Randy picked up after just one ring. "Hey there hero!" he shouted to me. "What's going on? You guys on the plane yet?"

"I'm not going to St. Louis," I said to him seriously. "I'm headed back home to Chandler."

"Is everything okay? Your Mom and Dad alright? Izzy?" Randy had some concern in his voice.

"They're all fine," I told him as I drove. "It's just me Randy. I'm done. These last two days have been amazing for me, but they also let me know that I'm ready for this part of my life to be over. It's the right time for me."

Randy then spent the next ten minutes trying to talk me out of retiring. Companies were calling for endorsements and commercials. TV shows wanted me for interviews. He said the Reds were thrilled and wanted me to stay. If I didn't want to be in Cincinnati, the Pirates owner called him and said the team made a huge mistake and they wished they had me back. Neither was enough to change my mind.

"I'm sorry Randy," I said to him. "It doesn't change anything for me. I hope I didn't disappoint you."

"It's okay, Wes," Randy said. "Hey, it had to end eventually, right? Go be with your family and pick up with your life. If things change for you down the road, we can talk again."

"They won't change," I said emphatically.

"Okay, fair enough. If you ever want to get back into the game, as a coach or manager or something, I'm sure we can work that out for you. Keep in touch with me, Wes."

"I will. Thanks, Randy." I hung up the phone and went back to concentrating on my drive home, what I would do, how I would tell Izzy, and how I wanted to surprise Kristin.

All that brought me back to lying in bed with Kristin at my side. She kept sleeping comfortably for about another hour or so before she started to rouse. I kissed her on the forehead and watched her eyes flutter open as she smiled at me.

"Oh good," she said as she stretched her arms. "It wasn't a dream. You're here."

"I sure am," I told her. I leaned down and kissed her on the lips. I looked at my watch and saw that it was nearly four. I sat up in bed while Kristin lay on the pillow.

"Where are you off to?" she said to me with a smile as she rolled over onto her stomach. I could see the fabulous curves of her body on the bed and was sorely tempted to crawl back in with her.

"I'm going to jump in the shower," I told her. "After driving all night and everything I think I need it. Then I thought maybe we could go down to my parents to see Izzy."

"That sounds good to me," Kristin said as she watched me walk towards the bathroom, whistling at me as I walked away.

I opened the shower door and turned the water on, letting it get hot and build up some steam before I climbed in. The shower had been custom-made when I had the house built, with an overhead waterfall shower and a bench seat along the far wall of the stall. The hot water felt great on my muscles and was just what I needed to revive me. I let the water rain down on me, but within moments I heard the shower stall door opening. Kristin climbed in with a grin on her face.

"I could use a shower too," she said to me, letting the water hit her as she stood in front of me. "I hope you don't mind the company."

"Not at all," I said with a smile. I grabbed the bar of soap from the holder and began to run it over her body, from her shoulders, down across her breasts and her stomach, up and down each leg, and across the downy strip of hair she had over her sex. Kristin then turned around so I could do the same to her back. I loved doing it, soaping her back and backside, cupping her in my hands, and touching her body all over.

Kristin rinsed off under the shower as I watched her run her hands over her body seductively. She looked over at me through the falling water and smiled at me. She reached over and took the bar of soak out of my hand and purred, "My turn."

I felt her work up the suds in her hand and glide the bar of soap over my shoulders onto my chest. Her fingers massaged my pecs, and I felt her thumbs rub across my nipples before she worked her way down to my abdomen. She made sure to cover it well, tracing each muscle with her fingers. She then squatted down and rubbed the bar of soap up and down each leg, from my feet to my thighs, before she slowly stood up again, bringing her wet body right up against mine so that I could feel her breasts run over my very stiff erection. She held the bar of soap up to my eyes as she slowly worked up a good lather on her hands, and then placed the soap back in its holder. Her hands then disappeared, going down to my waist, before I felt her take me in her soapy hands.

I gasped with each slow twist and turn she made on my shaft, each move and caress getting slicker and slicker with the mix of water, soap, and fluids. I could feel her gripping me, moving her fingers over me expertly, and drawing me closer and closer to exploding in her hands. She looked me in the eye with a smile and glanced at her hands.

"I think I need more soap," she said with an evil grin and went reached to get more before my hand grabbed her wrist to stop her.

"No, you don't," I groaned out. I kissed Kristin hard, pulling her to me. I wanted her badly and slowly moved her so her back was against the shower wall. I could feel her pressing hard against my body, rubbing her right leg and thigh against mine while we kissed.

I lifted her up, causing her to let out a gasp of surprise, and brought myself up and into her. Her gasp of surprise turned into a moan, and she wrapped her legs around my waist. I held her tightly against me, holding her up, while I felt her moving up and down on me. The combination of the warm water, the wetness all around us, and our bodies moving together was exquisite. I could hear Kristin panting, wrapping her arms tightly around me while she kissed my neck and shoulder until I felt her arms and legs squeeze on me tightly, trying to hold me in place as she came. I pressed her back against the wall again as I thrust one last time and came myself, my legs almost giving out beneath me.

Kristin looked at me with water coming down all around her, kissing me again and again. I put her back down, and her legs seemed as wobbly as mine. We both stood under the hot water for a bit before I looked down at her and smiled again.

"I guess I finally got to use this shower the way the space should be used. Thanks," I told her.

She smiled back at me, running her hands through her long, wet hair.

"I think we can find lots of good uses for all the space you have in the house if we use our imagination," Kristin said slyly.

After we finally brought ourselves to get out of the shower, we helped each other dry off, which almost led to another session on the bed. My hands were roaming all over her body when Kristin finally said to me "Wes, we're never going to get to your parents if you keep this up."

"And that's a bad thing?" I asked as I slowly dried off her left thigh, letting my hand roam and linger a bit.

"Hmmm," she moaned. "No, it's not a bad thing at all, but I promised Izzy I would help her tonight. She wants help picking out a dress for the dance tomorrow."

"Something down to her ankles and up to her chin is perfect. Maybe made of burlap or wool," I told Kristin as I playfully tossed the towels to the floor.

Kristin laughed at my suggestion. I watched her as she started to get dressed, sliding into her bra and panties under my gaze.

"Seriously," I said to her as I pulled out a pair of black boxer briefs from my dresser and put them on, "maybe she won't want to go, and we can do something else."

"That's not likely to happen, Wes, and you know it." Kristin lifted her dress over her head, and I watched her shimmy her body into it. "You had to know sooner or later she was going to start dating. It's a school dance, and he sounds like he's a nice boy. Izzy's a smart girl. Give her the benefit of the doubt."

"It's the nice boys you have to watch out for," I said to her as I put a t-shirt on and grabbed a pair of jeans.

Kristin came over to me so I could zip up the back of her dress. She then turned to me, slowly zippering up my jeans and then buttoning them with her hand. "I'll bet you were a nice boy back in the day," she said to me teasingly as she gave me a kiss.

"I was," I said to her. "That's what worries me."

"Everything will be fine. Let's go," Kristin said, taking me by the hand and leading me out the bedroom door.

We took a slow stroll down the hill to my parent's house, my arm around Kristin the entire way. I got a beautiful view of the farm and all around it. I could see a few of the horses out in one of the far pastures, running around. It reminded of just why Chandler was such a great place to live.

As soon as we walked into the house, Izzy ran over to us and gave me a big hug. She looked up at me smiled a broad smile.

"I can't believe you're home," she said excitedly. "This is perfect." She looked at me and then at Kristin, and took Kristin by the hand, racing off towards her room with her and leaving me in a lurch. Mom came walking over to me and gave me a kiss on the cheek.

"Welcome home... again," she said with a smile.

"I think that will be the last time you have to say that to me Mom," I told her.

"I'm glad to hear that," she said as she went over and sat in her chair.

"Where's Dad?" I asked her, sitting down on the couch myself.

"Down at the stables," she said as she switched the lamp on next to her chair. "He'll be back before dinner. Are you glad to be home?"

I was gazing down the hallway towards where Kristin and Izzy were before I regained my focus on Mom's question.

"I couldn't be happier," I told her as I sat back on the couch.

Kristin came walking out of Izzy's bedroom and sat down next to me on the couch, taking my hand in hers. Mom looked over at the two of us and smiled. Izzy came bounding down the hallway a moment later and sat on the arm of the couch next to me.

"Kristin helped me pick out my dress for tomorrow night," Izzy said excitedly. "She's going to help me with my hair and makeup too before the dance."

"Well she does have to work tomorrow too, Izzy," I said to her. "Maybe she won't have enough time."

"The dance isn't until eight, Wes," Kristin said, giving me a nudge. "I'll have plenty of time to help you, Izzy."

"Is makeup really necessary?" I pleaded.

"Yes!" all three ladies shouted at me.

"You're better off staying out of this, Wesley," Mom said to me as she pretended to read her book.

"Yes, Wesley," Kristin said to me sarcastically.

We had an amazing family dinner that night. The dinner itself was nothing out of the ordinary – just some beef and rice – but it was a treat for me to be around the table and see so much happiness around me, and to get the chance to take part in it. It was wonderful to see the laughs and smiles from everyone from the start of the meal to the end and to see Kristin be such an integral part of it all. By the time it was eleven, Izzy was heading off to bed, Mom was already in bed, and Kristin and I were both ready to call it a night as well. Only Dad looked like he could keep going strong.

I got up from the couch and took Kristin's hand to help her up.

"We're heading out, Dad," I said to him as I yawned.

"I'm surprised you made it this late. Have you slept at all in the last day or so?" He asked.

"No, I haven't," I told him. "But I have the rest of my life to sleep late if I want to," I said with a smile.

"Well some of us don't have that luxury, right Wyatt?" Kristin chimed in.

"You're right," Dad told her. "I've got plenty of work you can get up early for if you're looking for something to do tomorrow Wes."

"That's okay," I told him as we headed out the door. "Have a good night."

"Good night, you two," Dad said, grinning at us as he closed the door behind us.

We walked back up to my place, listening to the sounds of the birds, crickets, frogs, and insects enjoying the spring weather. I held Kristin's hand as we got closer to my house.

"Do you really have to go to work tomorrow?" I asked her, giving her a smile.

"Yes, I do," she said to me.

"I can drive you home if you want to stay at home tonight," I replied.

"Well, that would be more convenient for me," Kristin answered, "but then I wouldn't get to sleep in that great big bed of yours. Or take a shower in that shower in the morning," she said with a smirk.

"No, I guess you wouldn't." I held the front door open for her so she could walk in first.

"I think that means you're getting up early in the morning, Wes." My eyes followed Kristin as she walked over towards the bedroom.

"I'll try not to keep you awake too late tonight then," she said as she walked in the bedroom and sat down on the bed to face me.

Chapter 35

Wes

When I woke up Friday morning, I felt like nothing I had ever known before. I got up much earlier than I had intended, but it gave me a chance to be in bed with Kristin and be with her in the morning before she went off to work. I rolled over and wrapped my arms around her to hold her close to me. For the first time in many years, I felt comfortable, knowing I was with the ones I cared most about in life, and I would get to be with them for many days to come.

I gave Kristin a soft kiss on the back of her neck, causing her to lean her head back into me and giggle lightly as it tickled her. She rolled over to face me, pressing her lips to mine to give me a kiss and then nuzzle up under my chin.

"What time is it?" she asked groggily as she burrowed next to me some more.

"It's early, just after six-thirty," I said quietly to her.

"Why are you up so early? I don't have to be at work until nine," she said, getting cozy again.

"I know," I replied to her, "but I thought you might want to go to your place and have clean clothes to wear to the library instead of the same dress you wore yesterday."

Kristin peeked her eyes open at me. "Good point," she said with a laugh. She hopped out of bed, walking off to the bathroom without a stitch of clothing on, looking back at me with a grin as she did.

I got up and put a t-shirt and sweats on and went out to the kitchen to make some coffee for us. A few minutes later, Kristin appeared, wearing just one of my t-shirts, her long hair tied back into a ponytail. She came over and hugged me, and as soon as the coffee was ready, she grabbed a mug and curled up on one of the kitchen chairs.

"That t-shirt looks good on you," I told her as she stretched her bare legs out in front of her.

"Maybe I'll wear it home," she said with a grin.

"It's okay by me," I told her as I sipped my coffee, smiling at her. Kristin put her coffee down and ran back off into the bedroom, coming out a bit later wearing a pair of my shorts and carrying the rest of her clothes in a neat pile, including her underwear.

"This is all I need to get home with," she told me as she came back over to me to kiss me.

"Are you sure?" I questioned. "Seems kind of scandalous for the town librarian to go around dressed like this." I kissed her again, reaching down to cup her backside as we kissed, causing her to squeal a bit.

"Hmmm, we better get going, or I am never getting to the library this morning," she said to me as we broke our kiss. I grudgingly agreed and slid on my sneakers and grabbed my keys to drive Kristin to her apartment. We walked out to the car and Kristin certainly felt the morning chill on her body as she waited for me to open the car door.

"Yikes! It's cold out here in shorts," she said and felt it even more as she sat on the cold leather seats of my car with her bare legs. I smiled and turned on the seat warmers for her so she could be more comfortable, and then drove off to her apartment.

We were there in minutes, with no traffic in town just yet since it was still early in the morning. I didn't want Kristin to go but knew that she had to, and I gave her a long, slow kiss as we sat in the parking lot.

"I'll pick you up at work later to bring you to my parent's house to help Izzy?" I said to her, keeping my hands on her hips.

"That will be nice," Kristin said to me. "Have a nice first day of retirement," she said to me with a smile. I watched her climb out of the car and walk away up the stairs to her apartment. She looked back at me and waved as she got to the top of the stairs and then went inside. I let out a big sigh and realized something.

You're in love with her, Wes. You're acting like a schoolboy.

As I drove back home, I thought more about the idea. I had never felt this happy and comfortable with anyone, not even with Rachel, Izzy's mother. There was a time when we thought we were in love, but I don't think I ever felt the connection with her that I felt now with Kristin. The main thing was I didn't want that feeling to go away. I wanted to be with her more than I wanted to do anything else.

I got back home and finally unloaded my baseball gear from my car, bringing it all into the house for now. At some point I had would have to figure out what to do with it all, but I had plenty of time to figure all that out. Instinct told me I should be working out right now, but I was giving myself the day off.

I got enough of a workout yesterday, I thought to myself with a smirk.

I spent the rest of the morning making arrangements around the house. I wanted the place to look good since I figured now that I was going to be home Izzy would come back up to the house to live with me, and I hoped Kristin would be spending more and more time here with me as well. After that, I spent quite some time on the phone with Randy, ironing out a press release about my retirement, and lining up interviews and so on to explain everything. I didn't really care what other people thought of me walking away like I did, but I did all the press as a favor to Randy for all he had done for me over the years. Randy even said the Pirates had contacted him about holding a special day for me at the stadium later in the season when the Reds were in town. It was a great thing for them to offer, and I was touched by it and agreed we could work something out.

The rest of the day went by in a whirlwind as I went down to see Mom and Dad. Dad tried to talk me into going to the diner with him for lunch, but I told him I wasn't quite at the point yet where I was going to hang out with all the retired guys in town all day drinking coffee. Instead, I stayed at the house and had a quiet lunch with Mom.

Mom carried a couple of glasses of iced tea over to the kitchen table as we sat and had sandwiches.

She looked at me and asked, "Are you happy, Wes?"

"Mom, for the first time in many years I feel like my life is complete. Baseball always made me happy, but I know now that there was an empty part of my life outside of that. Now I have the chance to have Izzy more in my life, and you and Dad, and Kristin... I don't think there's much more I could ask for at this point."

"Good," she said as she sat back and sipped her iced tea. "We're going to miss having Izzy in the house all the time, but I think it will be the best for both of you so you can get to know each other again. And having Kristin... well, it's nice that you have someone to be in love with."

I coughed a little on my iced tea. "Who said we were in love?" I told her, feeling flustered.

"Wesley, please," she said to me. "I understand you haven't known each other very long, but I know what I see and hear. You clearly love her, so why deny it?"

"How do you know that?"

"I'm your mother," she told me. "It's my job to know these things. It's also my job to tell you that she might like to hear it from you because she clearly loves you too."

I sat and stared at Mom a moment as she ate her sandwich. "Do you think so?" I said. Now I really was feeling like a schoolboy.

"Honestly, Wesley, how did you survive all these years?" she said in her motherly tone. "A big, strong, handsome baseball star with everything in front of him, and you act like you haven't got a clue. Think about everything that happened. A woman doesn't go through all that and come back to you if her feelings for you aren't strong. Make sure you hold onto her."

"I'll do my best, Mom."

"Do better than that, Wes," Mom said as she cleared the plates from the table. "I like her. She's a strong young woman that brings a lot to all our lives, but you and Izzy especially. I think Kristin is just what has been missing from your life."

I spent the rest of the afternoon with Mom, laughing and being with her like I hadn't done in a long time. We told stories about the past and talked about the future, and it was nice to reconnect with her in this way. Before we knew it, Izzy was racing through the front door to see us. She tossed her backpack on the floor inside the front door and came over and gave Mom a hug and then gave one to me.

"What time are you picking up Kristin?" Izzy asked me anxiously.

"Izzy, it's just after two," I told her calmly. "Kristin doesn't get off work until five."

"I know, but I have been texting with her all day about ideas of what to do. I'm just so excited!" Izzy went off to her room to start preparing.

"Is this what I have to look forward to for the next several years?" I said to Mom.

"Enjoy it while it's here, Wes," Mom said honestly. "Before you know it, she will be off to college, and you will wonder where the time went."

When five finally came close, Izzy was begging me to go down and get Kristin, so I left the house just to satisfy her. I pulled into the library parking lot just at five, and saw Kristin and Karen out front, locking up for the night.

I got out of the car and walked over to the two of them as they slowly walked towards me. Kristin looked up and smiled at me as she got closer. She gave me a quick kiss as we met.

"Hi, Karen," I said, looking over at her as she watched Kristin and me.

"Hi," Karen waved. "I'll let you two get on with your romance here," she said with a laugh. "Enjoy your weekend, you two." Karen walked off, and I led Kristin to the car so we could head over to my parent's place. I noticed she had a case with her.

"What's with all the stuff?" I asked as I put the items in the back.

"Just some makeup and things that we might need to help Izzy get ready," Kristin said as she got in the car.

"All that to get her ready?" I said.

"Relax, Wes," Kristin said as I started the car. "It's a girl thing. It's her first date, and she wants to look perfect. "

"I know, but she doesn't need to look like a fashion model either."

"It will be fine, I promise," Kristin said as she flashed me a smile.

We arrived at the house, and as soon as we walked in, we could hear Izzy calling out to Kristin from her bedroom to come to her.

"You might want to go occupy yourself," Kristin said to me, "so you don't get yourself all worked up over this. It's going to be a while."

I sighed and gave Kristin a kiss as she walked down the hall to Izzy's room. An idea came to me as I stood there.

"How is Izzy getting to the dance?" I asked Mom.

"Your father was going to drive her there and pick her up," Mom told me.

"Tell Dad I'll take care of it," I said to Mom. "I'll be back later." I went out the door and up to my house to change.

I took my time getting myself ready, showering and shaving, splashing on some cologne, and then picking a nice suit out of my closet to wear. I looked at myself in the mirror and figured I looked pretty good, and I still had plenty of time before I needed to get Izzy. I drove down to Main Street and went to the flower shop and saw Dave there behind the counter. He had helped me yesterday with the flowers I got for Kristin, so I knew he would be able to help me out again today.

After getting what I needed from Dave, I had one more stop to make in town at another store. I then walked over to the diner and went in. The usual crowd was there, and Clyde Stuart and his buddies all greeted me with a cheer when I went in. I walked over to the table to pay homage to the crew and said my hellos as they drank what was probably their tenth cup of coffee of the day for each of them.

"Clyde," I asked as he sat at the head of the table. "Is your grandson here?"

"He might still be in the back before he goes home to get ready for the dance tonight," Clyde said as he pointed towards the kitchen. Just then, I saw the boy I had seen when I dropped Izzy off here last weekend came out of the kitchen. He stopped when he saw me, figuring he was in trouble.

"Are you Bradley?" I asked him with a serious tone.

"Yes, sir," he croaked, putting down his tub to collect dirty dishes.

"You're taking my daughter to the dance tonight," I said to him as I approached him.

"Yes, I am, Mr. Martin," He said quickly. "Sir, you have nothing to worry about, I promise..." he stammered.

"Relax, Bradley," I said to him. "I'm sure you'll be a perfect gentleman. I just wanted to give you this, to give to Izzy. I don't know if boys still do this, but it will make her feel special." I handed him the container with the white wrist corsage in it.

"Thanks, Mr. Martin," Bradley said, still looking at me nervously.

"We'll be dropping of Izzy at the school at eight," I told him. "Meet her outside and give it to her."

"I will," he said with a smile, putting the corsage down so he could pick up the tub and finish his work.

I strode towards the diner door, stopping along the way to answer a few questions from the gentlemen in the window.

"Wes," Clyde Stuart barked at me. "So, who is KA? It's Kristin Arthur isn't it?"

"Clyde, it would be ungentlemanly of me to speak of a young lady like that. You boys have a good night now. I have a date to get to."

I walked out of the diner with the men watching me and went to my car. By the time I got home, it was getting later, near to seven-thirty. I walked into the house and Mom and Dad were there in the living room.

"Just in time," Dad said to me. "They've been waiting for you to get here. You were making Izzy nervous that you would be late. Don't you look sharp."

"Thanks, Dad," I said to him.

"Is that Wes?" I heard Kristin shout from the bedroom.

"Yes," Mom yelled back. "We're ready."

"Okay, we're coming out," Kristin yelled. Kristin came down the hall first, walking over to me and standing next to me, taking my hand.

Izzy came out next, walking slowly out to make an entrance. She looked beautiful from the moment I saw her. Kristin had helped her with her hair, putting her hair up off her shoulders where it usually was. The dress she wore was a cream-colored tank dress with a floral applique top and a chiffon skirt, and it made her look very pretty. I could see my father taking pictures of her as she walked over to me.

"What do you think, Dad?" she asked me nervously. With the heels she was wearing she came closer to my height than she had ever done before.

"You look breathtaking, honey," I said to her, bringing a big smile to her face. "There's just one thing..."

Izzy interrupted me, and Kristin gave me a look. "Dad, I'm not wearing too much makeup, and we made sure the skirt wasn't too short..."

"It's not that," I told her. I reached into my suit breast pocket and took out a black velvet box and handed it to her. "You need this."

Izzy slowly opened the box and saw the pearl necklace inside and gasped. She picked the pearls up in her hand and held them.

"Oh, Dad," she said to me. "They're beautiful."

I took the pearls from her hand and helped her put them on, clasping them behind her neck. She looked at herself in the mirror, admiring them, and turned back to me and gave me a hug.

"Pictures!" my father shouted, so Izzy and I posed for several shots, and then Mom got in the pictures as well, and finally Kristin had her picture taken first with Izzy and me, and then alone with Izzy. Finally, it was getting late, and we needed to get going. Kristin and I escorted Izzy out to my SUV, and I drove the three of us over to the school.

The school was just a few minutes away from us on the other side of town, and we made it right on time. We pulled up in front of the school, where many other boys and girls were arriving at the same time. They were all dressed up for the dance and heading to the school excitedly. I got out and came around to the passenger side and opened the door for Izzy. Kristin hopped out as well and gave her a hug and told her to have a good time. Izzy hugged me once more at the curb.

"Thank you so much Dad," she said to me with a smile.

"Have a good time tonight," I said to her. I watched her walk over towards Bradley, who was dutifully waiting outside the school for her. They chatted briefly, and Kristin and I watched as he presented her with the wrist corsage, putting it on her. I could see Izzy blush a bit, and she looked back at us and waved as they walked into the school.

"Should we just wait here for them until they're done?" I said to Kristin, half-joking, and half-serious.

"Get in the car," Kristin ordered.

We started the drive back to the farm, with Kristin sitting next to me and taking my hand.

"It was nice of Bradley to give her a corsage," Kristin said to me as we drove.

"Who knew the kid had it in him," I said to her with a smile.

As we got to Martin Way, instead of going to my parent's or my house, I turned left and took us down the road towards the stables.

"Where are we going?" Kristin asked me.

"You'll see," I said to her. We stayed on the road beyond the stables, the same path we had taken our horse ride on until we got to the pond area. I parked the car close to where the tables were located and near where the hitch for the horses was. I kept the lights of the SUV on so I could see where the power was located and found the switch to turn on the lights that decorated the trees. The small white bulbs lit up in the trees like fireflies, and I came around and shut off the car lights. I walked over to the passenger side and helped Kristin out of the car. I then leaned into the car and turned on some music, putting on some Van Morrison to listen to.

"What are you up to?" Kristin said with a smile. I took her hand and led over to the clearing between the trees, so we were in the lit area. I then presented her with her own white corsage for her wrist.

"No reason we can't have our own dance," I said to Kristin as I put the corsage on her wrist gently. I then took her in my arms and started to slow dance with her as Van Morrison played in the background.

"I don't care what your father says," Kristin said to me as we danced. "I think you are very suave and romantic."

I laughed and smiled at her. "Well, I am glad you think so, but to be honest, I think it is you that brought it out in me. You make me want to be that way." I looked down into her eyes as we danced.

"I'm falling in love with you, Kristin," I told her.

"I'm in love with you, too," Kristin said as she put her arms around me.

As the song came to an end, I took Kristin's hand and led her over so we could look out over the pond. I put my arm around her and held her close to me.

"I'm so glad you came back for me," Kristin said to me.

I realized the last week had been filled with ups and downs and comebacks, but this moment was the highlight of them all. No home run could top this.

Continue Wes and Kristin's story in <u>The Home Stand Series</u> book two:
<u>Spring Fever</u>

Also By M. Geraghty

The Cosantóir MC

Small Town, Biker Romances

Finn
Preacher
Liam
Demon

The Home Stand Series

Small Town, Sports Romances

Change Up
Spring Fever
The Sweet Spot

The <u>Celtic Sisters</u> Series

Small Town, Dark Romances
<u>A Calm in the Storm</u>

Standalone Romances

<u>For What It's Worth</u>
A Christmas, Rockstar Romance

www.ingramcontent.com/pod-product-compliance
Lightning Source LLC
Chambersburg PA
CBHW020836260626
47169CB00003B/1010